TOMORROW'S GARDEN

TOMORROW'S GARDEN

Harriet Hudson

This first world edition published in Great Britain 2002 by
SEVERN HOUSE PUBLISHERS LTD of
9–15 High Street, Sutton, Surrey SM1 1DF.
This first world edition published in the USA 2002 by
SEVERN HOUSE PUBLISHERS INC of
595 Madison Avenue, New York, N.Y. 10022.

British Library Cataloguing in Publication Data

Hudson,   Harriet
    Tomorrow's garden
    1.   Gardens - Great Britain - Fiction
    2.   Vendetta - Great Britain - Fiction
    I.   Title
    823.9'14 [F]

    ISBN 0-7278-5838-6

Typeset by Palimpsest Book Production Ltd.,
Polmont, Stirlingshire, Scotland.
Printed and bound in Great Britain by
MPG Books Ltd., Bodmin, Cornwall.

Acknowledgements

Novels, like roses, do not flourish unattended; they usually require the input of quite a few people besides the author. Nutrition in the case of this novel was willingly and generously provided not only by my agent, Dorothy Lumley, and my editor, Amanda Stewart, but by my friends, Carol and Douglas Tyler, who rescued a wilting rose with their advice and help. My thanks are also due to my sister, Marian Anderson, and my husband, James Myers, who patiently plodded round rose gardens with me when he might otherwise have been at a car show.

H.H.

Prologue

*O*h, *red is for the roses, and red is for my love. Black lives but for the mourning day; roses for eternity.* Edmund Fontenay made no effort to control his grief, for here he was alone with his son, the only person who might in some measure understand.

Roses do comfort the heart, they say, and in this ancient garden of love do I leave mine, for naught can please it outside. Here in the centre by the fountain of life, I plant this damask rose, my Gertrude, who suffered so long, so cruelly, as does the rose itself by the pestilence that walketh in darkness. Here shall her name live for ever, even as the rose itself blooms in its loveliness by the side of Our Lady in Heaven.

At last he felt able to speak. 'Gerard, my son!'

'Sir?'

'Mark this well. I have a book of parchment, the book of my lady Gertrude's garden. When a Fontenay passes from this earthly life, a rose is to be planted here, where once Geoffrey Chaucer walked. In that book shall good record be kept so that Fontenay names shall not perish on earth as shall their bodies. And the first name therein shall be Gertrude Fontenay, born of the royal line of Scotland, Queen Rose of my heart. I have your pledge that you will obey, boy?'

Gerard Fontenay's eyes were red with weeping. 'Sir, you have.'

Edmund sighed. He had enshrined Gertrude's memory in this enclosed garden where no evil could enter. Yet the serpent found his way even into Eden, and the rose itself bore thorns, as did the crown of our Saviour Lord.

1

With His help, he must care for this blessed place so that Gertrude's rose might bloom for ever and, when God so willed, close by it, his own.

One

There were always roses at Fontenay, so David said.

No longer. A flying bomb had smashed the garden to smithereens during the Second World War, and it had never been replanted. That was a relief, since after his death I had enough family baggage to carry around with me without adding yet one more tradition. When I finally walked through the gates of Fontenay it was on my terms, not his. I had been a widow for nearly two years, and only now was ready to carry out his wishes.

David used to joke that he only married me because of my name, Rosanna, but he, like everyone else, agreed to call me Anna. I find roses overpowering – they make demands on you with their sweet perfume; they are flowers of beauty, but as they lure you into their possession, they stab you with their thorns.

Had the Fontenays never felt those thorns? Apparently not, for *The Book of Gertrude's Garden*, begun over four hundred years ago, seems to record only the deep love of a united family, and the remaining family portraits suggest nothing different. Surely, even the discipline imposed by hours of sitting could not entirely hide the stamp of a lineage at odds with life? And the pictures displayed roses everywhere, tucked in the folds of an eighteenth-century dress, wound into the symbolism of Elizabethan backgrounds, or clasped in the hands of enigmatic, unknown Fontenays. But who was possessing whom?

In theory, I now owned the Fontenay estate, but it takes a bold spirit to hold out against the Fontenays, and I was only one by marriage. With David, I had found freedom, and so I

3

assumed that when I came to Fontenay that freedom would continue. I came here for two reasons: firstly, because I made a promise to David that I would do so, and secondly, because of Gerard, our son. I had chosen to come here of my own free will – if he lives at Fontenay with me he can make his own choice whether to accept his inheritance or sell it after my death. It had seemed so simple – then.

I drove through the gates that first day with no intention of going near Fontenay Place. Instead, I went straight to install myself in my new home, the former grandiose Victorian lodge. I was alone as Gerard was away on a gap year. There, waiting for me, was Hugo Brooks, standing outside, keys in hand, for all the world as though *he* owned it and not I. Much as I liked him, he had an innocent way of putting his foot in my path that, for all our easy companionship, was irritating. It was no great problem, for I'd known him for years. He was the managing director and major shareholder of the specialist company that had leased Fontenay Place as a venue for conferences over the last ten years or so. I owed a lot to Hugo, because the school that had occupied it previously had more or less wrecked it and we had no money to restore it as the listed property authorities had demanded. Nevertheless, I was irrationally irked at finding his tall, cheerful, teddy-bear figure on my doorstep, grinning happily at my arrival.

'You said you needed a gardener,' he greeted me cheerfully, unlocking the door for me.

I forced a smile. 'You?'

He laughed. 'I wish. No, someone recommended this chap to me – did a great job at restoring those gardens at Cranhurst Court. His own master, but he's good and you can leave it all to him.'

Now, I didn't like the sound of that, one little bit. I would need a gardener – and how! – but I didn't want my control being questioned by some Napoleonic Capability Brown. 'I've a few candidates coming along for interview, but I'll certainly give him a whirl.'

Hugo knows me well. 'You lie in your teeth,' he informed me. 'You haven't got anyone yet, have you?'

'I shall have. Give me a chance.'

He shrugged. 'Give *him* a chance then.'

'Fair enough.'

Fair? What was fair about being dumped with Joss Foxley?

Let me explain about Fontenay Place. Back in the heady days of Norman influence, a right trusty knight called Rupert de Fontnoi galloped over the Kentish countryside to seek out an English home for himself. Very fashionable in those days. Odd that the situation is now reversed. Anyway, de Fontnoi established himself in the green Weald of Kent and built himself a state-of-the-art stone castle. It was on the smallish side, because by that time there was no need for massive defensive fortifications. Nor was it on a strategically hilly site; instead it was low-lying and close to water, with a river running through its grounds.

A couple of centuries later, the combined results of the Black Death and problems in the wool trade, plus a sneak burning and pillaging raid by the French in the Winchelsea area, had led to a downturn in the Fontenay fortunes, and by the time the family got itself together again, not much was left of the original Norman castle. The Fontenays rebuilt it in a style more suited to the modern living of the late fourteenth century, and the castle stumbled on for another hundred-plus years.

By Tudor times, the castle-cum-house needed renovating with red brick here and there, and the ladies of the house wanted decent chimneys, more rooms added, and so on. Another century or so later, the lords of Fontenay were dispossessed after a determined onslaught in the Great Kentish Rebellion of 1648. When, in due course, Merry King Charles II restored himself to the throne and Fontenay to its rightful owners (though there was, to say the least, some dispute over this) they decided the poor old castle wasn't worthy of their status.

Instead, Anne Fontenay and her husband built a grand new house in late seventeenth-century style, and this is the present Fontenay Place. They left what remained of the old castle to crumble, and there, minus quite a lot of bricks and walls, it is to this day, under the guardianship of English Heritage. Fontenay Place was let in 1960, along with its renovated stables, which

5

left the Fontenay family itself the use of the lodge, a few other outbuildings – and the grounds.

I use the latter word advisedly, since they can't be called gardens. After the Fontenays left their property in 1960, they went to live in London. David's father died five years later, after having been ill for some years. Nothing much had been done to the estate since the flying bomb in 1944. During the war, a large part of the grounds had been given over to vegetable and fruit growing. After it, there was more to think of than restoring and upkeep of gardens, especially since the bomb seemed to have knocked the stuffing out of David's father, as it had the rose garden. The cultivated land was grassed over and then ignored, the rest of it just left.

The grounds were huge, a lot of woodland, the grassland (some of which was let), the remains of late seventeenth-century formal parterre gardens, overgrown eighteenth-century pleasure gardens, walled vegetable garden – well, you know the sort of thing – and what used to be the rose garden. The public were allowed in by appointment to see the castle ruins, but there wasn't a great call for this service, because of the mini-jungle they had to march through and lack of amenities.

It was my bright idea, slaved over from all angles in the months since David had died, to restore the gardens, create new ones round the castle ruins, convert an old Tudor barn for teas and make myself some money! I was nearly forty years old, and saw it as 'A Great New Beginning'.

'You're crazy, Mum,' Gerard had said.

'Perhaps, but maybe you'll be crazy too, someday. If I don't do something about Fontenay now, it will be too late. Are you with me or against?'

Gerard had grinned. 'Neither. I'm open-minded. You're on your own.'

'Understood.' Just what I wanted – I was absolved from responsibility.

'Take care, Mum.'

'About what?'

'Fontenay. Even Dad admitted it can be an odd place.'

'The pestilence that walketh in darkness?'

'Precisely.'

'You're dotty.'

I forgot this well-worn Fontenay cliché in the excitement of my scheme. This was excellent, but was to prove to have two major drawbacks. The first was the rose garden. I had mentally renamed it the sunken garden, thanks to the bomb, and I had no intention of letting any rose come near it. I'd had roses up to here during my life with David. That was the reason I gave myself, but I think it was more complicated than that, even then.

The second drawback was Joss Foxley.

On that first day, I pretended to Hugo that I needed to be on my own to rearrange furniture, check electricity and so on – all the dull boring things I knew he would hate. Hugo was a townee-type by nature, and saw no need to pretend he was a do-it-yourself man. I lied to him because this was my first day at Fontenay. I'd visited it before, of course, but things were different now. It was to be my home, which changed everything, and I wanted to sniff it out.

I'm a great believer in taking time to sniff. Animals do it, although admittedly for less emotional reasons than us. Nevertheless, it proves there is an instinct to take one's time. First impressions are important. Of course, they can be false. David often talked of Chaucer's garden in his *The Romaunt of the Rose*, which family legend maintains he was inspired to rework from the French by his visit to Fontenay Castle. False-Semblant (false-seeming) was one of the allegorical figures whom the poet-narrator met in the poem, and who stood between him and his love, which was – wouldn't you just know? – a perfect rosebud in an enclosed garden.

Nevertheless first impressions can be right. It's one of life's little jokes that you have to make up your own mind. I like that.

So, I sallied forth to sniff. There wasn't much scope in the woodland, nor much to be done around Fontenay Place itself. Whatever ghosts remained there were kept in control by Hugo's business, I reasoned, and that applied to the now derelict formal gardens. I, Anna Fontenay, decided to plunge in at the deep end instead. I would start sniffing at the centre, where the story all began: the ruins of Fontenay Castle.

They are quite a walk from the Dower House, which includes the crossing of the former river, now a stream that divides the old castle grounds from the eighteenth-century park, which was laid out when desire for sweeping vistas and a 'return to nature' was replacing topiary and artifice. The path was a narrow one, a bare minimum trodden down through the woodland in front of Fontenay Place as far as the gravelled drive, then a grassy track across the meadow, barely maintained. Here wild flowers had triumphantly re-established themselves after years of banishment, and were revelling in their freedom. There were no ghosts here either. It was early June, butterflies and bees were everywhere, trees gloried in late spring greenery. Oh, the land was smiling, and confidently I continued across the stream and along the track to the old castle.

Here there was plenty to sniff. Much of the brickwork was covered with wisteria, and in one spot a rambling rose. I even smiled at it. I didn't resent its presence here, only in my life. David said that the castle had been ivy-covered for years until English Heritage saved it from its clutches, and planted more scenic and less harmful companions for the castle's old age. The air was very still today, and it was easy to imagine this a complete building, much larger than these ruins suggested. Here had walked one of Queen Elizabeth's chamberlains and some said the Queen herself. I am not over-fanciful, but there seemed nothing to fear here.

Fear? What on earth had I to fear save my own reluctance to get drawn into the web of Fontenay history? My background bore little relation to the Fontenays. My parents ran a small stationery shop in the south London suburbs. It was called Wickhams, since when they opened, it was still the custom to call shops after their owners, rather than cute names like Pen 'n' Pencils. The world of the Fontenays bore no relation to it, and when I met and married David in a whirlwind romance, they approached him with extreme caution. Whether living in it or not, he was the owner of a castle.

To me, too, Fontenay was somewhat unreal. It was easy to tell myself, in our London home, that history was past, and that I was only moving to Fontenay for the sake of Gerard's future. Once here, history might prove, I thought uncomfortably, rather harder to dismiss. The trick would be to treat history as a tool to shape the future. I thought of Sissinghurst Castle and its beauty; I even fancied I could be another Sackville-West, dedicated to creating a garden – no, Anna, don't go there, I told myself quickly. There was almost too much to sniff here, and I needed to avoid falling into it hook, line and sinker.

What I could sniff, I realized, was the English heritage itself, its ageless charm that doesn't shout at you; it just waits for you to enter its magic spell. The sense of age when one treads a centuries-old lawn. The way that old buildings merge into the landscape like growing plants. The plants themselves that accept their human carers as their regal right. Nothing definable, but it was there that first day, and definitely sniffable. Was there any harm in that? Surely not. If I was to run these gardens, I had to love them, too. Except for the roses. I had a problem with them.

My confidence began to return. Greatly daring, I even sniffed the pink rambler rose clinging to the pale red brick. There was no false-seeming here. It was as it seemed, and had been so for hundreds of years. This lovely place deserved that people should be able to come to see it, not as it might have been in Good Queen Bess's time, but as something of beauty in its own right. I had once been to Lesnes Abbey in spring – there the ruins were much more total than those of Fontenay, set on a flat field in south-east London. Behind were wooded hills, however, and in spring their slopes were covered with as many daffodils as Wordsworth himself saw so many years ago in the hills of the Lake District. Yellow and dancing, ageless like the ruin itself. Fontenay deserved this too, and it would have it, I vowed.

Before you think I was getting carried away – you're wrong. This had been a rational decision about something I could create for my own livelihood, and for Gerard's future, as well as for my own satisfaction.

There was, of course, one factor in my sniffing route that I had 'forgotten'. My route over to the grounds of Fontenay

Place would take me past the sunken garden, the former rose garden. I took it, though, pushing my way past bushes that overgrew the path, as though even they wanted to stop me. Careful, Anna, I warned myself, though why, I hadn't the slightest idea.

The undergrowth opened out, but I was so busy trying to push through long grass and tall flowers that only the sharp warning call of a blackbird made me raise my eyes. Ahead I could see more tumbled stones, more bushes, and thought little of it until I drew closer. They weren't stones, but tumbled red bricks, which here and there were covered with wild roses. The path had petered out, and brambles covered the ground. I had tough jeans on, so I pushed my way a little further. Only a little, for I felt the ground falling away at my feet, and ahead of me a great pit of bramble and wild rose. I stopped where I was, and looked around. Over to left and right I saw glimpses of what might be piles of bricks and in one or two places shrouds of ivy covering what might be ancient walls. At the far corner a golden yellow climber was struggling to survive.

This was it, I realized. I was in the rose garden of Sir Edmund Fontenay. My sniffing nose let me down badly that day, or was it that the atmosphere here was so powerful it obliterated any sense of what was to come? All I felt was that far-off whiff of unease, so slight it lulled me into false confidence.

In my nostrils was the smell of warm grass, in my ears the sound of bees humming in the wild roses. The walls were long since fallen, yet I felt closed in, trapped. Ridiculously, for I had only to turn to go out. I would not do so. I needed to see it, I told myself, even though there was no garden now, nothing of Edmund Fontenay's carefully planted roses.

Then I saw I was wrong: there were still two here, a red and a white, several blooms poking above the mass of wilderness, as if staring up at me. Were they willing me to turn tail, before the garden trapped me? Yet what was there here but sadness? The flying bomb crater brought thoughts of war and loss, the neglected roses those of a past beauty that had nothing to do with the gardens I was planning.

If the brambles were cleared and the overgrown flowers cut,

one could start again. It wasn't going to be a rose garden, even with the sun lulling me as it was today.

If this were Chaucer's garden, then Danger, Reason, False-Seeming, Jealousy and Shame would be here in spirit to try to prevent me from exercising my free will, yet there appeared nothing here but the sun and the signs of destruction. I would leave it so, I decided. And yet, and yet – *no*. I turned ready to retrace my steps. The narrator of Chaucer's poem had been taken into the enchanted garden by Bel-Accueil, Welcome. I suddenly realized I had a companion too, but it wasn't Bel-Accueil. I was not alone, as I had thought. There was a man perched on the ruins of the wall watching me.

'The castle is that way,' I said unsteadily, for he had given me a fright.

'Thanks. I've seen it.' He slid off the wall.

Was I going to trot out the 'This is private property' line? No. A curt nod was all it needed. I gave it – and it wasn't.

'Joss Foxley. I heard you wanted a gardener.'

A variety of emotions welled up inside me, but I decided on professionalism.

'Yes. I was going to ring you to make an appointment.' I managed to make it sound as though I was *still* planning to do so.

'I'm here now.' It was a statement of fact, nothing loaded about it, I had to admit.

'I have others to interview.'

'Of course.'

'But not now. It's not convenient. I've only just moved in. I'll ring you. Can you come back?'

He considered this. 'I could, or we could settle it now. First impressions—'

'Are often wrong,' I finished briskly.

'No. I'm sure I could work for you.'

I'd been wrong-footed. Bad sign. At first sight I'd thought there was nothing special about him. He was just a square-jawed man of about my own height in his early thirties, with the usual jeans and t-shirt uniform. A second look told me I was wrong. There was something special. His eyes fastened on me thoughtfully, summing me up. There was nothing sexual

11

about it, not even the quick appreciation of minds in common. What was unusual was that the look conveyed – I searched for the stray thought that passed through my mind – that I was a problem with which *he* had to deal, rather than the other way around. That translated into my being a particularly awkward plant which might ruin his scheme for the gardens.

His scheme – that was the nub of it. It was going to be my scheme.

I could tell him to get lost straightaway, or I could play fair as Hugo would want me to. 'You've good references apparently.'

'Yes.'

'Let me tell you what I have in mind then.' I waded closer towards him through the undergrowth. My words sounded strange considering I'd only just moved in, but it was as well to establish who was in control.

He listened in silence as I outlined my scheme for the castle ruins, and for the formal gardens, and the grounds in general, occasionally adding a comment which showed that he knew his garden history. I ought to have been encouraged, but instead it made me wary.

'So by the castle itself, you're looking for a romantic garden, but modern-style rather than Tudor.'

'Yes,' I said firmly. 'It deserves it. No point making it all paths and knots.' (I knew my history, too.) 'I want modern flower gardens with modern flowers.'

'Not too modern in style. It would need a fountain and some sense of the past.'

'We could compromise on that,' I answered too hastily. We?

His eyes flickered. 'Perhaps.' Then he asked one simple, but devastating question, 'And what about this?' He gestured to the sunken garden before us. 'Do you want to rebuild the Hermit's Retreat, for instance?' That had been the name given to the quaint summer house on one side of the garden built of thatch and beams sometime late in the eighteenth century when such conceits were the fashion. Joss Foxley was way ahead of me. I simply hadn't thought about it.

12

'I'm still considering it,' I told him grandly. 'It wouldn't sit well with my plans for this garden, though.'

'Which are?'

'A spring garden,' I said briskly, making an instant decision. 'All the sides of the crater covered with bulbs, and rhododendrons, and azaleas over the rest.'

'No.'

I felt my face growing red. 'I'm sorry you don't agree, but that's how it's going to be.'

'It should be a rose garden, as it always was.'

'How do you know that?'

'I've looked at the records in the Kent archives, Mrs Fontenay. It was always a rose garden. Even in Chaucer's time it must have had some roses at least. It should be a rose garden again.'

'Not if I don't wish it,' I said as gently as I could manage.

'That's irrelevant.'

'It is very relevant, Mr Foxley. I own this garden, and you do not.'

He simply slung his sweater over his shoulder, nodded a polite goodbye to me and disappeared.

I should have felt relieved, but I didn't. I'd handled it badly. He'd said enough to convince me that he was the sort of gardener I was looking for – in theory, at least. I told myself that there would be others, but I was proved wrong. I followed up Joss's references and they were ideal, to my annoyance. Nothing but praise for his work and character. So why had he made such a bad impression on me?

Over the next two weeks I must have interviewed two dozen prospective gardeners. None of them convinced me as much as Joss Foxley: some would need too much guidance from me, some knew it all, some knew nothing. Each day when I took them on a tour of the gardens, I found Joss Foxley sitting on the wall of the sunken garden. I had too much pride to tell him to get lost, so I simply ignored him, and he ignored me. Usually that was easy, because he was sketching. Was he sketching the castle remains in the background? Sketching what he saw before him in the sunken garden? Or sketching what he would like to see?

13

It became a battle of wits, which Hugo found vastly amusing. The Wars of the Roses, he called it.

'Ha ha,' I said savagely.

'Suppose I act like the Tudor rose and find a compromise between this warring pair? A trial period, for example.'

'It won't work. He wants his way. I'm going to have mine.'

'Sure you want him if he sees it your way?'

'Yes. He obviously knows what he's doing, but I won't be pushed around. I want that sunken garden turned into a spring garden.'

The meeting, which took place at Fontenay Place, was interesting, even to me. Hugo was a good negotiator, and we did reach a compromise. The sunken garden would be cleared, and reassessed once it was. With the land denuded of brambles, I could take an objective look – in time for the autumn bulb planting season. If Joss didn't agree with my decision, our ways would part. I wasn't happy, but I supposed there was a slender chance that it would work.

'Do you agree with that solution, Mr Foxley?' Hugo was doing his big managing director act, but Joss Foxley wasn't put off. Indeed, he seemed to treat Hugo as my equal partner in this – and that irked me, too.

'I'll need casual labour to help,' he told him.

'Of course,' I replied firmly, as though money were no object. It was, but he wasn't to know that. His salary – and salary it had to be, for this job needed full-time commitment – would absorb a large part of what I had to live on out of Hugo's rent and David's and my savings, plus a large overdraft facility. The sooner the gardens were paying their way, the better.

In the next few weeks, professional surveyors came and went, various labourers arrived, and Joss Foxley spent days at the Kent Archives office, then marched the grounds with English Heritage. I went with them sometimes, but often left them to it, deep in discussion about parterres, landscaping, and geophysical searches. I was looking after the conversion of the barn into tea-rooms. Sometimes in the evening Joss Foxley – we remained on formal terms, so I thought of him thus – would come to explain what he was doing. The table would be covered with ordnance survey and other historic maps, photocopied documents and plans, and his own charts covered the carpet.

Sometimes Hugo would come, too. I don't know why. He had little interest in the finer details of garden planning. Was he wondering what my relationship was with Joss Foxley? Unlikely. Hugo was divorced, and had no romantic aspirations towards me, so far as I knew. And I had none towards either of them. We remained, each of us, separate during those evenings, wrapped up in our own selves, united only by piles of paper on the table and floor, for they represented the future of Fontenay.

Early in July, after heavy machinery had been trundling to and fro for a while, Joss Foxley asked me to come to look at the sunken garden. It had to come sometime, so I braced myself, even though he explained it was only half-cleared.

The garden was beginning to look entirely different; the crumbled bricks had been neatened into piles, and in places the wall made good. The brambles had mostly disappeared, but a few dog roses still clung to the edges and the golden yellow climber was still there.

'I want your permission to leave those roses,' he said flatly.

It wasn't the climber he was pointing to. It was the two cascading shrub roses I had seen on my first visit. They seemed to be mocking me, the one a pale red, the other white, the colour they used to plant on graves in olden times. Why this thought should suddenly have struck me, I couldn't imagine, but I wish it hadn't.

'They must have been planted quite soon before the bomb. Otherwise they would have gone wild by now, or died of old age or disease. I'd like to leave them.'

'No,' I whipped back.

'But if you decide in the end to restore the rose garden—'

'We should start from scratch. You can put these in somewhere else.'

'You really want me to dig these up when they've survived here so long?' He was incredulous, and I suppose it did sound odd.

'Yes.' I don't know why I was so obstinate. I had no

15

reason for it, not even just to thwart Joss Foxley. It was merely instinctive, that this garden was going to be *ours*, a *new* Fontenay tradition.

He tried hard to persuade me. The muscles in that square jaw were working hard as he surrendered. 'I'll replant them somewhere else. Maybe by the castle.'

What the hell was the matter with me? I wondered afterwards. Usually I was a reasonable person. Perhaps even then the symbolic figure of Danger in Chaucer's Garden was laughing at my side.

I stayed away after that, until one day when I knew Joss Foxley would not be there. I had to see what he'd done with the roses.

The sunken garden was almost clear. I still called it that, clinging to my belief that it was going to be a spring garden. Only a small patch remained – but on it were those two roses. Cleared of the brambles, they seemed almost to be smirking at me.

'See,' they said, 'how glorious we look, spreading our tentacles out wherever we like. This is *our* garden, not yours.'

We'd see about that, I decided.

I felt almost sick, however, wondering what I was going to do. There would be another clash of wills coming, and I didn't want that. Fontenay had – until the bomb – been a place of quiet and beauty. There shouldn't be rows in it now, for it seemed disloyal to David.

The next day, I was talking to the builders in the barn when Joss Foxley came in. He had the grace to wait until the builder had finished talking and gone back to work, but I sensed it came hard.

'I've almost finished clearing the sunken garden, Anna,' he said.

'And those two roses have gone?' I asked, pretending I was busy with choosing stain colours.

'Yes – and no.'

I glanced at Joss for the first time, and was startled to see he was very pale. I'd never seen him look shaken before.

'What's wrong?'

'There's a skeleton buried between them.'

Two

T he thorn in the rose, was my first thought, after I recovered from my instinctive revulsion. There had to be one. One of my earliest memories was of standing in our pocket-sized garden staring at my finger, pricked by a rose thorn. A drop of blood, perfectly rounded, adorned my pudgy finger. My mother loomed above me, exclaiming at this calamity, urging me to suck it quickly.

'Why?' I had enquired.

'It could be dangerous.'

It left its impression on me; the beauty of a rose carried a dark, inexplicable threat. I used to listen to David's raptures about the Fontenay rose garden but, though I did my best, could never share them. Perhaps that was why I was here now.

David was only ten when he left Fontenay, but the impressionable years of his childhood had done their work and established Fontenay in his eyes as his Shangri-La. I had my doubts. His father was often ill, I gathered, and had an irrational temper. His widow Deborah, my mother-in-law, lives in America; she's still alive. I like Deborah. She married again after John Fontenay's death in 1965, went to live in the wilds of Alaska, and was widowed again. After that she opted for Washington, which made communication seem easier.

As an only child, David must have spent many hours alone in the grounds of Fontenay and this, fused with the normal rose-tinted glasses looking back on one's youth, made his passion for it understandable. So, too, was his desire that Gerard should live there, *before* the time comes for him to inherit it.

I was wrong, of course; this skeleton wasn't the first

thorn. It was the second. The first was with me right now, waiting.

'I'll call the police,' I said to Joss. 'Are you sure it's human?'

'What I can see looks that way. Shall I show you?'

'I'll wait for the law.' Anything to delay coming face to face with the unexpected in that garden of horror.

I made some coffee, and sat in silence with Joss. I belatedly realized he'd called me Anna. It must have slipped out under stress, but it suggested that's how he thought of me. I mentally shrugged it off. There were more important things, and to address him continually as Mr Foxley was becoming wearisome.

'Sugar, Joss?'

'No thanks.'

Four words and a relationship can move on. Not very far, it was true, but they indicated that there was something in common between us, in that we acknowledged a need to deal with this problem together. I suspected, however, that it affected us in different ways: Joss would see it as an interruption to his plans for the sunken garden, whereas I saw it as an excuse to insist on my own plan. How could a rose garden be planted where death had taken place, I could hear myself arguing? Roses were for love, weren't they? And for graves, an insidious whisper reminded me.

I pondered whether to ring Hugo. He would be good ballast against Joss, but why should I need it? In the end I did ring him, and he was surprisingly eager to join the party. When the police arrived, there were only two of them – the advance guard, they informed me, to judge whether the whole CID and coroner's team would be needed.

We picked our way through to the sunken garden. Strange how death, even of an unknown person, can affect one. I felt as if I was in a sheriff's posse as we marched in phalanx along the path. Lightheartedness passed as we reached the garden. One of the rose bushes had tumbled where Joss had unearthed it. The other was still standing, perched on the side of the hole. He had obviously had trouble in getting the roots out, for a pile of brick rubble and large stones lay on the ground too.

'I saw the arm sticking out,' Joss told the police. 'I –' he steadied himself – 'wasn't quite sure – it might have just been an animal bone, so I scraped away a bit more.'

We all stared – even me – at the half-exposed skeleton. It was crushed, with bits missing, and what looked like remnants of rotted clothes.

'A flying bomb casualty.' Hugo put a casual arm round me, and I was grateful.

'Odd it wasn't found at the time.' I spoke for the sake of it. The human voice reassures one that one is not alone.

'Underneath too much rubble probably. The bomb must have made a hell of a mess. Or maybe it threw up a skeleton from much earlier.'

We were just talking for the sake of it. At least, Hugo and I were. Joss was silent. I could hardly bear to look at him. He looked shattered, as though he, too, was having to come to terms with this intrusion into his dream of a garden. I am present even in Arcadia, as Death says in the mediaeval Latin tag.

The whole team *was* necessary, and yellow tapes had barred us from the site for several days before it was ours again. The roses had disappeared, and soil had been bagged up, together with every scrap of anything that wasn't earth or stone. Joss supplied sketches of how the stones had been laid, and the skeleton itself was of course removed for its post mortem. Meanwhile we waited in limbo. Joss obviously didn't want to work on the sunken garden yet, for I kept seeing him outside Fontenay Place, where he was to restore the parterre formal gardens. This led to the first overt dispute between him and Hugo.

The cause was nothing major; such things never are, they are the result of a pot finally coming to the boil. It stopped me in my tracks when I walked into the middle of it by mistake, I'd never seen Hugo really upset before. All because of a sundial. I was made to listen to both sides of the argument, which boiled down to having the usual stone sundial (Hugo) or the correct historical living sundial laid out in small bushes (Joss). I pretended to take it seriously, but I couldn't get that skeleton out of my mind. Reason told me I was being stupid, so I forced myself to give it thought. The restoration here was a big job because half a century later the formal gardens had been swept away by the landscape school, in order to provide sweeping views over meadow, wood and water. To restore it to the gardens designed when the house was built was a bold plan, but on the whole I approved. And with it went the living sundial.

Slightly to my annoyance, Joss didn't even seem grateful for my support. I suppose when someone considers so strongly that they are always in the right, they automatically assume others will agree with them and see no need for gratitude.

Two weeks after their first visit, the police called again to give me the news. The bones were those of a woman aged about thirty; she had been in the ground long enough to be consistent with her having been a victim of the flying bomb incident, but not long enough for there to be no need for the coroner. The bones had been crushed by rubble to a point where the cause of death was not possible to determine, but could now be buried. An open verdict meant an open police file however – temporarily at least. They questioned me about the flying bomb, but I could tell them nothing. David was not born until 1950, and apart from telling me the reason for the sunken garden, knew nothing about it. Nor would Deborah who married David's father after the war was over. I said I'd ring her, and I did give her a quick call but, perturbed though she was, she could tell me nothing.

Hugo nobly agreed to pay for the burial of the bones, and we had a brief, but moving, ceremony for this unknown woman. It was a closure for me, the land was ours again. Or so I thought. Perhaps even then I was deliberately blanking out the truth, for this woman must have had something to do with the Fontenay estate. I shut my mind to it. I had enough on my plate sorting out the future, without taking on the past as well. I gave the news to Joss and Hugo and prepared to get back to my tea-rooms.

I didn't see Joss again for some days, and it finally occurred to me he was deliberately keeping out of my way. Why? Apart from the question of the sunken garden, we had jogged along reasonably well over plans for the grounds, sometimes agreeing, sometimes disagreeing, sometimes agreeing to disagree. Time was passing, though. August had just arrived, and finally I decided I had to seek him out. Gerard would shortly be marching back to spend a few weeks before going up to university, and I wanted some quality time with him, not to be rushing around the gardens.

Joss didn't carry a mobile, and nor did I, so I couldn't track him down that way. I had to bury my pride and wait for him at the main gates one day. Even he couldn't just drive past me.

'How's the sunken garden going?' I asked brightly, as he jumped down from his Land Rover.

'I'm too busy to get round to it yet.'

'Come off it,' I said amiably. 'The truth please. Has what's happened turned you off the idea? You've come round to my way of thinking?'

'Not exactly.' He hesitated. 'In fact, I'm even keener on the idea. It only needs a little more work to be ready for adding topsoil and planting.'

'Bulbs. And for the spring garden, it remains sunken.'

'Roses. They'd have to be in by November to give them the winter to settle down. That's not a lot of time if we have to design the garden, choose the plants, and get them delivered.'

'Bulbs,' I repeated even more firmly, fighting back an irrational panic that I was losing ground. Then I relented. 'What's holding you up, Joss?'

He shot a glance at me. 'I can't plant roses over a mystery. It would be at odds with what the garden was created for. There are ghosts there, Anna, and they have to be laid to rest. Are you trying to find out whose the skeleton was?'

'That's the police's job,' I said defensively. Ghosts? I couldn't pretend I didn't know what he meant. 'Do you mean if you can't plant roses, you'll make it a spring garden?'

'No. I mean I want to find out so that I *could* create the rose garden. At least then we could have a fair fight – your way or mine. This way it's unfinished business.' Then he shot the arrow. 'I get the impression you don't much like roses.'

I fired up. 'Just because I don't agree with you—'

'It's not that. You don't like them, full stop.'

Well, why not tell him? 'You're right, I don't. I take it you do?'

'Yes. They're survivors. They go back millions of years, and they're still here, ruling the roost.'

Not, I thought, in my backyard. What I *said*, however, was, 'Okay. I'll make enquiries about the skeleton.'

I had no real intention of doing so. I'd pay lip service to it, of course. I needed to concentrate on having some sort of gardens that I could open to the public for next season. They wouldn't be finished, nothing like it, but there would at least be flowers round the castle ruins, and other gardens in progress.

'I already have made enquiries.'

Taken aback, I was about to hurl 'Mind your own business' at him, but held it back. It was his business as much as mine, if I were to respect the fact that I was dealing with a gardener and not an odd-job man.

All the same, I couldn't resist muttering, 'You should have told me.'

'I am telling you. There's an old chap in one of the almshouses in Cranden who was an under-gardener here in the Second World War. I thought you might like to meet him.'

'Have you?'

'Not yet.' He grinned as he saw my suspicious expression. 'I play fair, Anna. Do you?'

Joe Hendricks was in good shape for a man in his early eighties. He might be in an almshouse but he was spry enough to be looking after its gardens very effectively, and that's where we found him. Cranden is only a mile or two away from Fontenay, and the fortunes of the village had once depended heavily on the estate. No longer – though if my plans worked, the tourist trade would most certainly increase.

'August,' Joe remarked with disgust, looking at the greenery around him. 'The waiting month, I call it. Autumn flowers aren't out, summer ones gone. Come along my lovely,' he addressed a yellow rose bush. 'You're supposed to be blooming, continuous flowering, remember? Time to get moving. I'll be giving you a helping of potash tonight for supper. And some nice water, too. There –' he turned to us with satisfaction – 'that'll do the trick. Now what can I do for you two? Fontenays, are you?'

'I am by marriage,' I said. 'This is Joss Foxley, he's restoring the grounds. My husband was John Fontenay's son, David. Do you remember him?'

'Course I do. Fine lad, he was. Broke his heart to leave Fontenay, I reckon. Still, children that age recover, don't they?'

Not always, I thought. There can be an unhealed wound, papered over with time. Had David had one? I had never sensed it, but perhaps his insistence that I should fulfil his dream of living at Fontenay again was a balm to such a wound.

'And I remember him when he used to come on visits. Mind you, I've been retired nearly twenty years.'

'Then you stayed on when the Fontenays left?'

'I did. Tim Parsons, my gaffer, he was head gardener here, he retired. I took over his job. Wasn't the same when that school was here. No feeling for the place. Just chop it down or stick that in, and mow the lawns. And the kids! Like they pick the wings off flies, they did with my trees, hanging on them, tearing off the branches, never thinking of the harm it does.'

'You heard about the skeleton?' Joss said.

'Whole village heard about it.'

'We're trying to find out whose it is.'

Joe took a careful look at him. 'What's the interest in skeletons for you then, mister? Mrs Fontenay's, I understand.'

'It was in my garden,' he replied simply.

I didn't interrupt. I wanted to play fair. If Joss saw it as his garden, I could live with that – up to a point.

'Ah now. In the old rose garden, they said.' They shared a look which I – correctly, I'm sure – interpreted as gardeners bonding.

'The sunken garden,' I corrected resignedly.

'Names remain as you meet 'em,' Joe informed me. 'I was Joey when I was growing up, so though all the world and his wife call me Joe now, inside me I'm still Joey. See?'

I saw. 'The rose garden,' I agreed. For today, I mentally added.

'What do you want to know then? Who this skeleton

was? If so, reckon I can take a good guess. It was Mrs Jennifer.'

'Who was she?' I asked blankly.

'Mr John's first wife.'

I hate being caught on the hop and this was a corker. 'I didn't know he had one.'

'Oh yes. He didn't marry Mrs Deborah till after the war, forty-seven if memory serves me correct.'

'But David never mentioned her.' I still couldn't believe it. Nor had Deborah ever breathed a word about it.

'Perhaps he never knew. Mr John didn't talk about her after she'd gone, and Mr David was only a kid when he left Fontenay.'

'But my husband was so keen on family history, so he'd know. There'd be wedding certificates, it must have come up.' I floundered helplessly, a beached whale from the one sea I thought I knew – David.

'Perhaps he did know, perhaps he didn't.' Joe looked at me sympathetically. 'About this time,' he said carefully, 'I usually fancies a pint in the Crown.'

We took the hint and escorted him to the local pub, finding a quiet corner in the garden. He had suggested this to give me time to recover, and I appreciated it. Joe looked at the garden scathingly. 'Look at them gaillardias there. Crying out for sun and they plant them where they only sees it maybe an hour a day. And that poor hosta, scorching to death poor thing.'

'Tell me about Jennifer,' I demanded, as soon as the beer began to slide down his throat.

'Mrs Jennifer loved that garden, she loved all the grounds, but she was specially interested in roses. Mr John didn't care for it, so he left it to her. It was like her baby, having no children.'

So at least David didn't have a brood of half-brothers or sisters. That was some relief.

'My gaffer and she,' he continued, 'spent a lot of time there. "That Clarence Goodacre has had its day," she'd say. "It's too old to bear. Needs replacing." Or, "You can't do that, Tim. That's Emily Fontenay. Died at 18 she did." Course, I didn't understand then, thought she was off her head, but Tim did.

There was a lot of roses past their time then, some of them planted in the First War like Mr Percy.'

'A rose for every Fontenay that dies,' Joss said.

I blanched. He had done his homework. I didn't realize he knew that tradition. I thought only the Fontenay family did. To the outside world it was just a rose garden, no plaques, no nothing. Just a garden. How did he find out, I wondered.

'And more during that war,' Joe added. 'Tim told me Mr John's father had a rose planted for them as worked here, and that was a lot of them in those days. Rising thirty, working outside and in. All the menfolk marched off to war, and those that came back weren't in no state to work at Fontenay. A lot of roses planted then there were. Mr Edward, Mr John's father that is, insisted they were planted, though the men weren't no Fontenays. "All part of the family in war," he said. And then comes the next war, and more folk dying. The doodlebug put paid to roses for them, though.'

'So what happened when a rose tree died?' I asked hastily, seeing him wrapped up in some private sad memory.

'Mrs Jennifer would say whether it should be replaced after the soil recovered. Tim Parsons said that old Mrs Fontenay before her – Mrs Jennifer were only here eight years or so – said she'd leave it all to him, but you couldn't do that with Mrs Jennifer. Nice about it, and she knew her roses, so Tim went along with it.'

'Was the garden full then?' I decided to let him ramble on. It was the best way of seeing the whole picture.

'There were roses everywhere, standards, rambling, climbing, bushes, shrubs, miniatures, oh it were a sight. And in the middle always a red shrub rose, and a white one not far away. That never changed. Whenever a Fontenay died, the close family that is, they had a planting ceremony and another if a dying one were taken out for good. Some roses seem to live for ever, others die at twenty. Like folks, I reckon.'

'What happened on the night of the flying bomb? Were you there?' I asked, anxious to get away from roses.

'No. It were my afternoon off, it was. One of the other under-gardeners, George Timms, he died there. They found his body though. The bomb shook the village. My home then was a cottage at the back of the estate. Sold off, now they are. Alice – she was the wife – and I heard the doodlebug cut out overhead. "See you at the pearly gates, Alice," I roared out, pushing her under the table. No time to get to the shelter. The whole house shook, but we were okay. "Reckon that's the house gone, or the old castle," I says. I went up to have a look to see if I could help, but they said it missed the house. Only the rose garden copped it, so I went home. They didn't know about George then. They found him after I'd gone. I felt bad about that. It was like abandoning him. There was no damage to the house or the lodge, a few more walls of the old castle tumbled, but the crater was dead in the centre of the rose garden. You'd think old Hitler planned it that way, jealous of our having a bit of loveliness around. Huge crater it was, bigger than you'd think, because it's all grown over and some of the loose rubble and earth shifted down the sides.

'Tim called me that evening. "Joe," he said, "bad news for you. Young George has had it." I wanted to have a go at Hitler myself, for his sake, but they wouldn't have me in the army. I've got this leg shorter than the other, see? I've gardened with it all my life, but that wasn't good enough for the army. "You stay where you are, Joe. There's work enough at Fontenay." And there was. Most of the blooming grounds were dug up for cultivation, only the bit round the castle left and the rose garden. I became Farmer Joe and the gaffer with me – when he wasn't on fire-watching duties. I was in the Home Guard,' he added without enthusiasm. 'Any German who came near me could be attacked with my broom handle.'

We dutifully laughed. 'And what about Jennifer?' I asked again. 'Why wasn't her body found? Didn't anyone realize she was missing?'

'No one knew she was there. Not even Mr John. She'd gone to visit her sister near Sevenoaks that day, so he didn't worry when the doodlebug fell here. Then when he heard about the doodlebug where her sister lived, he rang up. When he managed to get through, he was told she left just before the bomb fell, so he realized she might have been caught. Quite a number were killed and very messy it was. The air raid wardens assumed she was one of them. Far as I know they never thought of looking in *our* rose garden. What would she be doing there anyway late in the evening, and what would have killed her? I reckon she must have heard about the buzz bomb here, gone straight to her beloved garden, and been killed by a falling rock or summat. The Hermit's Retreat falling in, most like. Pity to think of her lying there all that time. I liked Mrs Jennifer.'

'It might not be her of course.' There was a gentle note in Joss's voice I hadn't heard before.

'No one else missing? None of the indoor servants?' I asked.

'Servants? Didn't have none, not in wartime. There was Polly Pink, but she was too old to count as a servant, and she's long since gone to the great kitchen in the sky, so you can't go bribing her with drink.' Joe held up his empty glass triumphantly, and Joss and I both moved to oblige. I won.

'Why didn't you tell me?' Hugh said indignantly, when I casually mentioned our visit that evening. He'd invited me to dinner in Fontenay Place to discuss the tea-rooms and how this might fit in with the conference centre. Fontenay did possess at one time one of the very earliest dining rooms in an English country house, but this was not it. The modern dining room is the old withdrawing room, and the original room is now the bar. A pity because it has a pleasant informality about it, that the current dining room lacks. It's not Hugo's fault, merely the demands of a modern conference centre, and each step was thrashed out with David first.

I took a leaf out of Joss's book, when I replied to Hugo's question. 'I'm telling you now.'

'Rather late. Just because I rent the house and not the grounds, it doesn't mean I'm not interested. I know this house and grounds inside out, so skeletons in the garden are in *my* closet too. I paid for the burial.'

'Come on, Hugo, be reasonable.' I was taken aback at how ratty he was. His face was quite flushed. 'We can't go dancing down every path in a threesome like *The Wizard of Oz*.'

He must have seen me looking at him oddly, for he managed a grin. 'No. I'm just being a spoilt child left out of an interesting party. Tell me all about this Jennifer.'

27

I related to him what I had told the police that afternoon, and he listened, frowning.

'Odd that David didn't know about Jennifer. He never mentioned her to me either, and it would surely have come up in conversation sometime, since we used to talk a lot about the house. After all, he'd lived in it as a child until he was ten. There must have been some record of her existence there if they were married for eight years.'

'Not necessarily. We're not talking seventeenth-century, but thirties Britain. Unless you decided to be very grand and have a portrait painted, there would only be the odd photograph to record your presence. The Fontenays weren't into keeping up with the aristos by that time.'

Some of the family pictures still hang at Fontenay Place. When the family left and the school took over, the paintings and good furniture were taken away into storage by John and Deborah, and only a few were taken out by David and myself. When Hugo moved in he asked if he could have them and any other Fontenay memorabilia back in the house if he paid the insurance, and a nominal rent for them. 'For atmosphere,' he'd explained. 'It gives my conference parties a secure feeling.' I think he genuinely likes them around too, for he has a feeling for history. None of the paintings are by great names, but most of them have some interest. There are one or two Elizabethan miniatures, an early Gainsborough and some Gainsborough and Reynolds lookalikes, the stately gloominess of Victorian portraits, and a couple of Edwardian offerings with distinct twinkles in their eyes. David kept back one photograph album, but I'd seen that, and there was no photograph of Jennifer. Of that I was sure.

'Keep me in touch, Anna.'

Hugo spoke carelessly, but he laid his hand over mine on the table to emphasize the point. At least I presume that was the reason. For a fleeting moment I wondered what it would be like to be in bed with Hugo, and found the idea rather appealing. David's debilitating gastric trouble, which finally turned out to be cancer, had meant that our sex life had been patchy, to say the least, in the few years before he died. My body had gone to sleep, where it still remained. I was not quite forty, however, and I was beginning to be aware that sooner or later it would either have to be awoken or would awaken itself. I hastily put that thought to one side. There was too much work to be done first, and I didn't want emotions getting in the way, not sexual ones anyway. I had more than enough to do with gardening passions to welcome any others.

'Of course.' Guiltily I was aware that I was not going to play fair by him, just as I wasn't with Joss. I had something I wanted to follow up first. How had Joss known about the Fontenay traditions? I supposed, on reflection, there must be books that referred to them, but he would have to have made a positive bid to track them down. Why should he? Why not, I answered myself, not altogether satisfactorily.

I had promised to report to Joss on the police's reactions to my telling them of Jennifer, however, so it slipped in quite naturally, and I received a quite natural answer.

'I found references to it in the archives. I told you I'd been there. The Fontenays are a large family, there were servants and gardeners – they all knew about it.' Then he added a rider, the one thing I thought I *could* keep to myself. 'Do you have *The Book of Gertrude's Garden*?'

'No,' I said too quickly, so he knew I lied. I took a deep breath. 'Well, I do, but—'

'I want to see it.'

He assumed I played fair, but I didn't. I hadn't even played fair with myself, and now it was crunch time. I stalled. I wasn't ready for this.

'I'll make a bargain with you.'

'Another?'

'Yes.' My face felt bright red, a sure sign that I was on dicey ground. 'We must soon decide about the garden. If, and only if, you have your way to restore the rose garden, I'll show you the book. *That's* fair, isn't it?

He didn't answer. Or rather he did, but the reply didn't seem relevant. 'Has Hugo Brooks seen it?'

No one had seen it. Not even me after the first time that David showed it to me. It had come with me, part of the family collection that meant so much to him, and it was tucked away inconspicuously amongst books of Redouté rose paintings, family albums of one sort or another, and books of splendid bindings but dull contents.

I went home to the lodge, had a shot of whisky to give me strength, and went to the chest where they now lived. I had to face it sometime, even if I finally decided against the rose garden, otherwise I would feel I was betraying David. Even had I been a rose lover, it would have been a difficult task. My ghosts were just as real as Joss's, even if they were different to his. The future was where I wanted to live, and there are no ghosts there.

I took the book, enclosed in its safety metal box, and opened it. I felt slightly sick, and it had nothing to do with the whisky. I stared down at the first recto with *The Book of Gertrude's Garden* inscribed in beautiful calligraphy, surrounded by small pictures of the garden, like the illustrations in Chaucer's *The Romaunt of the Rose*, and on the page facing it a small, lovingly detailed illustration of a red rose. Underneath it were two lines from the Chaucer poem.

So was I full of joy and blisse
It is faire such a floure to kisse.

The first entry page was also ornamented and gave the barest details of Gertrude's life, followed by the words 'Deare Rose'. Opposite, was a full page illustration of a pale red damask rose. I'd seen such a rose recently. It was one of the pair that had survived in the sunken garden. One of those that had guarded the skeleton.

On following pages came all the succeeding Fontenays, headed by Sir Edmund, their names, their deaths, their relationship to the family, and a whole paragraph about each of their lives. I could not bear to look in more detail at the book. I repeated to myself that I wasn't ready for it, and it was true. First must come the question of the rose garden itself. Had the skeleton swayed my feelings one way or the other? Time was running out, for Joss, encouraged by my temporizing, declared he would return to the garden tomorrow. In a few days I must take my decision.

Regardless of what that decision was, one day I should show Gertrude's book to Joss, and perhaps even to Hugo. And one day I must pass it over to Gerard.

But even the book did not play fair. There was no mention of the Sinclairs.

1943

'I can't think why you don't like coming here, John.' Jennifer finished deadheading the Mrs John Laing Hybrid Perpetual planted for her late mother-in-law, Adelaide. It was July now, but there would be bloom until autumn. Then would come the barren twigs of winter before it burst into green growth once more. Couldn't John see there was beauty in the bare twigs, that expectation was as important as blossom? That the perfume from this rose would last in the nostrils until spring came again?

'There's a war on, Jen,' he grunted. 'Roses are not relevant. Crops and food are.'

'But so are roses, John. They're relevant to your family. And after all, our baby is recorded here.' She glanced painfully at the pinky-mauve *Rosa Mundi gallica*, for the child that was stillborn, who could never wander through this garden as did she. To Jennifer, the baby was always Rosamund, the rose of the world, who lived forever within her heart.

His face went black. 'That's why, Jen,' he said savagely. 'I can't bear the place. If only you'd conceive again, if we had a living child, it would be different. If I had my way, I'd dig the whole garden up. But I can't do it alone without Parsons, and he's dead against it, so I'll have to lump it. But don't ask me to enjoy it.'

Jennifer realized she'd gone too far and John was well on the way to one of his tempers. She hastened to smooth things over. 'I'll make some rose petal jam. You like that.'

'Yes,' he added, grinning because she'd won the round after

all. 'By the way,' he added, 'I've invited someone to dinner tonight.'

'I hope he's bringing his coupons,' she replied blithely. 'Who is it?'

'A chap called Michael Sinclair.'

'Sinclair?' she repeated incredulously. 'I thought you told me that the Fontenays had some kind of long-running feud with the Sinclairs – or isn't he from the same family? I know it's a common enough name.'

'I've no idea. Anyway, that story's rubbish.' Slow anger took hold of him again. 'We're living in the twentieth century now, not feudal times. He's in the RAF, day fighter squadron, just flown in to West Malling.'

John walked out of the garden, but she remained. Here was peace, here was one place from which the glory had not yet departed. She guessed why this man was coming. John was too old at forty-five to be in the army, and compensated for it by entertaining all the servicemen he ran into. This one would be no different, even if he was a Sinclair, and even if he were one of *those* Sinclairs. John was an odd mixture. He acted as though the Fontenay traditions meant nothing to him, and yet sometimes she suspected that he was as firmly entrenched in them as his father.

She decided to gather the first of the beans for tonight, but still she lingered for a few more minutes. This garden would survive the war. She knew it would. It had survived the Battle of Britain and so it would survive anything that Hitler might throw at it. It might not be her family recorded here, but she had made the roses her own, and from them drew her strength to carry on. Roses were survivors.

Three

The Sinclairs had been at the heart of my doubts when David had given such a glow to the Fontenay family history; they were the thorn of the rose. He had happily told me about the feud between the two families, but didn't seem to think this conflicted with the nostalgic image he presented of his heritage. For a start, some of the anecdotes he told me made his forebears sound half-mad, though admittedly time might have embellished them in the retelling.

I suppose, looked at from the grand omnipotence of the twenty-first century, a feud in itself has a romantic air; it is something of which costume films can be made, something that suggests cardboard emotions played out through dagger and duel, not a reality that affects the lives of the real people involved.

What had sparked it off in the first place? Sinclair was originally a Scottish name, but it has spread much further afield, and so far as I knew the Fontenays had no connection with Scotland. Probably, I had laughed with David, the feud had been ignited by something really important like a border post moved half an inch, rather than a clandestine love affair.

David couldn't answer me; it had been his father who used to talk broodingly of the Sinclairs and how no good ever came of letting a Sinclair into the house. To listen to him, David said, you would have thought they laid siege to Fontenay for hundreds of years, ravishing daughters, slaying sons and stealing the family silver. In fact, he had since discovered, the historical record only revealed three conflicts – admittedly, what one could term major. Firstly they claimed Fontenay land was originally theirs, and secondly it was the Sinclairs who made it their business to burn the castle down in 1648. It was an own goal, since the Fontenays were dispossessed and the Sinclairs given the devastated land as a reward. By the time they'd made it presentable again, the Fontenays were back in possession. The third conflict I couldn't remember, which annoyed me since I seemed to recall it was the most interesting.

Written records seldom talk of feuds; they deal with laundry bills, of sacking butlers for incompetence, of the servant shortage problem, of births, of deaths – but not of things that a family takes for granted as shared knowledge. I suppose that the Sinclair feud – if one indeed existed as a continuous threat – would come under that heading.

'What did your father say about the Sinclairs?' I had asked curiously. 'He must have indicated the kind of menace they still presented, if any.'

David had frowned. 'He died in 1965 so I was only fifteen. It's not that I don't remember what he said, but it didn't make sense so I can't bring it to mind just like that. It'll come back to me.'

It did, in the middle of one night, when he kindly shook me awake. 'I've got it,' he announced. 'I knew it didn't make sense. There was a lot of stuff which I dismissed as boring history, and he finished up with: The Sinclairs are the pestilence that walketh in darkness, the terror by night.'

'One of the Psalms. Very lucid,' I murmured.

'I asked what he meant,' David continued. Having got David going on something, I could never stop him until he'd finished. And that could take some time. It looked as though the Sinclairs were going to run and run. 'So far as I recall, apart from the major blips, he said he'd heard some story about the Sinclairs and the Fontenays fighting over some woman, and presumed that was the pestilence meant. After that, he only railed in general terms.'

'That seems likely.' David's father came from an age when sexual entanglements were not referred to in explicit terms, particularly to a child of David's age.

Just thinking of David now brought a hard lump to my throat. I haven't said much about David, simply because I was trying so hard to make that fresh start. But I missed him greatly. I loved him, you see, and loving through those years of illness steeled me not to agonize with him, but to cope for him. At times such as this, however, I wanted his strength at my side, not to lean on, but to be aware of his presence, to know that together we could face the dragons of life by spitting fire back at them.

I sat in the window of the lodge two days later looking at the badly tarmacked lane that led to the present main Fontenay drive. The entrance guarded by the lodge was rarely used now, and then only for private use, or deliveries. The lane was pitted with holes from last winter's frosts, for there was no money to pay for its upkeep. Hugo had said he'd do it, but I refused. This was my responsibility. Everything, it seemed, was my responsibility, just as I'd wanted. Mine to keep the house in the family, mine to care for the whole Fontenay estate for Gerard, if he should want it, mine to bear the duty I owed to heritage – and mine to make the decision about the sunken garden today.

I was going to say no. I needed to build on the past, not recreate it. You might think this sits at odds with what I have just said about a duty to heritage, but to me it does not. A sterile replica of what has gone would achieve less than a loving contribution to the overall history of Fontenay. History does not stand still, today is tomorrow's history. The skeleton had made up my mind for me. The flying bomb with that pitiful human relic had put paid to one era, but my spring garden would start a new one. A resurrection of life where death had struck so terribly.

I dreaded telling Joss what I'd decided, yet we had made a bargain. Would he leave? I hoped not, because Fontenay needed him. That had to be his hard choice to make, as I had made mine.

I had even dreaded telling Hugo, since he too favoured the rose garden reconstruction – though perhaps he was thinking of its appeal to conference delegates rather than heritage.

'You could have a spring garden nearer the house,' he had pointed out. I'd asked him to dinner last night feeling it only fair to break the news to him first. We had been sitting in the

35

garden on one of those rare summer evenings when the heat of the day graciously lingers till nightfall. 'Why does it have to be where the rose garden was?'

'I don't know,' I answered honestly. 'In my mind's eye, though, I see that great hole of nothing covered with bulbs, violets, primroses. It will look lovely. A rose garden would mean filling the crater in.'

'Not necessarily. It could be stepped. But being so near the river, a spring wild garden would surely look unnatural. It's too small to appear a natural valley.'

He had a point, and I considered it, partly because he was easier to argue with than Joss. 'Then we'll make the hole bigger.'

'Stubborn, aren't you?'

'Why shouldn't I be?'

'You never were with David.'

'When you see a couple, you don't judge either of them as individuals, only as their working partnership suggests, consciously or unconsciously. Wearing your company hat, Hugo, even you're speaking for two, not one.'

'Very profound. Have you told our Mr Foxley yet?'

'No. I said I'd look at the site with him and I will. But nothing can change my mind now.'

'He'll try. He won't want to leave this cushy job.'

'If it comes to his walking out, I'll have to live with it. There are other gardeners.' I spoke more bravely than I felt.

'I won't be sorry, even if it does mean we lose the rose garden.'

I looked at him in surprise. 'I know you don't get along too well with him, but even you admit he's a brilliant designer and gardener.'

'He's a creep.' He laughed when he saw my astonished face. 'I don't mean a wimp, just that there's something odd about him. If this were a century ago, I'd say he wasn't one of us.'

'I'm sure he knows which knife and spoon to use.' I spoke rather coolly, defensive of Joss, because of this weird remark.

'That's not what I mean and you know it. His face doesn't fit, that's all.'

Joss wasn't of Hugo's world, that was true. I considered this as I dished up the lasagne and salad. I wasn't either, so was there any more to Hugo's dislike other than Joss's extraordinary self-containment? I had, now I came to think of it, little idea about Joss Foxley the man, because it wasn't relevant. Was he married? Was he gay? No, that I was sure about. What was his background? I had a vague recollection of a CV he gave me; it looked standard, university horticulture degree, diplomas in this and that, all essential pieces of paper nowadays. Joe Hendricks wouldn't approve of that, for bits of paper told you something, yet nothing. And the nothing tended to be the crucial part.

'My lease comes up for renewal next year, Anna.'

'Why was Hugo dropping that into the conversation? Instantly I wondered whether this was leading to something specific.

'You'll renew, I hope,' I said politely, though I most certainly meant it.

'Yes. I'm sure you'll be a tough negotiator, but you'd have a hard job shifting me. Or do I deal with Master Gerard?'

'With me,' I said shortly. Gerald had told me he didn't need to be consulted until and unless he had to be. So far as he was concerned, Fontenay was mine completely, not just legally. Sometimes my son is remarkably sensible. It's so easy to slip one's head in a noose to see what it feels like.

'Do you know Cranhurst Court?' Hugo asked.

'Where Joss restored the gardens? Yes, I've been there.'

'One of my conference delegates runs a local charity and offered me tickets for an opera in the grounds next week. Like to come? It's *Cosi fan Tutte*. One of those picnics in the interval events.'

'In the rain?'

'That's part of the fun.'

'Yes, I'd like to. Thanks. I'll bring the picnic.' I like to have a stake in such circumstances. It was the first time Hugo had invited me in the evening, apart from the odd business dinner, and I always play cautious.

'I'll warn you, there's a snag. The charity is looking for

37

fresh venues for the opera for next year. Do you think Fontenay could be ready?'

'Damn you,' I said amiably. 'I'll think about it. What about acoustics, size, stage, bushes for hiding entrances – all the paraphernalia?'

'I'll help with that.'

'Done,' I promptly agreed, blithely ignoring the fact that a year was very little time to create a paradise out of chaos – especially if I had no gardener. Then, 'Hugo, did David ever talk to you about the Sinclairs – or is there anything in the house about them?'

'Not the famous feud? I know about it, I can't think why. Perhaps David told me, or I heard some other way. Why do you want to know?'

'Tomorrow I'm going to have to tell Joss he's not getting his rose garden. I wanted to know whether the Sinclair feud was a modern one, or merely an ancient legend.'

'You're not making sense, luvvy. What does that have to do with our Mr Foxley or with the rose garden?'

'I suppose I'm still thinking about that skeleton. If the feud continued up to modern times, I wonder if it could account for David's father being so reticent about his first wife.'

'I've no idea, but I have the impression it went back a long way. I'll check the inventory again – I expect you have a copy of that anyway. Maybe a Sinclair portrait has popped in, but I wouldn't think it likely.'

Looking back on last evening, I felt now as if I were lumbering around in one of those fogs so beloved of filmmakers of Victorian London. I had to haul myself speedily out of it, for it was time to go. I picked up a sweater as the warm weather seemed to be cooling down, and set forth. Hugo had wanted to come, but I wouldn't let him. He'd be siding with Joss and two against one would be twice as hard to combat.

As I walked over the bridge over the river, I noted it was getting rickety. I'd have to talk to Joss, I thought automatically – then I realized that there probably wouldn't be a Joss after today. Never mind, I told myself. Stick to your path and it'll land up somewhere. It sure did.

Gardener Joe was both right and wrong about August.

Garden flowers were in a lull but there were plenty of wild flowers in our open meadows. Bindweed was in full flower, Rose-bay Willow-herb stuck proudly up, pink and glorious to the view, and daring anyone to call it a weed. And here was I on my way to ring the death knell for the rose garden. I just about managed to convince myself that it was a rational decision.

As I approached, I saw the walls were inching upwards. They weren't just piles of stone and brick anymore, but had been relaid to my dismay. My spring garden wouldn't need high walls or hedges, it would be open. Wordsworth didn't have to walk through a gate to admire his daffodils. This was Joss's doing, I realized, suddenly angry. He was inching those walls upwards, so sure was he that I would relent, and he'd get his way. That did it. I was now distinctly bloody-minded.

I could see Joss there already, arms crossed staring into the sunken part of the garden, back to me. That back looked proprietorial.

'Joss,' I called, gearing myself for battle.

He turned, but then I saw that he was not alone. A girl of perhaps eighteen, who had been hidden from me as she had been sitting on the ground by one of the walls, scrambled to her feet. Like me she was jeans-clad and t-shirted, and she gave me the quick appraising look of one assessing the likelihood of competition. Presumably sexual competition in this case since she must know who I was. She was attractive in a way, with blondish hair hanging down to her shoulders, but she was no picture postcard otherwise; she was dressed, as I was, for work, even if she were his girlfriend.

The point was quickly settled.

'This is Sarah Dodds, Mrs Fontenay. She's doing casual labour here.' Joss had several helpers, but this one was new to me.

The girl smiled – at least her mouth did, for the gesture didn't reach her eyes – obviously having sized up my age and realized I could be no competition. 'During the holidays, Mrs Fontenay, before I go to college.'

'I'm glad to have you here, Sarah.'

I sounded genuinely cordial, and indeed there was no

problem – except for its timing. I expected to be alone with Joss and I wasn't. I suspected that he had brought her deliberately, though it seemed a crass move on his part, which I wouldn't have expected. Did he think I wouldn't be outspoken in front of the girl? If so he was wrong.

'Let's look at the problem then,' I said briskly. I stepped across a piece of fallen wall onto the track of trodden down weeds that Joss had left round the wall, and walked to join them. There we were lined up on that track like Hear no Evil, See no Evil, Speak no Evil looking out on the bare earth. It seemed enormous now that it was an empty canvas. I could see the crater's shape now that it was cleared of everything. No weeds, no roses save for that one yellow climber still bravely producing one or two blooms in defiance of scythe, fork and pickaxe. I wanted to tell it I had no quarrel with it. That it could stay when this was a spring garden, even turn wild to complement it, if it felt the need. But I couldn't – not with Sarah present.

While I was staring at the ground, wondering how to phrase the blow I was about to deliver, Joss took the initiative. He took my arm as well, as if to ensure my attention.

'Look,' he said, 'use your imagination, Mrs Fontenay. There at the far end, raised above the level of the rest of the garden is a bank of roses and grassy paths with an arbour covered with pink ramblers in the middle, with steps up to it. In front of it are grassy lawns, borders and beds. Nothing formal, nothing too cultivated, just a mass of cascading roses everywhere. All the old ones, the damasks, the albas, the Apothecary's Rose, the *centifolias*, and more *gallicas*, *moschatas* – the lot. Round the sides are the climbers, tea roses and noisettes, and the rose walk – a pergola of roses rambling over wooden frames, with an archway in the middle left clear – will divide the old garden from the other part.'

'What other part?'

'To carry the newer roses – comparatively. The old roses are more uniform in colour: reds, white, deep pink and mauve. This part will have a riot of China and tea roses from the eighteenth and nineteenth centuries, descendents of the famous Parsons' Pink China, Old Blush, Hume's Blush, Parks' Yellow and so on. The middle archway will be echoed by a resited main gateway arch – giving a view of the old castle, lined up with the arbour. It must surely have been planned so, originally. Oh, and the Hermit's Retreat over there—'

'Does Gertrude get a look in here?' I tried to keep a rising indignation at this hijacking of the Fontenay rose garden out of my voice. Reason told me it was illogical and I was being unfair.

Joss didn't seem to notice anything amiss. He was caught up in his own dream. 'Gertrude's rose would be the focal point of the garden, and Edmund's would be next to it.'

'What have you done with those two surviving roses in the garden. The ones –' I swallowed – 'by the skeleton?'

'They're waiting to go back in.'

'Not here,' I said immediately. 'Put them in somewhere else.' I didn't want a constant reminder of that horror. 'Plant them near the castle.' I quickly changed the subject. 'Would you want a fountain as in Chaucer's time?'

'Probably, but that's your decision. Oh, and incidentally, we'd leave room for more roses to be planted.'

'By the time I pop my clogs,' I pointed out, 'some of the ones you plan to plant would be dead.' The nervous joke gained me time to gather strength. The thought of those two roses had dispelled any lingering doubt in my mind. I wasn't going to have Gertrude's damask staring at me from my spring garden.

'It depends how far you extend the eligible family,' he replied.

'Stop, Joss,' I managed to say. I had to put an end to this – quickly. Those two roses might just grab me by the throat otherwise. Already I had an image of them triumphantly hogging centrespace again, their tendrils reaching out to suffocate me with their perfume like chloroform. 'I can see what you're planning, and it would be beautiful. But you can create most of that round the castle ruins itself. I'm sorry but you haven't changed my mind. I want this as a sunken spring garden.'

It was as if I'd hit him in the face, although he looked astounded, rather than pained by it. Slowly his hand left my arm, but he said nothing, until Sarah gave a nervous giggle. Then he asked stiltedly, 'Can you tell me why? Perhaps I haven't—'

'You have, and I can't, altogether,' I answered honestly, though not with the whole truth. How could I, a grown woman, admit roses gave me the heebie-jeebies, that I was even afraid of them? 'Only that I want a fresh start to this garden. That skeleton clinched it. I have thought about it a great deal, but each time I come back to that. The old rose garden needs an ending. I'd never look at any restoration without thinking of that contrast of rose and death. A spring garden would overcome that, and provide a new start for the Fontenays.'

He looked defenceless for once. Then he grew angry. 'You can't mean it. All that history, all the possibilities, all lost.'

'Then plant a rose garden on the other side of the grounds,' I found myself shouting. It was my way of being defensive. 'This is just bare earth here. Gardens are all about change. One century tears down what another has created. So we're starting something else for the twenty-first century. Can't you see that?'

'No.' He was shouting too. 'I can't live with it. It's desecration.'

'The garden is *mine*,' I hurled at him. 'I take the responsibility. I am master of my fate, I am captain of my soul and I'm bloody well captain of Fontenay. Are you hearing me?'

'I think the whole world must be hearing you, Anna.' Hugo had arrived out of the blue, suitably clad in parka and wellies, and amused by the slanging match.

'What the blazes are you doing here, Hugo?' I turned on him in my fury. Later, I'd regret this outburst, but just now anything went.

'Taking a breath of air. If I'd known it was going to be this hot, I wouldn't have come.'

'Can't you persuade her?' Joss asked. His appealing to Hugo as a last resort made me feel almost sorry for him. It can't have been easy.

'Tried. She's as immovable as stone. More in fact.' Hugo

glanced at me thoughtfully, then acknowledged Sarah's presence. 'Who's this? The face is familiar.'

'Sarah,' she answered for herself. 'I was a waitress for you last year.'

'Ah yes. A bad one I seem to recall.'

'Gardening's my thing.' Sarah was not a whit perturbed.

'And now that seems closed to you too, as Joss will be leaving,' Hugo remarked.

'Are you, Joss?' Sarah gave me an inimical glance.

'Looks that way. I'm sure there'll be work here for you if you want it. Ask Mrs Fontenay.'

I wasn't going to give in to Joss on the main issue, despite three pairs of eyes on me, but this was a minor matter. 'Certainly you can stay on, Sarah.'

'All right,' she said ungraciously. 'Mind you, I agree with Joss, this ought to be a rose garden. In remembrance like.'

'Of whom?' I asked. 'The flying bomb, the gardener, the skeleton or the Fontenays?'

'My great-great-aunt.'

'What on earth are you talking about?' I asked wearily. I'd had rose gardens up to here. All I wanted was to get away.

'I forgot to mention it,' Joss came in apologetically. 'Sarah's family is related to Jennifer Fontenay.'

He said it as though it were a mere detail, but it changed the whole picture. The atmosphere was suddenly and inexplicably different. Was it me the emotion was coming from? From Sarah? Hugo? Or Joss?

'How related, Sarah?'

'Told you. Mum reckons she was my great-great-aunt. Mum's grandma Elsie was her sister. They came from Sevenoaks way.'

I hesitated, uncertain where to take this conversation, but Hugo had no such problem.

'What does your mum think about the skeleton? Does she think it could be her great-aunt's?'

'Yeah. Police came to ask her to take a DNA test. Told us the other day there was a match. No doubt about it.'

Did all the world know more about the Fontenays than me? The police had yet to come to tell me about it. But then why

43

should they? Jennifer had died in a bomb incident over fifty years ago.

'Why Mum and Gran were interested,' Sarah continued casually, though I noticed her eyes were gleaming, as she tossed us this bombshell, 'was that there was always a rumour in the family that poor old Aunt Jen was murdered.'

She had us all staring at her. 'Murdered?' Hugo repeated blankly. I was incapable of stuttering anything, and even Joss looked fairly shell-shocked.

'Yeah, crime of passion, they reckoned. That Michael Sinclair dunnit.'

1943

'Here it is,' laughed Jennifer, 'this is what you wanted to see, our rose garden.'

'Bloody mad, both of you,' John grunted.

Michael Sinclair entered the garden and gazed at its enchantment. He hadn't realized gardens like this still existed in wartime. Most had been dug up for vegetables and fruit crops. Not this, probably because enclosed as it was, entire of itself, it could add little to the vast acreage of the Fontenay estate now given over to cabbages, potatoes and flax. He was happy that it had escaped, that it could still contribute its beauty to the scales of war. They said that birds had still sung in the mornings at Passchendaele, and when in this new war of horror he flew his Spitfire up into the blue heavens, he often thought he was invading space that God had meant for peace.

'After all,' added Jennifer, 'it's only right that you should see it. The Sinclairs have been bound up with the Fontenays over the centuries. Shouldn't we be feuding now, not enjoying an after-dinner stroll? Isn't that what our family legend would want?' She glanced at John, almost nervously, Michael thought.

'Maybe.' He didn't know. Ancient feuds had little relevance in today's war.

He listened as Jennifer explained that there was a rose tree here for every dead Fontenay. If all his mates who had gone for a burton had a rose tree planted they would fill the poppy fields of France. Nevertheless he found he was charmed, not only by Fontenay Castle but by Jennifer. John was a stuffed shirt, but his wife was a corker. It was good to be able to talk, and she was interested in what he had to say, interested in his family, sensed when he wanted to talk about his flying in the RAF and the war, and when he didn't. John was the opposite. He'd seen a bit of the first war, survived, and couldn't stop talking about it. Things were different now and Jennifer understood that. She was more his age, in her late twenties he thought, only five years or so older than him, and beautiful with her dark hair and pale complexion. She was like one of these roses herself, lovely but untouchable, with thorns for unwary hands.

'This is John's mother.' Jennifer pointed to a soft-pink rose. 'She died last year. Isn't it glorious?'

'She's buried here?' Michael wasn't concentrating. He was still thinking about Jennifer Fontenay, wishing that Hazel were as natural and warm as this woman, and then quickly dismissing the thought.

'I mean the rose tree planted for her. And this pale red damask is for Gertrude. We don't keep all the old names going, only Gertrude's. She was the first, the wife of Edmund Fontenay who started the tradition. It seems only fair to replant his white rose. Do you think I should? A white alba perhaps. Some say the garden itself goes back to the time of Chaucer.'

Michael was only half listening.

'. . . his *The Romaunt of the Rose*. The poet enters the Garden of Mirth and falls in love with a rosebud. All fearfully symbolic of course. And all the allegorical personages try to stop him, Danger, Jealousy, False-Seeming, but he beats the lot, with the help of the God of Love, but then falls prey to Jealousy and builds a wall around his beloved.'

'That's nice,' Michael murmured. He meant it. Not the poetry, but the whole Fontenay tradition. 'Where do the Sinclairs come in?' Perhaps he'd ask his father about his

45

lineage. After all, he might be one of the Sinclairs linked to the Fontenays.

'We don't know. The feud's being going on a long while, that's all. Everyone seems to have talked about the feud, but no one mentioned who started it.'

'The pestilence that walketh in darkness,' John suddenly said.

'What does that mean?' Michael laughed. 'Rose blight?'

'Goodness knows.' I remember my father telling me. He wouldn't have a Sinclair in the house.'

There was an awkward silence, until Jennifer hastily said, 'And this is the oldest rose we can trace. Montague Fontenay who died in 1887. He must have been a cad because the book merely says, "Montague Fontenay: He did his duty". What man deserves that as an epitaph?'

What book, Michael idly wondered, as Jennifer chattered on. Not that it mattered. All that mattered was today and possibly tomorrow. All the same he could see the appeal of yesterday. Not that he'd have long to consider any of them. The survival rate for pilots was very low, and things were going to get worse before they got better. He was sure of that. He wasn't going to last much longer himself, however lucky he'd been so far. These rhubarb and circus operations that sounded vaguely fun to the outsider, had been grim reapers in the death toll, as they made their individual forays over occupied France. Now the heavies were coming in, Halifaxes, Lancasters and Liberator bombers were flying in to West Malling, and American USAAF uniforms were mingling with RAF blue, as the big bomber offensive was getting under way.

'I envy you this place,' Michael said sincerely. 'Make sure you keep the garden safe and sound, both of you. And if I find out anything about the Sinclairs, sir, I'll let you know.'

'Do. I don't believe in feuds,' John said cordially. 'Come over any time. Mind you, don't believe all you hear about roses, they've got nasty thorns.' He grinned, but a sudden coldness in his eyes made Michael wonder. Then he realized he must be imagining the dislike. After all, he'd just invited him here whenever he cared to come.

46

'Surely they don't dare to prick in this garden.' Michael forced a joking tone into his voice.

John guffawed, waxing good-humoured again. 'That's all you know. There's a family legend that one of the Fontenays was murdered here in the eighteenth century.'

Jennifer shivered. 'You've never told me that, John.'

'Haven't I? One of those crimes of passion. Probably some husband did his wife in.' Another laugh, but there was no humour in it this time, as John glanced at Michael. 'Jealousy's a powerful thing, stronger than bloody roses.'

My stomach churned with shock, and Joss and Hugo looked stunned too. That skeleton wasn't going to go away. It was there, with its own story, its own demands. Sarah might or might not be right, but whichever, the cracks could not be plastered over. How could this rumour be right, however? Jennifer died because of the flying bomb, and to prove it we'd found the skeleton buried, crushed by masonry. Yet an insidious thought crept like an earwig from a plum; what better place to hide a body than a bomb site? Especially afterwards, when all the digging for bodies was over. If it had been an accident, as Joe Hendricks speculated, the body could not have been buried so deep. It would have been found by the first passer-by.

I stared out at the barren earth. It might still hold secrets. It seemed like a dark drawing board waiting for the rest of the story to be laid upon it; Fontenays, past and present, were all symbolized in that one skeleton. The perfume of the rose still lingered, but it had become a stench. Ghosts? Joss had asked, and the answer was yes.

How could Joss still maintain he loved roses, still want to go on with this charade? Because roses were survivors, as he'd said. To me, they were the enemy, and with that skeleton they had thrown down the gauntlet. *And I was proposing to give in to them.* No way. I'll do it, David, I vowed. I'll take up their blasted challenge. You'll have your rose garden, I promise.

'I've changed my mind.' The words came out clearly, as a

clarion call, and Joss looked at me as though he could not be sure what I had said or what I had meant.

'Anna?' Hugo must be glad too. And Sarah. So why were they all staring at me? Why weren't they rejoicing?

'About the garden? Why, Anna?' Joss asked as though he needed a reason . . .

'Yes.' If he did need a reason, I could give him one. It wouldn't be all of it, but it would answer him. 'If I make this a spring garden, it would merely plant bulbs over the cracks. The crater would always be here, reminding me that it was once a rose garden. I was wrong in what I said earlier. The rose garden will be the new beginning, not the spring garden. Whether the skeleton is Jennifer's, whether she was murdered or not, the garden can begin again with her as the first rose.'

'And Gertrude's?'

Joss wasn't giving me an inch. I hesitated, and yielded on my terms. 'Yes, and Edmund's. But not the ones you've planted near the castle. They can't have been the original ones, anyway. We'll plant *new* ones for them.'

Joss still looked uncertain. 'There's more to this than just a new beginning, isn't there?'

Did I have to bare my soul here now before everyone? No way. 'There's one condition,' I told him. 'I realize you have to go ahead now, but before everything's planted, Jennifer's story must be rooted out, no matter what the police decide to do.'

A long slow look from Joss, an amused one from Sarah, a shrug from Hugo. He strode off with a few polite words, but the look he gave Joss wasn't polite at all. Joss despatched Sarah to the village to order topsoil, he said, but I knew he wanted – now at least – to be alone with me, and I was right. 'You told me you didn't like roses. You're sure about this?' he asked me.

'Never been surer, though I'm going to challenge you about the design of the garden and its contents, I expect. I don't know why Sarah's little bombshell changed everything, but it did.' Belatedly I realized that Joss might have hoped for this. 'Did you put her up to telling that story?'

'Yes.'

'Is it true?'

48

'Yes. I didn't know about the murder rumours though.' He looked over the now cleared garden for a few moments. 'You know, the geophysical search suggests that if we dig deep enough we'll find some of the original Tudor paths, even the beds.'

'New, Joss, *new*. Remember?'

'I remember. Tell me why you don't like roses. I'm sure it's not just an overdose.'

'Tell me why you do,' I retorted lightly. 'I'm sure it's not just that they're survivors.'

'Actually it is – expanded into a wider context. In an age of symbolism, they stood for the root of life itself, the Almighty Power – flower and thorns together. Every time I see one, smell one, I want to make it perfect, and know it can't be, but that I will keep on trying. How's that for an explanation?'

I seemed to be frozen inside. Stiltedly, since I had to say something, I told him about the blood on my childish finger so long ago. It was a poor return for his confidence, but he seemed satisfied.

Joss understood me better than I had thought, but so what? Did it alter anything? No. In fact, far from feeling manipulated, I was almost grateful to him. I was ready for a fresh start, and able to talk eagerly of willows, of shrubs, of hybrid teas and apothecary roses.

Like the garden, my body was on the threshold of coming to life again. I thought of Hugo's hand on mine, I thought of the way Joss's hand had gripped my arm, but for the moment at least my body cared for neither of these. It was afire with the story of the Fontenays, and the resurrection of the rose garden. I would fight those roses on their own terms – for better or for worse.

Four

Which came first, the rose garden or the Fontenays? Joss was quite rightly going to be after me to see *The Book of Gertrude's Garden*, but even in my euphoria, I could see the hitch. Should we be replanting roses in memory of the hundreds of names in the book, or did we start anew? This would result in a rose garden with either nothing or just two roses in it, those for Gertrude and Edmund Fontenay. No, I was wrong. There should be another three at least, David, his father, and Jennifer. I recalled David's father had a sister Esther who lived in Australia. Would she qualify?

There were questions to be answered, but I wanted to consider them myself for a day or two. I could tell Joss I was busy with preparations for Gerard's return, but in fact I was anxious to meet Sarah's granny. Moreover, I wanted to speak to Gerard since this concerned him whether he liked it or not. I itched to ring Deborah, too. She, more than anyone must know something about Jennifer. For some reason I decided to postpone this, telling myself the more I knew myself before ringing her, the more I'd ask the right questions. On the other hand, if Sarah told Joss I'd had time to see her grandmother, he'd know I was avoiding him. To hell with that. I reminded myself I was the captain of this ship, and I would sail it my way.

By ill luck Sarah was with Joss when I set out to ask her for the phone number, so I received that enigmatic look from him, whether I deserved it or not. He didn't offer to come with me, thankfully.

'Here it is . . . Mrs Fontenay.' As she handed me the scribbled note, there was a pause before the Mrs Fontenay

50

as though she were pointing out that I now owed her one. Or was I getting paranoiac? 'She lives just outside Tunbridge Wells, East Grinstead road.'

Sarah's grandmother, Amelia Wilson, sounded friendly enough, and I agreed to meet her the next evening. She was still working at a farm shop during the day, she explained. It wasn't a long drive from Fontenay to Tunbridge Wells, but long enough to reflect I was hardly playing fair by Joss, or Hugo come to that. I reminded myself that I was being ridiculous; at this stage, this was my business not theirs.

Amelia was a much older version of Sarah, lithe for her age, cropped dark hair, lively eyes. Only the lines on her face spoke of sixty-plus years, not eighteen. She was in trousers and smock, so I was glad that I'd chosen comfort over appearance myself, with trousers and sweater.

'Come in,' she welcomed me. 'A touch of the non-alcoholic alcohol?' I settled for a spritzer, and decided I liked Amelia Wilson.

'Sarah said you wanted to sniff out the Fontenay family secrets,' she began after we got the civilities out of the way. 'It's my guess there were quite a few of them.'

'Guess? I was hoping you could tell me.'

'Rumours, Anna. You don't mind if I call you that, do you? After all, Jennifer was my aunt, and your father-in-law's first wife, so that makes us somehow related, doesn't it?'

We chatted amicably, each getting our bearings.

'Do you mind my asking why you want to know about Jennifer?' she eventually asked.

'I'm not sure I can explain it precisely. I'm sure Sarah told you that we plan to reconstruct the rose garden where Jennifer's skeleton was found. All that I can say is that it seems necessary.'

'Past influencing present?'

'Part of it. After all, I've a son who's entitled to know what lies in the Fontenay closet. It seems wrong to go on planting roses, if there's some nasty blight on the ground.'

'Aunt Jen wasn't a blight.'

'You knew her?'

'Depends what you mean by knew. I was seven when the

flying bomb struck in '44. I remember her. She and my mum were close and – before you ask – I lost Mum five years back. You don't *know* people at seven; you see them, and you know what they mean to you. Mum married a gardener, Jennifer married the lord of the manor so what I saw on the rare occasions we went to Fontenay was my idea of heaven. Fancy china, big gardens, treats for tea – even in wartime. And Jennifer was a beauty. Clever too, Mum said, but then Mum was as well.'

'Was her marriage with John Fontenay a happy one?'

'Mum reckoned it was, but he had a temper on him, and the question of kids lay between them. She had a stillborn baby, a girl, but then years went by without her conceiving. John wanted an heir. Bloody Fontenays,' she said without rancour.

'So what about Michael Sinclair?' How does he come into it? Sarah said the family rumour was that he murdered her.'

Amelia gave me a long look. 'This is hearsay. That doesn't mean it's true. Right?'

'Understood.'

'What Mum told me was this. Michael Sinclair was a Spitfire fighter pilot stationed at West Malling, and John Fontenay invited him down to dinner one evening in the summer of '43. Mum remembers Jennifer telling her about it and how nice he was even though he was a dastardly Sinclair. Joke, as I'm sure you know. He was really interested in her rose garden and John wasn't. This was wartime, so Mum was working her socks off with a part-time job, growing vegetables and trying to bring up us kids, and Jennifer was running the estate like a commercial farm, with land girls and whatever. They'd see each other on special occasions, birthdays and that, but travel wasn't easy. That's why she was over at Mum's the day of the bomb. It was my birthday, thirteenth of July. I was seven. I remember that all right. It was about seven o'clock. Jennifer must have gone, and I was just going up to bed when we heard a doodlebug up there. I remember Mum's face to this day when it cut out. That's how you knew you were for it. Mum grabbed me, no time to get to the shelter, just flat on the floor and pray. Well, it missed us, and we thought Jen might

52

have got home because she'd mentioned she might get a lift back. When Uncle John rang to say she hadn't reached home, we told him the bomb had got the bus queue, which was true. But she'd gone a bit too early for that, so when we heard the news Mum reckoned the lift had been from Michael Sinclair and he had taken advantage of all the bombs falling to bump her off. Now, with her skeleton turning up at Fontenay, it's my guess that's what did happen. Michael Sinclair picked her up by car, and drove her back to Fontenay.'

'Why drive her back there if he was going to murder her?'

'I've got an idea about that. But curb your impatience,' Amelia grinned. 'I'm getting ahead of myself. In the autumn of '43, Mum said, it was Michael this and Michael that, and how interested he was in the roses, and how he really understood her love for them. How he'd brought her an old copy of Gertrude Jekyll's *Roses for English Gardens*. I don't know how he had time, the amount of flying he had to do. Then it all went quiet for some months. In the spring of '44, however, he came back. He'd had a crash landing, Jennifer told Mum, and hurt his spine, so he'd been posted back to West Malling with a desk job. He went over to Fontenay as often as he could, only Jen warned Mum that John wasn't to know that. They met in the rose garden; there was some sort of summer house there which must have been handy. I expect that disappeared with the bomb, too.'

'Did she tell your mother she was having an affair with him?'

'People weren't so forthcoming in those days. Mum asked her whether she was doing anything she shouldn't, but Jennifer just laughed and said no, absolutely not. Anyway, Michael was married, she told her. And he had a baby son by his wife.'

Now this was interesting, I thought. If it was true, it raised all sorts of possibilities, and certainly the glimmerings of a motive for murder which so far had been absent.

'Mum asked Jennifer why he was coming over in secret if there was nothing to hide,' Amelia continued. 'Mum was always on the straight and narrow herself. Jennifer just said they had interests in common, which John didn't share. Mum assumed she meant sex. Michael was a looker apparently.'

'Did your mother meet him?'

'Once. There was something between them, Mum said. She could always tell.'

'It could have been unhappiness,' I commented fairly.

'So it could.' Amelia's turn to laugh. 'In a rose garden in the spring? Come off it. Anyway, then came summer and D-Day and the whole of Kent was clogged with military vehicles and so forth to make it look as if we were going to attack France from here. Michael was involved in that, of course. Fontenay Place was taken over as a dummy headquarters, the army moved in, and guess who their liaison officer was with the local RAF? Michael Sinclair. What a surprise.

'There was a fine old rumpus, Jen said, but there was nothing John could do about it. There was a war on. So it was Michael this and Michael that, on the phone. We went over for Jennifer's birthday not long after D-Day. I vaguely remember it. Jennifer was blooming and her husband looked grumpy. Next time Mum saw her was the day of the bomb, my birthday, thirteenth of July. She brought me a doll's house. Toys were hard to get in wartime, and I thought it was the cat's whiskers. That was the day Mum said that she told her she was three months gone.'

'Pregnant?' I exclaimed. This was beginning to make sense now.

'Mum was pretty surprised too. "A proper little Lord Fontenay, is he, Jen?" she asked. Jennifer said of course, but from the look she gave her, Mum said she knew she was lying. It was Michael Sinclair's all right. She was convinced that's why he killed Aunt Jen, and I agree. I reckon she told him on the way back to Fontenay, and they had a first-class row, which ended up with his killing her. Then he panicked, wondering what to do with the body. Maybe he had some idea of burying it in the grounds of Fontenay. Anyway, my guess is that when he got there he found the flying bomb had fallen and the place was swarming with people trying to work in the blackout, so he had the bright idea that if he hung on to Jennifer's body until the crater had been dealt with, he could bury it there.'

'But *why* kill her, even in passion?'

54

Amelia shrugged. 'Jennifer was head over heels about him. He wasn't happy in his marriage, nor was she. She may have thought he'd marriage in mind.'

'Did she say so to your mother?'

'Yes, Mum never forgot because they were almost the last words Jen said to her. She said, "John knows now. It'll have to be goodbye."'

'A row, yes, but it seems a big step to Michael killing her.'

'Mum said Jennifer was the type that could come on strong. Michael wouldn't have wanted a scandal ruining his career. Divorce wasn't acceptable if you had ambitions to climb high in the establishment, and he had a young child, too.'

The cards seemed to be stacking up against Michael Sinclair. In one way it was a relief to me. A solution meant that I could forge ahead with the new garden. In another it opened new lines of moral obligation. Michael Sinclair might well, after all, still be alive.

1943

'What do you think?' Jennifer asked gently, as she brewed up the tea on the paraffin stove. The Hermit's Retreat was a pleasant place to be on this late summer's day.

Michael jumped. 'What? Sorry, I was miles away. I think you're right. The caterpillars have been at it. Give it a spray.'

Jennifer laughed. 'You haven't been listening to a word I say, have you? I was talking about the skeleton John told us about. Was it a murder being covered up, a suicide maybe, because they couldn't be buried in consecrated ground, or a loving burial?'

With a great effort Michael concentrated. All he really wanted to do was relax in this place of peace, with Jennifer at his side. He'd just come back from leave – if it could be called that. Hazel went through the motions of welcoming him, playing devoted wife and happy mothers and fathers, but he saw them for what they were. Empty. Yet for William's sake they had to continue. He was only three years old – too young to know of the tortuous relationships men and women could find themselves in. He suspected Hazel had a lover, he could almost smell his presence in the house, but he said nothing and she said nothing. Hazel would be very careful to provide no evidence. She was too strong-willed ever to want to compromise what she saw as her social position with divorce. She had her life – and his future career – mapped out and nothing would change that. Nor, with the baby to consider, would he wish it too. The child had to come first. The war had made him see that.

And what a war it was. People thought with the Battle of Britain won, the pressure was off for the fighter boys. If only they knew. Escort duties sounded so bland. The flak didn't, nor the sight of bombers and fighters crashing before your eyes, only balls of fire where once there had been men.

He roused himself to play a part in this guessing game. 'Murder is my guess. Otherwise there would have been more signs of a coffin, or memorabilia around. Pity we don't know whether it was man or woman.'

'I could look into it,' Jennifer said thoughtfully, handing him a cup of tea.

'You stay in your rose garden.' He wanted her here, not in a stuffy library.

She sighed. 'Was it any better?'

She meant his leave. He laid his hand on hers.

'No. I still think there's someone else. After all, why not? I'm in the same boat.'

Jennifer hesitated, obviously longing to ask about the child, and as so often he seemed to guess what she was thinking.

'The kid's mine, though. My mother said she'd know those Sinclair ears anywhere. Anyway, he was conceived when we both thought we were in love.'

'Good.'

'Is it?' Michael wondered about that. If the baby was his that *was* good, but it made divorce all the more difficult if he did eventually decide to tackle Hazel. Would he? His parents' marriage hadn't been a happy one, and he'd been so determined to make a success of his own. People should stick together, especially in wartime. He watched Jennifer sweep her long hair back from her face, and thought again how lovely she was. She wore it dragged back in a net most of the time, as all women did if they didn't cut it short. He was glad she hadn't.

Jennifer changed the subject. 'Don't forget you said you'd help with the autumn spraying and pruning. Oh, and I need a hole dug for grandfather George. His Old Yellow Scotch – highly suitable for him, I gather – died early in the war, and I've a new one coming tomorrow. Over here.'

She led him to a far corner of the garden and studied the ground for a moment. 'The old rose, according to the plan and my memory, was roughly here –' she indicated a position near to the gravel path – 'but I think it might look good further back towards the wall. How about here? Feel like exercise?'

She indicated a spot further back towards the corner. 'Leave a little distance, though, from the wall. I pulled a dying *Rosa moschata* out from there a couple of years ago and I'm thinking about replanting one. Of course, I couldn't get an original white musk rose, but I could get one of its noisette descendants, a Madame Alfred Carrière. You can put your manly foot on the fork there.'

Michael laughed. 'Digging will be better than a cold shower for taking my mind off things. Besides I feel I have a stake in this garden now.'

'Useful,' she quipped. 'There's a Crimson Glory over there could do with it.'

He squeezed her hand. 'Emotional stake, I meant. I asked my parents about my Sinclair forebears. They got suddenly very cagey and talked about looking up family bibles and so on. Finally they confessed. Lo and behold, I am indeed one of those dreaded Sinclairs that walketh in darkness. Indeed I have a nasty feeling my ancestors were responsible for that.' He pointed towards the ruins of the old castle. 'Will you ever speak to me again?'

Jennifer exclaimed, half joking, half serious, 'Don't tell John. Are you *sure?*'

'I'm afraid so. Dad said Kent had a little civil war of its own in 1648. There were plenty of king's men left in Kent, wanting to see an end to the republic and the monarchy restored; Sir

Robert Fontenay was one of them. The rest of Kent wasn't exactly pro-Puritanism and parliament either. The County Committee set up by the republican government managed to keep a careful balance until Christmas 1647 when they tried to enforce the injunction against celebrating Christmas. All hell broke loose, and a rebellion of king's men began, starting with petitioning and ending in violence. I regret to say Mr Rupert Sinclair took his opportunity to settle old scores against the Fontenays. Down came the castle, Fontenays and all – until the monarchy was restored years later and gave their lands back to them. We Sinclairs didn't like that at all.'

'What old scores?'

'Who knows? Maybe Rupert just disliked Robert Fontenay and decided to burn his house down. They were stirring times.'

Jennifer did not reply, but he guessed what she was thinking – that so were these stirring times, and here was she welcoming a Sinclair into Fontenay territory. As though it mattered now. He picked up the spade and fork and obediently went to work on the deep hole that Jennifer required, while she busied herself with deadheading.

He thought nothing of it at first. It was just something long and white, disturbed by the fork. He bent down to investigate and found himself staring at bones. A strange feeling came over him. A cat, a dog, he told himself. But it wasn't, and for all the grim evidence of death he had faced in this war he felt like vomiting as he scraped away more of the earth. Finally he was in little doubt.

'Jennifer,' he called unsteadily, and she came to stand at his side, squinting in the autumn sunshine.

'What is it?'

'I think I've found that skeleton.'

Joss was standing on my doorstep. My heart sank. I had to face it sometime, and it wasn't because of Joss himself that I was putting it off. It was because it was a kind of commitment to something that hitherto had just been verbal.

'You're here about *The Book of Gertrude's Garden*, aren't you?' I adopted my cheerful but bullish pose.

One eyebrow shot up. 'Part of the bargain.'

'Don't worry. I won't go back on my word. We'll make a date if you like. Come over to lunch on Sunday.'

It was a test and he knew it. Did his interest in the garden (not in me) extend further than the working week?

'Can't, I'm afraid. I'll take a rain check though. Tomorrow?'

'Gerard comes back. That's why I'm busy.'

'Making up one bed?'

One to him. 'Trying to get everything sorted.' I hesitated, with an odd sense of wanting to establish a bridge again. 'Come in for a few minutes now, and I'll tell you what I discovered from Sarah's grandmother.'

He was in like a shot, and listened quietly as I regurgitated Amelia's story.

'Seems to me the jury's out,' he then pronounced. 'No hard evidence at all as regards the Sinclair involvement. I agree with your reasoning that murder is more likely than accident, though.' He hesitated. 'You say Jennifer was pregnant. And this Amelia thinks it might have been by Michael?'

'It's hardly likely to be John's child, as they'd been trying so long for another baby. The book records a stillborn daughter in 1937, one of the last entries in it.'

Joss did not comment. Instead he asked, 'Does this affect the rose garden plans? You said I could go ahead, but do you intend to delay that until you know everything there is to be known about Jennifer and Michael Sinclair? If so, suppose you never do? Time is running out, and you still haven't said whether you agree with my plans for the garden. I've brought a chart of the layout, but it has to be your decision whom the roses are dedicated to. Only then can I order suitable varieties.'

It was a fair point, and it made me think. He was right. Decisions in principle over the rose garden had to be made quickly, whereas it could take months, years even, to be sure I knew all there was to know about Jennifer's skeleton. I took a quick look at the chart, although it was hardly necessary. I'd

59

been thinking about it for a while, and knew I had to broach my only main objection.

'What about having the central part of the main garden slightly sunken, with a fountain and Gertrude and Edmund's roses as the central feature, and a few shallow steps down to it on all sides, with urns and pots carrying roses?'

To do him justice, he considered it carefully. Then, as I expected, he shook his head. 'Not good for roses to be in a sunken area.'

'Slightly sunken?'

'I'll think about it, but I'm doubtful.'

Big of him, I thought crossly. 'About the choice of rose trees, Joss—'

He almost visibly bristled. 'What about it?'

'Is there any way we could delay planting?'

'For your sake or the roses'?'

I glared at him. 'Mine.'

'You could delay planting them until the spring.'

I grinned. 'All right. What about the roses' sake?'

'November planting at the latest to give them time to get established, and more resistant to disease.'

'No Sinclairs to creep in by night?'

He laughed politely, and I wondered why I was being so difficult. 'Come tomorrow morning,' I suggested amiably. 'Gerard isn't coming till late. I warn you though, I still think of it as a garden of new beginnings.'

In a spirit of goodwill, he even offered me a pub supper. I turned it down, but only because I had my own plans for the evening ahead.

I wanted to read through a few letters that Amelia had offered me, the only ones her mother had kept from her sister from that period. I opened them eagerly, though without great expectations. If Jennifer had been guarded in what she told her sister, she would have been even more guarded in what she wrote. There were about twenty in all, some of them relating to a time before Michael Sinclair first came to Fontenay. About twelve covered the years 1943–4. Most of the content concerned family affairs. There was talk of remnants of material she'd picked up, which might be a help to her sister, of

60

she'd been murdered. She vanished, and he thought she'd been killed in the bomb that hit Amelia's mother's village.

'What kind of woman was Jennifer?' I asked.

'Rose garden crazy, I gather. Very lovely, and caught the eye of any attractive man going.'

'Did she return it?'

A pause. 'I'm trying to be fair. I really don't know. That's what John said, and he also said she more than returned it. Michael said it wasn't true.'

Michael did? Something wasn't making sense here.

Deborah must have realized that needed explaining for she continued smoothly, 'I was a Waaf – didn't you know? I met Michael at West Malling. I didn't marry John till after the war. It's nearly sixty years ago, and I'm getting to be an old woman. I can't help you over your skeleton, Anna. I'm sorry.'

She didn't sound old. She sounded like someone who didn't want to go on talking.

'Is that what you told Hugo?' something made me ask.

'Hugo wasn't asking me about Jennifer's skeleton. He was interested in the other, much older one.'

Five

S o much for my being the captain of the Fontenay ship. I
was highly irritated. What was going on here? First the
gardener I employ assumes he has equal rights in deciding what
is or is not to be done, now my tenant considers he's as much
a part of Fontenay as I am. Why was Hugo ringing Deborah
about *my* skeleton, especially one I'd only just discovered
this evening? How did he know about it? David had never
mentioned it. Grumpily, I slept on my grievance. I had no
choice in fact, since Hugo didn't live at Fontenay, he only
worked there. His home was about ten minutes' drive away
in a village called Leahurst, and though I had the number I
considered it out of bounds to ring, save in emergency.

So I played it by the book. Early next morning I rang to
make an appointment for eleven o'clock. I kept my voice as
neutral as I could make it, but he seemed slightly surprised at
my formality.

'What's all this that couldn't wait, Anna?' he asked when I
turned up in the bar. 'Trouble with Gerard?'

'No, Hugo. He's due back early this evening.'

'With Joss?'

'No.'

'Ah. Must be the builders.'

'Let me buy the drinks, and then you can tell me how you
knew about the second skeleton in the rose garden. The one
that Jennifer Fontenay found.'

Hugo laughed. How dared he? 'One's sins will find one out.
Or rather Deborah will reveal them. There's no mystery about
it. All this business of Jennifer's skeleton in the garden brought
back a half-memory of David saying something to me about a

skeleton being found in the garden yonks ago. It didn't mean much at the time, so I didn't follow it up, but when I recalled it, I realized it couldn't be Jennifer's, so I thought I'd find out more for you.'

'Good of you.'

He gave me a searching look. 'Going somewhat overboard, aren't you? You don't own history.'

'I do own Fontenay though,' I flashed.

'Implying?'

'I don't like the feeling that things are going on behind my back.' The minute I said it I felt ashamed, even though there was a genuine grain of truth in it, so I apologized. After all, Hugo was the other half of Fontenay. He had the house, for which he paid a fairly stiff rent, plus all the paintings, the main library, and some of the memorabilia. He was custodian of all that, whereas I had been an absentee landlord.

Hugo was still annoyed. I watched the fingers drumming on the table, and the muscle in his cheek working overtime.

'I accept the apology,' he said at last. 'But I could say the same, you know. I rent the house, and so it gives me an odd feeling that everything is being changed around me without my being consulted. Are you telling me I should keep out of everything except Fontenay Place itself? Keep out of the rose garden, the plans for the new tea-room and shop, and the rest of the gardens? I thought we'd made a good partnership up till now.'

'We have.' I remembered the umpteen details I'd bothered him with already during my time here. 'I want to be kept in the picture, that's all.'

'And so, Anna, do I. Over the rose garden, for instance. Quite apart from my emotional if not proprietorial feelings about Fontenay, it has a commercial aspect for me. The more it's developed as a tourist attraction, the more customers I get for conferences, so it affects me directly, whether you like it or not. If you decided to grant planning permission for a motorway through the grounds I presume you'd consult me?'

'Yes.'

'So what's different with a rose garden?'

'I can't consult everyone at the same time.' I was back in

control now. 'I'm boss of Fontenay, not the chairman of a committee.' There was no point in my pulling punches, and I still felt tetchy, even though reason had reasserted itself.

'I see. Master Joss Foxley.'

'What's that supposed to mean?'

'Think about it, Anna. He behaves like the bloody lord of the manor himself. Whatever you decide, he'll take no notice, assuming you'll never sack him after your climb-down.'

'He's entitled to his say.'

'Then so am I.'

My hackles shot up, firstly at my rational decision being seen as a climb-down, secondly at the thought of having to plan the garden as a threesome.

'Hi, Mum!'

Unexpectedly, and for once in his life early, my gap-year son strode into this moment of silent tension, a long-haired skinny hero to save the day. Only he didn't. He merely grinned at the warring parties.

'Awkward moment?'

'You could say that.' Hugo stood up, as Gerard peeled off his anorak. He and Gerald had always got on. No matter. A wave of emotion hit me as I rushed over to welcome him. I hadn't seen Gerard since last Christmas. My awkward, uncommunicative spotty son now had – even to my eye – such an ease and confidence that it took me a moment or two to see him as the same lad. And then, as they say, he kissed me. A son's kiss can mean every bit as much as a lover's, and this one told me he was glad to see me, even if he wasn't glad to be here at Fontenay.

'Where's your luggage?' was the only endearment I could think of to utter.

'Dumped it in the lodge garden. Some bloke I ran into at the barn said he thought you were up here.'

'What bloke?'

Gerard shrugged. 'Almost as scruffy as me, and almost twice as old. Dark hair. Does it matter?'

I supposed not, but I wondered how Joss knew I was up here. Only Mary Filkin could have known where I was. Mary kept the house running on some kind of organized lines for a few hours each week. She had a key, today was one of her days, and she must have overheard my telephone call. She'd have gone by the time Gerard got there though. But how did Joss know – the terrible truth hit me. He'd arranged to see *The Book of Gertrude's Garden* and I'd forgotten to cancel the date. Great, Anna! Well done, I fumed. It seemed to be my morning for apologies.

'What will you drink?' Hugo asked Gerard, and then went off to get the requested beer.

The odd e-mail, postcard or telephone call was all I'd received as my son had made his way round half the world. It had been useless to worry. I'd had to dismiss it from my mind and hope. And now he was back.

I glowed with pleasure. 'Welcome home, Gerry.'

'Home?'

'Let's hope so.'

'Seems to be a lot going on,' he ventured enquiringly.

'There is.'

'Do I want to know about this?'

'Probably not. Especially today.'

'Right, then.'

I reasoned that Gerard would have seen so much on his travels that the minutiae of the rose garden would seem petty. Only when he had settled again would he see it in context, and realize that this was as important as anything else, if one saw it as such.

'Fontenay must seem small beer to you.'

'A large one will be better,' Hugo quipped as he plonked a pint in front of Gerard.

'Now this,' my son said appreciatively, 'is what I miss about Britain. You can drink wine anywhere, but this is the true nectar of the gods. Um – have you finished your discussion before I launch into tales of Timbuctoo?'

'Yes.'

'No.'

The yes was mine, the amicable no Hugo's.

'I'll get going then.' Gerard drank speedily.

'Have lunch,' Hugo offered. 'Easier than going home.'

I have said earlier that my son is sometimes percipient.

67

'Thanks, but I guess Mum can whip up her rat risotto, can't you?'

'I can, with a plentiful supply of spinach, Popeye.' Gerard hates it.

'I'll go on ahead, then.'

'Anna,' Hugo said immediately, 'you'll tell him about the rose garden, won't you? It will need discussion as to whose roses go into it.'

Damn and blast Hugo. Why did he have to raise this *now*, and why put his finger so adroitly on the problem I still had to sort out with myself, let alone agree with Joss? Was I going for dictatorship in Fontenay decisions, or for a governmental cabinet approach?

Gerard looked from one to the other of us. 'Did I hear the dreaded word *rose*? I'm definitely off.'

'You heard it,' Hugo said firmly.

I made my mind up quickly. 'You go, Gerard. I'll catch you up in ten minutes.'

I used those ten minutes to build bridges. I told Hugo all I'd discovered about Jennifer and Michael Sinclair, and that I intended to find out about the other skeleton. Anything he could do to help would be welcome.

He listened, frowning slightly. 'This doesn't make sense, Anna. You want to do all these investigations into history, but you keep saying the future's more important than the past for the rose garden.'

'It does make sense to me. I want to create a clean slate for Gerard.'

'Hand him the unblemished rose?'

'Yes.'

'There's no such thing as a perfect rose, Anna. They're all grafted on to the past, as we are ourselves.'

'But the rose was a *symbol* of perfection. That's what David told me. The home of the Almighty, a symbol for the Virgin Mary too, and a symbol of Paradise.' It didn't seem polite to mention Joss had much the same attitude.

'And no serpent in Eden?'

'Not in my garden,' I whipped back. 'No pestilence shall walk in darkness there, no Sinclairs will come marching into my garden by night or by day.' Then I wondered what on earth possessed me, and laughed shamefacedly at my vehemence.

Hugo rewarded me by giving me such a sweet smile that I felt guilty all over again. For the moment at least, he had spared me further argument over the one thing I dreaded fighting about. I couldn't take on both Hugo and Joss together, even if Gerard miraculously joined in on my side. I was all too conscious that *The Book of Gertrude's Garden* still had to be faced. It, too, had a say in the matter.

Gerard let me talk at last that evening. It was only fair. I'd listened to stories of Tibet, of China, of Russia, and Turkey, and quite a few places I'd never heard of. I was fascinated at the way words poured out of him. A year ago, with the future still locked up inside him, it was difficult to get an answer to 'Do you want lunch?' Now, with a little bit of his future safely under his belt, it was a different matter. He had something to offer and he gave of it generously.

But it was tit for tat. If he could spill out words, then so could I, and I did. I explained I too had had roses up to here with David, that I'd never liked them but that I'd come to realize that they could be considered a symbol for Fontenay's future. It was a battle I had to fight, and since he would inherit it, I did want to hear his opinion even if the final decision were left to me. I was apologetic about it, telling him I understood that to him a rose garden was of little consequence at present.

'Why?' he asked me to my secret amusement at how much gap years can achieve. 'There are enclosed gardens of paradise all over the world in ancient history, and today. Why should Fontenay be any different to them?'

And so he got the whole story, and at last I reached the skeletons.

He was, he informed me, gobsmacked. 'Now you're talking. Tell me, *tell* me about them.'

So I told him all I knew. The probable adultery of Jennifer and Michael left Gerard unmoved. The idea of the Sinclairs creeping in by night fascinated him, though of course he too had listened to David on the subject. He even reminded me of the other major Fontenay–Sinclair clash, which I'd forgotten.

How could I? It was in some ways the most important. There was a legend that the famous Gertrude herself had died of a broken heart because of the Sinclairs. It left a bitter taste in my mouth, as if the whole rose garden had been based on a lie, and reconfirmed me in my belief that the garden must be for the future, not the past.

Gerard seemed to be to the same way of thinking, for what fascinated him about the Sinclair–Fontenay feud was that it might be a *living* legend. After all, he pointed out, World War II must seem not that long ago for oldies like me.

'Thanks,' I murmured.

'Are there Sinclairs about now?'

'I've no idea. Michael might still be alive, but where would we start looking?'

'Can't help. So tell me the problem over the rose garden again. Hugo seemed to be making sense, if you don't mind my saying so. The past *is* part of Fontenay.'

'I knew you'd take his side. Joss thinks the same.'

'Who *is* this Joss?'

To my horror, I realized I'd been jabbering on without explaining Joss's presence, which implied that he'd become so much part of the Fontenay fabric that my subconscious hadn't clocked up the need for such information. Quickly I rectified it.

'But he's a gardener. Why does he have a say?' Gerard asked, reasonably enough.

'Because,' I grappled and lost, 'he's like that.'

'Have you taken leave of your senses, Mum? You never let people get to you like that. Do you fancy him?'

'No, dear child. You can't reduce *all* the problems of the world to sex. Joss understands gardens, he understands Fontenay, and he knows its history, and he's genuinely interested in its future.'

'He understands you, if you ask me. He sounds too wonderful to be credible.'

'You'd better meet him before you dismiss him lightly.'

'I did, if he's the bloke I met earlier. Seemed ordinary enough to me.'

'He'll probably be coming here in the morning to look at

The Book of Gertrude's Garden.' I'd left a message on his home answerphone to apologize.

Gerard's eyebrows shot up in amusement. 'Hey, get the white gloves and disinfectant, like Dad always insisted on. No heated words either, in case they affect the parchment.'

'Do you want to be in on this?'

He thought this through. 'I'd like to be a fly on the wall.'

'Not possible. Your boots are too heavy.'

'OK. I'll stay half an hour, and then scarper. Things to do. You can fight the battle from there.'

'Don't you have any view on what I've said?'

'Sure and I agree with Hugo though not for the same reason. Forget all this rose symbolism stuff. You're right to go on looking into the story of the skeletons, but you can't have a tourist attraction with no roses until one of us pops their clogs. Even if you planted one for Dad it would look a bit lonely.'

Trust Gerard. Just what I'd been thinking of course. 'We'd put underplanting flowers in at first.' It sounded feeble even to me.

'Hogwash.'

'It's a beginning.'

'You know what I think, Mum?'

'You're telling me fairly plainly.'

'This whole thing about rose gardens and skeletons is about something else altogether.'

I groaned. 'Pestilence?'

'No. Maybe you don't fancy Joss, but does he fancy you?'

'Gerard, he's at least six years younger than me, and probably more.'

'That's no answer.'

'Then, hand on heart, I have felt no sexual vibes, seen no sexual signs, nothing. He does *not* fancy me.'

'Hugo does. That's what's behind it, you can bet on it. Sex.'

'You could have fooled me.'

'Seen the way he looks at you? He's probably waiting for you to take the iron belt off.'

'*What?*'

'The old chastity belt lords used to fix on when they

71

galloped off on missions. Maybe he thinks Dad fixed one on you.'

I felt my face redden. 'Gerard, you don't know what you're talking about. Neither Hugo nor Joss fancies me, is that clear?'

'Do they fancy Fontenay then?'

I stared at him, as my stomach seemed to dive down to my trainers.

Then I tried to pull myself together. 'You've been reading too many tales of derring-do,' I replied quietly enough. 'And you're the heir anyway. It would be a temporary ownership on Joss or Hugo's part, if that's what you're worried about.'

'You're not too old to have another kid. You could leave it to both of us.'

'Thank you, dear son. Any more rubbish you'd like to dream up?'

'No. I'll leave you to ponder it.'

I yelled after him as he marched out in some kind of triumph. 'My sex life is nothing to do with you, do you hear? I don't ask you about yours.'

Next year I'd be forty years old, but I was blushing like a schoolgirl when I let Joss in the following morning. Luckily, I calmed down. This was just Joss, not some Casanova who, but for the presence of my gangling son, would smother me with kisses and pin me to the floor in ecstasy. Even as the thought passed through my mind, it transformed itself into an image of that same scene – and hence brought back my blush.

'You've met Gerard,' I said brightly.

They shook hands. Gerard was fortunately on his best behaviour.

'I've heard a lot about you,' he lied.

Joss glanced at me. 'Mrs Fontenay has been *forced* to talk a lot about me. We may still have to do battle over the rose garden. It's good of her to let me in to see *The Book of Gertrude's Garden*. You don't mind?'

'Go ahead. I'm only an interested observer. You and Mum can fight on regardless.'

'No one –' Joss said softly, looking at the page for Abigail Fontenay – 'could fight over something as beautiful as this.'

The book was bound in old vellum, and I had opened it at random. Joss had actually brought transparent disposable gloves with him, and I couldn't resist a glance at Gerard to see if this scored a point with him. From the innocent look on his face, you'd think he had nothing but roses on his mind.

I turned over the page to one in honour of her husband Stephen, born 1710, died 1791, commemorated by a Blush rose, beautifully drawn on the left. The calligraphy was easier to read than that earlier in the book, and the words 'full of wisdom and knowledge of roses' caught my eye. Austere compared with Abigail's 'beloved wife, dear lady of my heart', his wife's brief tribute on the page before. She had died in 1790, and the ink was slightly smudged as though a tear had fallen. I stared at it, wondering what right I had to deprive these people of their memorial. This, if I stuck to my guns about its being a new garden, is what I would be doing.

Gerard had his bright-eyed stare firmly fixed on Joss, but no one could have mistaken the look in Joss's eyes as he peered over my shoulder, as anything but genuine. It was the book he fancied, not me.

'What are your views, Mr Fontenay, on the rose garden?' he asked formally. 'A garden of the future alone, a garden of the past alone, or both.'

'I don't have a view, or at least it doesn't alter anything. I can't believe Mum's really dotty enough to create a completely empty rose garden.'

'Not entirely empty,' I interrupted, not wanting my ground to be ceded by Gerard.

'The garden has to record those remembered in this book,' Joss said.

'How would we know who's worthy?' I asked sharply. 'What criteria would we apply, where would we put limits? Or would we put all of them in, saints or sinners? Wouldn't we have to apply some kind of historical aspect? We could be including a murderer, after all.'

'If it's to be a true record, all of them should be in.'

'Some were dropped over the centuries, when the roses died

and they weren't replaced. *That's* historical judgement. Why couldn't we do the same?'

Joss stared at me. 'There'd have to be a careful record of what you're doing.'

'Not me, Joss. I want to start afresh.'

The more I fought my corner, the more impossible my position seemed, even to me. Yet I was damned if I was going to include all the Fontenay monsters.

'I think I'll retreat.' Gerard saw the signs of war on my face – and thus provided me with my perfect answer.

'The Hermit's Retreat,' I shouted, before he could do so. 'We're building it up again, aren't we?'

'Yes, I've got the architect's plan here.' Joss made as if to move, but I stopped him.

'Scrap it. We'll build it bigger and stronger so that can be a tourist attraction. Long, low, and thatched.'

'Expense no object?' Gerard enquired.

Joss said nothing – yet.

Thus encouraged, I continued, 'You can have your way about putting in the ancestors, but inside the Retreat we'll put a record of all the people commemorated in the garden, plus a photo of the rose, plus a biog. We could have saints and sinners then, because visitors could make their own judgements.'

A silence.

'Sounds good to me,' Gerard said offhandedly.

I looked at Joss. A nod, even it could be said, an enthusiastic one.

'Agreed.'

'So that's that,' I said happily.

'Except for Hugo,' Gerard put in.

All my good intentions about cabinet rule vanished. 'He'll have to lump it.'

'He'd hardly object,' Joss said. 'It'll be ideal for his business.' His face was so deadpan I couldn't tell whether he was being sarcastic.

Gerard grinned, because I'd told him about the antipathy between the two men. 'You could use the portraits in Fontenay Place for illustrating the biogs in this Hermit's Retreat.'

'A lot of thumping crooks get their pictures painted,' I

pointed out. 'And a lot of unsung angels get overlooked. I fancy keeping the two separate, and having a Rogues Gallery.'

'No one will look at the saints then,' Gerard pointed out.

'True. So where shall we start?'

'Selecting roses,' Joss said immediately.

'How?' I asked.

'Flower-bed roses didn't make it big till Victorian times, after all the China roses had been introduced in the late eighteenth and late nineteenth centuries. Our climate meant that on the whole they didn't grow as big as in their native soil, though. Up till then, roses here were chiefly ramblers and shrubs, and we'd need to select what we can find of the older roses to match the Fontenay ancestors. What would Chaucer have seen, for example, or Good Queen Bess? What would the seventeenth- and eighteenth-century Fontenays have seen? We need to get variation. That's why I divided the garden into two parts. The old roses and the new. The really old roses would have much less colour variation, the ones from the late eighteenth century on would have far more. Each garden would have its own splendour and style. And what's more, there's so much going on in the rose world, we'll need space for the future.'

'Not the famous blue rose everyone's aiming at?' Always a good plan to show one knows a *little* about a subject.

'Perhaps. It would need a place to itself – that couldn't be popped in between a *centifolia* and a *gallica*.'

'People first,' I objected. 'I don't like the idea of separating the generations.'

'Only saints and sinners,' Joss shot back at me.

A polite cough from Gerard. 'I'm off,' he said. 'Sounds like heavy duty on the way.' He ambled off, and after he'd gone, Joss pulled up a chair and sat at my side at the table. 'Doesn't he mind what we decide to do?'

'No.'

'In that case I must have been found worthy.'

Startled, I looked at him, as he continued, 'If I were his age, and found my mother battling with a problem the size of this estate on her own, I'd be anxious to see no one took advantage of her. Ergo, his early departure is a good sign for me.'

I laughed. 'You're right. He was anxious to see that neither you nor Hugo has designs on my person and his inheritance.'

How could I have *said* that? I'd relaxed my guard too soon. I suppose I thought that was in Joss's mind when he spoke. It hadn't been.

He was completely shell-shocked. 'You're not serious? Do *you* think that?'

'No.' I made amends as fully as I could. 'I might as well spell it out now. I've no intention of marrying again – ever.' Once one sinks in a bog, it's a long way to struggle out to land, and I wasn't doing very well. 'Anyway, I'm enough my own person for it to not be relevant.'

'It *is* relevant.' Joss frowned. 'Very, if Gerard thinks that way.'

I was cold with shock at what I'd said, and furious with myself, and in a trice our whole relationship had changed. I was the pleading one now. I needed to make it to safe ground quickly. 'The only thing that is important is the rose garden, Joss. I know nothing of your life outside. You could have six former wives and ten kids for all I care.'

He shrugged. 'Maybe I do. Shall we look at the book again?'

I'd hurt him. It had been incredibly rude of me to imply he was a fortune-hunter. Not that I had a fortune in the normal sense, but to Joss – maybe to Hugo – Fontenay might be fortune itself. I'd meant it jokingly, but the very fact that I'd said it at all suggested that Gerard's words had taken their toll. Now I had to recover lost ground. I battled to put it from my mind, and as with Hugo, I told Joss about the other skeleton. This at least was shared territory.

'Interesting,' he said when I'd finished.

'Perhaps. It isn't necessarily a Fontenay though.'

'It's hardly likely to have been anyone else. The rose garden would be under regular cultivation – not a good place to bury a body unless it had some special meaning, even if it was in a corner. There might be a clue in the book as to who it was.' His gaze strayed back to the book. I took the hint.

I should explain that in addition to the book itself, there were two other vital records for the garden bound into one which David had called *The Book of Roses*. One was an index of all those remembered in the garden, with their dates, and the roses planted. Each entry had extra space in case the roses had to be replaced, and each had a number. The other record was a series of maps, of where each rose was planted, indicated by an outlined rose shape with the relevant number in the middle. Any change of position of a rose was noted, and in due course incorporated on a new map, roughly every fifty years or so. These two records were compiled from earlier rough records and detective work in the early nineteenth century either by Charles Fontenay, who died in 1818, or his son St John, or both.

It was Gertrude's book though which Joss was naturally eager to look through further. As I turned to the first page, the page to Gertrude, I felt as though I were seeing it for the first time. Looking at it with David, I had of course admired the sheer beauty of the whole idea, and of the rose flower illustrations and calligraphy. I had listened patiently (most of the time) to his explanations of who these people were, how they tied up with the surviving portraits and their relationship to one another, but that had been at one level only, my eyes and my brain.

What I saw now, for whatever reason, was striking deeper than that, as it called for an emotional response that I was beginning at last to give. Perhaps it was because Joss was so patently captivated by it, but I don't think so. It probably had more to do with the fact that I was now involved, part of the story myself; I had a role to play.

'"Good wife, a just mother",' I read out of Matilda Fontenay, 1610–69. Fairly chilling compared with the nearby Abigail's 'dear lady of my heart'. I decided I would look at the family tree again next time I was in Fontenay Place. This was begun by Charles Fontenay, and finished by David's grandfather, Edward, and hung in the entrance hall.

'Look at this,' Joss said. 'A *gallica* called Crimson Joy. That's odd.'

'Why?'

'I've never heard of it.'

He smiled, when I laughed. 'I think I would have done,' he

continued. 'Firstly, the name doesn't sound right for the late eighteenth century, and secondly, why would they choose an old rose like that and not one of the new China roses?'

'Goderic Fontenay,' I read out. 'Born 1763 and departed 1796.'

'Why departed, not died, like all the others? And what's more, he's out of place. He comes after Mary who died in 1799, and Charles who died in 1818.'

'Maybe he wiped the dust of Fontenay off his feet.'

'Why put him in at all?'

I looked through his brief biography. 'Son of Stephen and Abigail Fontenay, brother to Charles. Married Elizabeth Sayles.'

'No clues there,' Joss frowned.

'I stick by the wiping dust off feet theory. Fed up with the Fontenays.'

'It's true it's just possible they weren't all perfect.' Josh kept a straight face. 'After all, there are two skeletons to explain.'

That switched me to the skeletons again. 'We know Jennifer isn't in the book. John's mother is the last entry. So there's no help in the book on that one, but the second skeleton dates from approximately between 1750 and 1850, if Jennifer's letter is right.'

'Let's see if there's a girl who fits the description.'

'Or young man. She wasn't certain. The index would be the quickest guide.'

Our search produced two suspects. A girl Henrietta, who died at 21 in 1845, and a boy Thomas who died in 1762 aged 18.

'How many are there in this index?' Joss asked me.

'A hundred and sixty-one, I think.'

'Not that many, when you take into account the infant mortality rate and larger families. That would suggest that the book was for the Fontenays who actually lived in the house, their spouses and children.'

'So?'

'The early skeleton might just have been a Fontenay who never lived here, and never made the book.'

I considered this. 'No proof. Why bury the body there? Anyway it could be someone entirely outside the family.'

'Not from the way Jennifer describes it – carefully positioned near a corner of the wall near the rose. It must have been someone who *meant* something to someone in the family. Henrietta and Thomas are recorded in this book; we're looking for someone who isn't recorded, in my view.'

'That's simple then,' I answered brightly.

He gave a faint smile. 'Perhaps.'

We worked our way through *The Book of Gertrude's Garden* and the index again, and studied the maps of that period. We passed George Fontenay with his three wives, Jasper Fontenay, priest of this parish, Cecilia Fontenay, who made music for our hearts, and finally worked back to Sir Edmund Fontenay and Gertrude. Another story that might never be known.

'Some Fontenay somewhere,' Joss remarked, 'lost the "Sir". Who was that, do you think?'

I knew that one. 'Sir Robert. The time of the rebellion. The Sinclairs burned down the old castle, claiming the land upon it to be theirs by right since time out of mind. When Charles II was restored to the throne, he appeased both sides by turning the Sinclairs out but rescinding the knighthood after Robert's death. He only had daughters, and Anne, the eldest, inherited. It went to some second cousin Fontenay after that.'

'Good for King Charlie.' Joss sat back.

Finally, after a lot more fairly amicable bickering over the new garden, I closed the book, and with my terrible faux pas still in my mind, asked him bluntly, 'Have you forgiven me?'

He managed a smile. 'No.'

I hesitated. 'Would it help if I said that the book has made me change my mind? That your instinct may be right – to keep saints and sinners together in the garden, and to keep the centuries roughly divided. We'll choose the roses, and the positions after I've consulted Hugo on portraits and relevant family papers. We don't want arch enemies next to each other.'

Joss looked dubious. 'Are you doing this simply to please me? If so, it's a bad decision.'

'I don't think so.' I struggled to find the right words. 'And if I am, it's because we need to work together.'

'Is that all?'

'No. You know, Joss, I hated this book while David was alive. This morning it has meant something, at last. We keep Fontenay's past and plan for a future.'

'Which is?'

'The more recent roses, and *something*. I don't know what it is yet, but it will come to me. Is that okay?' This sounded so weak, I half expected Joss to say no or at the very least to think I was completely round the twist. Strangely, he didn't.

Instead, he thought it over, and gave an abrupt nod. 'Let's do it. But Anna –' he got up to go – 'tell Gerard he need not worry about my making a play for Fontenay through you.'

'Why?'

'I'm gay.'

It was totally unexpected and the shock kicked into me with dire results.

'You're not. I know you're not. I wouldn't feel—' I stopped in horror at what I'd blurted out and what it implied. How could I have thought I felt no sexual vibes? I did, and thanks to his sneaky tactics, I'd revealed them all too clearly.

Joss cupped my face in his hands, and kissed me lightly on the mouth. 'Forget it. I will.'

1943

'Michael!'

Jennifer greeted him eagerly as she entered the Hermit's Retreat, disappointed not to find him waiting at the gate for her. 'Thank goodness you're here. I thought something must have happened.' She always did, every time there was the droning of aircraft engines in the sky. He kissed her in welcome. A kiss could mean so much, and John never kissed her like that. It was friendly, comforting and companionable. She needed all these things.

'I've been working my way through Gertrude's book trying to find someone who might turn out to be our skeleton,' she told him. 'None of the Fontenay women during that hundred years seem to have died in their early twenties. They either died much younger as children, or older, often in childbirth.'

'Perhaps she was a black sheep daughter.'

'Did they have them in those days? In any case, if I know the Fontenays, they would have hidden the black sheep aspect. Why not bury her in the cemetery with a suitable pious message? No one would have objected.'

'So what do you make of it then?'

'My theory is that she wasn't a Fontenay at all, and was buried there because she became a threat.' Jennifer shivered. She'd always suspected there was a dark side to the Fontenay story, and this to her was confirmation.

'A servant? After all, it could have been one of the gardeners burying the remains of his former sweetheart.'

'With the hands folded over the chest, and tidied away in a corner, by a long-dead rose? It's too planned to be a stranger, yet there's no one in the family tree who relates to it. Woman *or* man.'

Michael tried to grapple with this. 'Perhaps it was a servant whom the current Fontenay fell in love with. It would have to be someone who died *after* the skeleton, if you see what I mean – whether he was lover or murderer.'

'Murderer?' Jennifer was aghast. She hadn't got this far.

Michael shrugged. 'It's almost got to be some violent death, hasn't it? One to be covered up, whether it was accident, suicide or murder.'

He shivered and Jennifer noticed. 'I'm sorry. All this talk of skeletons when you're surrounded with death every day can't be fun.'

'No, you're wrong.' Michael frowned. 'I distance myself from it every time I come here to the rose garden, and so this skeleton too, I suppose, is an escape.'

Jennifer slipped her arm through his. 'We'll forget about it. I bought that new golden climber I told you about. We can plant it together, and then bid farewell to the poor soul.'

'Good idea. It's not only the war we need to get away from occasionally.'

'I agree,' Jennifer said quietly. The rose garden was her escape from John's uncertain temper, and the ever present questioning as to whether she'd ever have the child she longed for and over which he was obsessive.

'How is John? Still as bad?'

'Broody. We discuss the vegetables in the evening. And he *watches* me.'

'Do you think he suspects us?'

'Who knows?'

'Live only for the day, as we do.'

'But you're fighting for the future,' she pointed out.

'And so are you. A baby.'

'Is that so bad in wartime?'

He smiled. 'You are a romantic, Jennifer. Rose garden, beloved mistresses laid to rest?'

'What's wrong with being romantic?'

'Nothing.' Michael was suddenly light-hearted again. 'Here's another romantic idea for you. Suppose that skeleton was one of my lot, one of the dreaded Sinclairs, who crept in here by night and never returned.'

By the time I went to Fontenay Place to see Hugo that evening I was still feeling shaky. If ever I was to feel on firm ground on my own property, I had to do as Joss suggested. I had to forget what Gerard had said and what *I* had said; most of all, I had to forget what Joss had said. I couldn't – and I wouldn't – believe he was gay, though I did not dare to investigate why it was so important.

This made seeing Hugo all the easier, for his normality was much easier to bear than the sense I had with Joss that our partnership was being run on his terms – and I wasn't being permitted to know what they were.

'What's the plan of campaign?' he asked, after we'd had an introductory drink.

'I think I'm looking for a mistress.' I laughed at this idiocy.

Hugo laughed, too. 'That's me out then. I take it you mean that this second skeleton might have been someone's mistress. It would be easier to find a Fontenay who didn't have a mistress around that time rather than who did. Are you looking for a dirty old man or the squire's son?'

I hadn't thought of that aspect. 'I rather fancy the squire's son.'

'Let's go and gaze at the family tree.'

Edward Fontenay, the last person to tinker with this sacred object, had died in 1935. The saddest thing was that his son John's entry had a careful marriage symbol entered with no name, since Jennifer had not yet come on the Fontenay scene, and equally careful lines to show the descendants from such a marriage who never came. If Jennifer had been forced to look at this every day of her married life, I felt very sorry for her indeed.

Hugo and I studied the list and came out with a short list of six possible candidates for a putative lover of the second skeleton (assuming the latter was a woman, as Jennifer had said was probable) of which Thomas Fontenay was the most probable if one took the young squire route, Stephen Fontenay if one took the dirty old man route, and his sons Charles and Goderic if one were being more charitable over age.

'I'll do some more rooting around in the library,' Hugo offered. 'Shall we look at the portraits?'

'If she's a mistress she's unlikely to be there.'

'Not necessarily, but actually I was thinking of who's to be remembered in the garden angle, assuming that some may have to be dropped.'

'We'll get them ordered, in case it influences the numbers we can choose from a particular century.'

'Roses before people? Sounds like the great Joss's idea to me.'

'Not a bit of it. It's common sense. After all, there are various siblings and stillbirths that need not have a separate rose each. One rose to record them all perhaps. And a record will be kept in the Hermit's Retreat.' I told Hugo my ideas for that, and he nodded politely.

'I'm sure Joss agreed as well,' he said blandly.

'Yes.'

'Shall we look at the portraits?' he asked.

Here we worked off our mutual ill humour, and felt highly pleased with ourselves, having chosen thirty obvious candidates. I would now, it was agreed, check these against *The Book of Gertrude's Garden* and *The Book of Roses*, and Hugo would check other sources to see whether their records suggested something more should be added. A known villain should not be immortalized with just 'A good husband' as epitaph. We beamed at each other in high approval as we listed John Michael Wright's portrait of Robert Fontenay and family, painted long before Robert died in 1875; Sir Peter Lely's portrait of the formidable Anne Fontenay who inherited after his death; an early Gainsborough of Abigail, a miniature of Sir Edmund's daughter-in-law Arabella – and glory be – an unexpected find, a miniature of Gertrude herself who stared at us, pale and wan, surrounded by her ruff. I could see she was a beauty, but she looked unhappy which sat ill at ease with the devotion the book suggested her husband lavished on her, but confirmed in my mind the Sinclair legend of secret love. Did this affect their two roses in the new garden? I had decided not, eventually. The love Sir Edmund had for her was valid reason enough for them. I was even more glad Joss had moved those two roses to the castle. The new ones we would order would provide the clean sweep I wanted, which was preferable to unsolved secrets – as Gertrude's and Edmund's would surely be.

Then Hugo asked, 'How are the design plans going?'

I pulled a face. 'Joss now says he's doubtful about the sunken garden paved area, in case the roses don't flourish there, but I'm determined to have it. It would set off the fountain, and draw the eye to the roses we plant for Gertrude and Edmund.'

'Did Gerard agree?'

'He wasn't asked.'

'And did Joss give in?'

'He will.' I felt my face flushing.

'Don't get too close to Foxley. There's something odd about him, if you ask me.'

'I didn't, Hugo. Thank you, though.'

He pulled a face. 'Anna,' he added awkwardly, 'just be careful. I'm very fond of you.'

I stiffened. 'That's nice of you, but I'm a big girl now. I don't need a minder.'

'Don't you?' He sighed. 'A pity. I'm rather good at tea, cream cakes and sympathy. Remember that if you need them.'

'They'll wait.' I relented, and added, 'but I might come anyway.'

'Good. We can swap theories about ancient skeletons.'

Six

1795

'My dear, shall we enter?'

Charles Fontenay offered his arm to his wife. Mary, the folds of her brocade dress arranged to her satisfaction, took it as they entered the New Assembly Rooms. Both actions were automatic, as was the courtesy endearment. Society demanded it of them, as of everybody. Behind them came his brother Goderic, ten years his junior, and on his arm his recently betrothed Miss Elizabeth Sayles, a beauty and an heiress. Charles hoped that would lead at last to Goderic's contentment. The role of second brother was not an easy one, but with Elizabeth's fortune and the house they proposed to purchase in Oxfordshire – well away from Fontenay – there was a chance that Goderic might at last come to his senses. Charles envied him, not for the money, nor even for the beauteous Miss Sayles, but for the new life that awaited him. The unknown instead of the known, now there was a thing.

This season in Bath had provided an opportunity for Mary at least to seek the unknown. He had hoped that she would be diverted from her normal melancholy, and that the social atmosphere of Bath with its theatre, concerts, Pump Room and meeting rooms might even provide that which they both wanted so much: a child that might be carried full term and survive its birth. Fontenay needed an heir, otherwise it would pass to Goderic and, unless Elizabeth could work miracles with her husband, Fontenay would be sold. Goderic hated Fontenay, jealous of his brother's inheritance. To look at him now, however, it was hard to believe in Goderic as a malcontent. His handsome looks, the elegant cut of his blue coat, his sparkling gaiety – oh, yes, he was a winner of hearts indeed.

Charles looked round the crowded rooms. Was it only he who saw, not the unknown here, but the dull known of everyday life, and that Bath had nothing to offer but that he had experienced a thousand times before?

'I fear,' Mary said, 'that the concert room may be full. How shall we be seated?' She turned plaintively to Charles.

'There is room enough on that bench.' Goderic indicated seating on the far side of the room, and the party made its slow way towards it. Slow, because one must be noticed. It was all mere vanity, Charles thought, longing for the familiarity of Fontenay.

He and Goderic both saw the girl together, as they approached the bench.

'Pray allow me to be seated first,' Goderic said anxiously to Mary, 'so that you ladies may converse together, as I know you would wish.'

Charles knew full well that Goderic had no such concern in mind. He thought only of how he might be seated next to the fair-haired, pretty young lady of perhaps eighteen or nineteen. Her head was turned from them, as she talked to her companions, presumably her parents. Then distracted by their arrival, she turned her head slightly towards them before resuming her conversation.

'What have we here?' Goderic muttered quickly to his brother as he prepared to take his seat next to her.

Charles could not answer. Never had he seen such deep blue, almost violet eyes, set in such a jewel of a face. No fashionable starch on that shining hair, no need of rich brocades for that delicate figure. The girl was perfection stepped forth from a painting, a rose of Sharon.

Naturally Goderic, as the party took their places, made great play of attention to his own ladies, but Charles knew him well. He thanked heaven that this was a mere passing encounter – if it could even be deemed that since the girl was a stranger to them both. Nevertheless, he found it hard indeed to concentrate on the hour of ballads and musical pieces before there was an interval for refreshment. The young lady's party moved off instantly, but Goderic was forced to remain while Mary adjusted her hat and skirts once more. Charles was mightily pleased.

His pleasure did not last long, however, for once outside the concert rooms, he was almost immediately accosted – there could be no other word – by the very party he had hoped to avoid.

'By heaven, Mr Fontenay, I do declare.'

Charles, taken aback, frowned first in displeasure at this lack of etiquette from a stranger, then from a disturbing thought that this *was* no stranger. He had seen this fellow before, a hearty, overdressed – and overfed – gentleman of forty-odd years.

'Why, sir, I have provisioned your tables with fine wines and sherries these ten years or more. Joshua Kendall at your service. My wife, Mrs Kendall, and my niece Miss Gwendolen Sinclair.'

Charles presented his own party without a thought – save for the overpowering effect that Miss Sinclair was having upon him.

Mary greeted Mr and Mrs Kendall in the gracious way she maintained for those of lower breeding, and Charles pulled himself together, remembering a little about Mr Kendall's establishment and that he was a good-hearted man.

'It is strange, is it not,' he remarked, 'that though we dwell close to the excellent watering place of Tunbridge Wells, we meet in Bath?'

'Indeed it is, sir, but these young folk, like Miss Gwendolen here, think nothing of home pleasures. They must see Bath.'

Gwendolen smiled, and instantly Charles's heart was won.

'Are you enjoying Bath, Miss Sinclair?' Mary's arm stiffened in Charles's as though he were about to seduce the girl. He was well aware that she was percipient where he was concerned.

'I am, thank you, ma'am.'

Charles saw that the beauty of her face was not an insipid one. Miss Sinclair knew her own mind, although she was younger than he had at first thought. Eighteen, at the most.

'I believe I have seen you in the Wells, Miss Sinclair.' Goderic's eyes held the warmth in them that Charles dreaded. He had seen it before, and had hoped, now Elizabeth was here, not to see it again.

'Indeed, it is possible, sir. My father is a schoolmaster, and

I assist him. Perhaps you may have seen us with the children on May Day.'

'A schoolmaster's daughter,' Mary echoed. The tone of her voice indicated that Gwendolen was dismissed. Charles was furious, and hastened to make amends.

'Your pupils are fortunate,' he said, with exactly the right tone of polite flattery.

'To have a teacher with your beauty,' Goderic added, with such calculated objectivity that no one *could* object.

Charles felt his temper rise. 'Shall you take the waters, Miss Sinclair?'

'I have already, sir, though I must confess I consider our Tunbridge Wells waters far superior.'

'I find Bath more . . . *elegant*,' Mary contributed, then she turned to Charles. 'My dear, we must not take up more of Miss Sinclair's time. I believe the concert recommences.'

As they took their places once again, Charles could see that Elizabeth looked troubled, and his instinctive feeling was confirmed when she, and not Goderic, took pains to seat herself at Gwendolen's side.

In the days that followed, Charles endeavoured to put the girl out of his mind. He was a middle-aged man of forty-two, married these ten years. Eighteen-year-old girls had no place in his life.

And yet he could not succeed in dismissing her image. Those eyes danced before him; he found himself contrasting the sweet gentleness of her look and the nature to match, with Mary's sour humour. It was amazing how often he glimpsed Gwendolen in the distance, just as he thought he was managing to forget. He avoided contriving a meeting, however, until the night of the Assembly Room ball. Elizabeth had taken a chill, and he, Mary and Goderic went alone. To his dread, the first thing he heard on entering was Joshua Kendall's loud laugh, and it was compounded by the fact that Goderic danced not once but three times with Miss Sinclair, including the supper dance.

'Take care, Goderic,' Charles warned him.

Goderic smiled. 'You are such a boring man, Charles. I

am permitted to dally until I am actually married, am I not?'

'Not so, and not with a girl such as Miss Sinclair.'

'Could it be, Charles, that you are smitten yourself with the fine Gwendolen's charms? She holds her fan before her face with her left hand. This new language of the fan is spreading rapidly amongst society. Miss Sinclair's fan is indicating she is desirous of further acquaintance with you.'

Charles flushed. 'I am a happily married man.'

'Married, yes,' Goderic agreed.

'And forty-two years of age.'

'Just the time for foolish thoughts.'

'But with the wisdom to suppress them.'

Goderic sighed. 'Now I, alas, lack the maturity to do so. That must be my excuse.'

'You are impossible, sir.'

'I am indeed.'

'It is fortunate we leave Bath in a week's time.'

'I am eager to do so. By the way, dear brother, I have reserved a dance for you with the beautiful Miss Sinclair.'

'*What?*' Surely even Goderic would not be so mischievous.

'The lancers will provide plenty of opportunities to touch the fair Gwendolen's hand. You need not fear. I shall do my duty by Mary for you. She'll not notice.'

'There will be nothing to notice.' It sounded weak even to Charles. How extraordinary dancing was, he thought in a dream, with Gwendolen at his side as the lancers began shortly afterwards. Dancing was parting and coming together, like life itself. The exquisite touch of the fingers a glimpse of what might be. The arm round her waist a symbol of the possession that could never be his.

'Are you enjoying the dance, Mr Fontenay?' Gwendolen said. 'You do not speak.'

In another girl such a statement would seem a demand for flattery, but in her it was a mere statement of truth.

'Forgive me, Miss Sinclair. My thoughts were far away.' Charles lied. They were in fact all wrapped up in her.

'You have a fine rose garden at Fontenay, do you not?'

'You have heard of it?'

'And seen it, sir. I have visited the grounds with my father. He knows much about Kentish history. He has told me about the old legends.'

'The rose planted for every Fontenay on death?'

'That – and the one about the Sinclairs.'

To Charles that name was a terrible jolt. How could he not have registered the name before? His father had rammed it down his throat often enough. The old story about harm coming to the Fontenays through the creeping pestilence of the Sinclairs. It was a common name, however, and perhaps Miss Sinclair did not mean what he feared.

But she did. 'My father told me,' she explained, as they danced, 'that he believes we are descended from the family that did yours much harm in the Rebellion of 1648. But that is long ago now, nearly a century and a half. And we had good reason, father says.' She laughed as though he, like her, saw this as ancient history to be disregarded. 'It was once our land, we were dispossessed, and it was given to the Fontenays. So you see,' she stopped suddenly as she saw the look in his eyes. 'I have displeased you, sir.'

'No,' he replied fervently. 'As you say, it is a long while since those days.'

He thought of the entries in *The Book of Gertrude's Garden*, and remembered it had been the redoubtable Sir Robert Fontenay who possessed Fontenay then. Would he ever have imagined that one of his successors would be leading a Sinclair in dance and with such pleasure? 'You like roses?' He hastened to change the subject.

'I do, sir.'

The dance was ending now. Charles bowed and heard himself voice the fatal words: 'You must permit me the honour of escorting you round our rose garden one day.'

'I should welcome it, sir.'

It was over. Charles heaved a sigh of relief. Two formal sentences committed one to nothing. True, Gwendolen (for so he had come to think of her) lived not so very far away, but back in the security of Fontenay, back into everyday life, he could forget her. Forget the way he imagined her hand had rested longer than it should have in his, forget the way her eyes

91

had shone when he so stupidly offered to take her round the rose garden. If only, dear God, if only it had been possible.

He was right. Back at Fontenay it was easier to at least seem as though all was normal. That was so for three months, until the day he realized that normality had gone for ever.

'Charles.' Mary had been brooding. He could see it from the look on her face.

'My dear?'

'I saw that Sinclair girl this morning. I am almost sure. She was in the village, as I rode by in the carriage.' The faint emphasis on carriage was intended to point the difference in their two stations.

'I daresay you are mistaken, my love. What would she be doing in Cranden?'

'I ask myself that very question. Do you know the answer, Charles?'

He was perplexed. 'No.'

'I do. I made it my business to enquire.'

'Of her?'

'Naturally not. She is not the class of person I acknowledge in the street.'

'What class of person is that?' he could not resist asking.

'Do not rile me, Charles. You know full well. To continue, that girl is now an assistant in our village school, if you please. This is your doing.'

'*Mine?*' Charles blinked in astonishment, even as the warmth slowly entered his life again. 'How could it be mine?'

'I saw the way you looked at her.'

'What way is that?'

'Desirously,' Mary proclaimed in triumph.

Charles sighed. This had happened before and doubtless would again – though not with such cause, he admitted. 'We have been wed for many years, Mary. Have I shown in any way that my feelings for you have lessened? They remain unaltered since the day I wed you.'

Another lie but it would placate her. Another part of his brain was intent on wondering whether it were true that Gwendolen was or had been in Cranden, and how it had happened. 'I assure you,' he continued, 'I have no idea how the girl came to be here.' Had she taken a position just to be near Fontenay's rose garden, to be near – he hardly dared think it – to him?

He quickly realized there was another more likely answer, however, and his burst of fantasy died quickly away.

He went in search of Goderic, whose apartments were on the other side of the house. If only Goderic would wed quickly and be gone from here. These rooms were for a nursery, not to nurse an infantile brother.

'My dear Charles, how pleased to see you!' Goderic reclined on a day bed reading a newspaper.

'Mary tells me that Miss Sinclair is in the village, working at the school,' Charles said without ado.

'Is she? Dear brother, what have you been up to?'

'Nothing, as you know full well. Are you mad, Goderic? With your wedding even now being planned?'

'I shall not be wed for a year. Elizabeth's parents wish it that way. They would spend the coming winter abroad in Italy with their darling daughter.'

Charles's heart sank. 'But the marriage will still take place?'

'Indeed. Elizabeth adores me.'

'That is not quite the same thing. You paid Miss Sinclair too much attention and it did not go unobserved.'

'Only by you. I was polite, that is all.'

'And now politeness has led you to find the girl a job in the village?'

He shrugged. 'Why not? She is interested in roses.'

'But let it stop there.'

Goderic grinned. 'There are long summer nights, brother, and next summer is far away.'

Charles felt a great chill. 'I will warn her.'

'Do as you please. I doubt she will listen – *now*.'

'What have you done?' His breath came in short bursts. The significance of the 'now' was all too clear. Goderic meant to imply he had seduced the girl. Had he done so or did he but taunt him? Rage, such as Charles had never felt before, consumed him. He would turn Goderic out of his house. No, that would be worse. There would be no control then and the scandal would break. He would have to find out from Gwendolen herself, Charles decided.

'This is beautiful indeed.' Gwendolen's cheeks were as pink as the rose itself. Her gown was of pale blue and all the roses in the garden could not produce so lovely a sight.

'One of the new roses from China, a Parsons' Pink Blush, planted for my dear mother Abigail who died five years ago. We are near the end of the season now, yet it stays blooming in her memory till winter frosts are with us.'

He watched her as she bent over it, and his heart turned over as her lips rested lightly on one of the blooms in a kiss.

'It is glorious, Mr Fontenay, and yet my heart is with our English roses that grow so sturdily. My favourite is the simple white musk rose, the *Rosa moschata*. This bloom is too perfect, and life cannot always be so, can it, sir?'

'No, Miss Sinclair. You are very wise.'

'I trust so, sir.' For a moment her face was sad, but then the shadow passed.

He had held out as long as he could against extending this invitation, but during the past weeks, with the schoolchildren occupied in harvesting and not at their lessons, he had not even been able to catch a glimpse of her at the schoolhouse. Had she been there – or returned to her parents? Or worse, was she with Goderic? Finally he could hold out no longer and had written the long-delayed suggestion that they should meet here.

Charles had still battled with his conscience. After all, Gwendolen had wanted to see the garden again, and he had had no option but to try to discover what her feelings for Goderic were. His voice revealed nothing of his inner anguish. 'This is Sir Robert Fontenay's white alba rose. As you perhaps know, it was he defended the castle in vain in the rebellion.'

Gwendolen hesitated, then drew confidence from the smile on his face. 'Against us wicked Sinclairs.'

'I fear so.'

'But you Fontenays are strong. You came back when the king returned, and we Sinclairs lost all we had *again*, just as we did in earlier times. Perhaps you do not know that the land was held by King Malcolm of Scotland, among other estates in England; he gave it to the Sinclairs who at Malcolm's behest paid homage to the English king for it. Then it was seized with the king's permission by Rupert de Fontnoi, and we poor Sinclairs dispossessed.' She laughed. 'Do not fear, Mr Fontenay. I shall make no bid for your land.'

Charles tried to think of some urbane remark, such as Goderic would give, but he could not. All he could think of was his delight at her closeness. 'There will be no more war between Fontenays and Sinclairs,' he said grandly.

'We have peace in England now.'

'With the Revolution and Robespierre's death in France? Not for long I fear.'

'But Captain Nelson is succeeding so well against the French fleet.'

'I suspect this young Bonaparte is intent on conquering England. So we Sinclairs and Fontenays must stick together.' There was a heartiness in Charles's voice which he hoped would cover his racing heart.

'You are very good, Mr Fontenay, to ignore my teasing.'

'Pray do call me Charles.'

'I cannot.' She looked alarmed.

'Just once.' He held her hand, in panic that he had gone too far.

'Charles,' she whispered.

'I would do anything for you, Gwendolen. You must come to me if ever I can be of service.'

'This red rose,' she faltered, 'what is this?'

'For true love. This one is for a man who loved a maid but could not tell her so because he was already married, albeit childless and unhappy.'

'And what happened?' She looked steadily in the opposite direction.

'He could not with honour even speak of his love and so he never knew whether she could have loved him as he did her.'

'Oh, Charles. She could not.' She took his hands, and kissed him on the cheek. 'She could not do so for she loves someone else.'

'Someone close to him?' He could not bear it, he could not.

Gwendolen flushed. 'Yes. You will think badly of me, Charles, but he, Goderic, has explained. He was trapped into an engagement with Miss Sayles, who is delightful, but whom he cannot love as he loves me. He has asked her to leave the marriage for a year while she travels on the continent on the grounds that he is older than her and she must be sure of her own mind. Goderic is sure she will forget him, so that we may be wed with honour.'

'Wed?' Charles groaned. 'He will never do so, Gwendolen.'

'Oh, yes,' she smiled. 'I know he will. I am –' that blush again – 'already Goderic's wife in all but name.'

He could not speak. He could not even look at the innocence of her face, and see the happiness there, the confidence in what would never happen. He covered his face with his hands. She put her arms round him and kissed his cheek again. 'Do not weep for me, Charles. I am so happy.'

But he did weep. And blinded by tears, he did not sense the third person, who crept away from her hiding place by the gate, unable to hear their conversation, but well able to see their embrace: Mary.

'Charles, I would speak with you.'

'My dear?' Charles looked up at the unusual softness in Mary's voice. She had been exceptionally withdrawn this last week, which suited him for since his meeting with Gwendolen his heart had been too full of his own grief to cope with Mary's supposed ills.

'There is something I must tell you. I have good news.'

'I am pleased. Your sister is coming to stay?' Such polite platitudes might conceal his aching heart.

'Far better. I am with child again. I am sure of it.'

He looked at her astounded, unable to believe his good fortune. This was indeed something to rejoice at. 'My dear love,' he said as he kissed her, 'our Bath visit followed by the summer sun must have produced what we have so long hoped for.'

'Was it not a delightful visit, Charles? How happy we shall be now.'

A child. He clutched the thought to him with relief. All would be well, if Mary could but carry it full term. 'When?'

'In early June. A spring child. It will come with the roses.'

He took her in his arms. 'Dearest Mary, indeed we shall be happy. But you must take every care.'

'I shall, Charles, I shall.'

I debated over what I should wear. A dance in the assembly rooms at Tunbridge Wells called for a certain amount of formality, so I put on my black trousers and top. I then looked in the mirror and decided I looked like a halloween spectre. To wear all black is not a good idea for me, and so I ended up with my black velvet skirt and blue blouse. An evening with Hugo was a velvet skirt sort of occasion, I decided. It wasn't exactly a date, because Gerard was coming too, plus Sarah Dodds, with whom he seemed to have struck up a friendship. I hoped that was the right word. It was a charity do, so we had all bought our own tickets, which in practice meant I bought three and Hugo bought one. It was hardly an eighteenth-century-style occasion even though that was the skeleton on my mind as we arrived in Tunbridge Wells. It was nevertheless quite formal. After all, this is an eighteenth-century town with its Pantiles and spa.

'What about Joss?' Gerard had teased me when I first broached the idea to him.

'I haven't the slightest idea. I shouldn't think he's a charity dance person. More into preserving woodlands, and the like.'

'Even they have to have fundraising ventures.'

'Look, I'm going with Hugo. Okay?'

He spread his hands in surrender. 'Suits me. He's the sort of guy to order champagne or nothing. Mind you, he's also the sort of guy who won't want to buy his former waitress champagne, unless he has seduction in mind.'

'You're the future lord of the manor. You have the prerogative. Anyway, he won't purloin Sarah, since Hugo's also the sort of guy to want to keep in with you.'

'And you.'

I lost it. 'Get stuffed, Gerard,' I yelled at him.

'I intend to.' So that answered my question.

It did prove to be champagne, as Hugo had organized it. Gerard shot me a triumphant look.

'Isn't there something wrong about making profit on champagne to give to the starving?' Sarah demanded.

'Don't have any if you're worried. I'll drink it.' Gerard is always practical.

'How's the hunt going?' Hugo enquired, after we had toasted Fontenay's future success.

'Which skeleton?' My voice was somewhat dry, despite the champagne.

'There's more than one?' Sarah asked curiously.

'One from the past,' I explained. 'Possibly early nineteenth-century but, in my mind at least, more likely late eighteenth. It was dug up by your great-aunt.'

'Poor old Jennifer. Didn't have much luck, did she?'

Hugo asked Sarah to dance (almost as if setting out to confound all Gerard's theories) and Gerard stared gloomily at me. 'I hope you're not going to ask me to waltz with you, Mum.'

'I am.'

'Absolutely not.'

'If I can, you can.'

'Joss wouldn't like it.' He was looking over my shoulder.

Before I could launch myself into another tirade I turned round to see a stranger approaching me, who slowly reformed himself into Joss. I couldn't be blamed for not instantly recognizing him. He was in evening dress, not jeans, and his hair was organized into some sort of shape.

'Shall we dance?' he offered politely as Gerard leered.

'I can't find my dance card. It may be full.'

'I'll risk it. The irate punters can drag me away from you if they feel strongly enough. Anyway, it's obligatory for the boss to dance with the staff.'

'Only at the New Year's Eve servants' dance.'

'Are you propositioning me?'

'Sure,' I tried to quip, deciding I wasn't much good at this. 'You, Sarah, the milkman and the men who come to clear the cesspool.'

'Glad I was here first then.'

It was weird dancing with Joss, not least because I'd never been hot on ballroom dancing and couldn't remember how to waltz, apart from the fact that one-two-three came into it somewhere. Joss, unfortunately, appeared to be black belt or whatever its equivalent is in ballroom dancing.

'Just relax against me,' he purred. 'Leave it to me. I'll steer you.'

Only one way to deal with this. I accepted. Anything else would play right into his hands. Mind you, this did too, almost literally. Once I'd commanded my body to relax, it was relatively easy to dance. It was not relatively easy to forget how close I was to him, or that my body fitted all too comfortably against his. I even – no, forget that, Anna. Forget it right away.

'We ought to talk serious roses tomorrow,' I said quickly to distance myself from the physical.

'We have to, if we're going to get them in time.'

'The eighteenth-century ones in particular.'

'Ah. We're on skeleton number 2, are we?'

'Yes. I've been looking at the map again, and I'm sure I know in which corner the skeleton was found.'

'Which is?'

'I'll tell you tomorrow.'

The dance ended and he thanked me politely.

'Drink?' I offered.

'I should return to Gemma.' He looked vaguely round, apparently spotted her and vanished. Gemma? Wife, sister, girlfriend, or aged aunt? I craned my neck, but in the crowd I lost him, which was just as well, because Hugo returned to claim me.

'I see the roughneck is looking relatively presentable tonight.'

'Amazing how these commoners ape their betters, isn't it?' I remarked companionably.

He laughed. 'It's very easy to stir you up, Anna. I can't resist doing it. Dance?'

This wasn't a waltz but a sixties pop session, so I knew where I was with this. Hugo did too, and we wriggled, jigged and spun our way through, thoroughly satisfied with ourselves. By the time he twisted me back into his arms for a final united jig, I really felt comfortable with him – far too comfortable.

As I disposed of my make-up later (alone, as I'd thwarted an overt offer by Hugo to join me) I reflected that the evening had taught me one thing at least. My body, and increasingly my heart, were ready for love again, but that I'd better be darn careful whom they picked.

All signs of Joss, the dinner-suited gent about town, had disappeared when he turned up at the lodge next morning, armed with catalogues, notepads, and design plans. Once more we pored over the latter with their detailed comments on sun, shade, and space available. The village stonemason was already at work on the fountain and would soon be transporting it here. He was a bit of an amateur historian, it turned out, and was keen on producing his own version of a description of a Tudor fountain at the palace of Nonsuch, beloved of Queen Elizabeth but now, alas, no more. In effect we were getting two fountains, not one, each spurting water round its companion, and both adorned with carved stone birds with more water pouring forth from their beaks. Joss and I both liked the idea, especially since the two elements of the structure balanced the two roses of Edmund and Gertrude which would be either side of it.

We were still at odds over whether the fountain should be in a sunken paved area or whether the garden should be levelled. To my relief Joss appeared to be in a mood of compromise for once, and this issue was settled by the choice of roses flanking the steps coming down to the fountain, with only a handful of hardy roses on the lower level itself. I wanted Jennifer's to be there, as well as Gertrude and Edmund's, but Joss was dubious.

'Why not skeleton number 2's then?

I had the perfect answer to this. 'I think the skeleton was in the far left-hand corner, and that the yellow climber still there is the remains of the rose Jennifer planted for it. Her letter spoke of buying a Rêve d'Or and the skeleton all in one paragraph. She probably replaced an earlier rose that had died. It would have lasted a hell of a time otherwise.'

'What's your proof? The *Rosa moschata* that Jennifer pulled out of the ground goes way back into late Tudor times at least. You've got an eighteenth- or early nineteenth-century skeleton.'

'Who liked old roses,' I retorted.

'Not convinced. The China roses were coming in from mid-century on, once the East India Company got established. They weren't all big on perfume like the English roses, but they flowered and flowered again. That was a big deal then, and likely to have appeal for rose gardens.'

'Can you get them now.'

He looked at me kindly. 'Masses of modern roses are developed from them.'

'I still think that yellow climber is Jennifer's replacement, and that the far corner is the right position. Look.' I produced my coup de théâtre, the map of the late eighteenth century. 'Something struck me as odd when I looked at it again last night. You see this rose shape in the corner, indicating a rose has been planted there.'

'Yes.'

'It bears the number 57. Number 58 is Mary Fontenay who died in 1799 and 56 is Charlotte Fontenay, a stillborn baby of 1787. Both their roses were in the south part of the garden. Number 57, according to the index, is Matthew Fontenay, twin to Charlotte, and also stillborn. Planted in the north-west corner.'

'So? I can see it's odd that the babies would be separated, but what does it mean, if anything?'

'I don't know.'

At that very moment, since the two of us began to laugh at the absurdity of our detective instincts, Hugo walked in. We'd been sitting in the conservatory, which from Fontenay Place is in the first room of the lodge that you see, so he came straight through the garden.

'Tell me,' he asked plaintively, seeing the Fontenay books spread around.

Obligingly, Joss did.

'There's one obvious explanation,' Hugo said when Joss had finished. 'And that's the maker of the map intended to cover up the true identity of Number 57.'

Joss and I looked at each other.

'The map-maker?' My mind clicked into gear again.

'Yes. We can assume that the rose was planted at the time of death.'

I agreed. 'No need for secrecy otherwise.'

'Then there's an obvious choice,' Hugo announced. 'Either Charles or St John Fontenay, and I seem to remember David telling me Charles did the early ones and this one shortly before his death in 1818.'

'I don't remember his being so specific.'

'Ah, but you, darling Anna, were never exactly enthusiastic on the question of roses.'

'Checkmate,' I surrendered.

'I'm still on the board,' Joss remarked here. 'If Charles Fontenay drew up this map, why did he need to conceal the identity of the skeleton?'

'Because he murdered it,' Hugo rejoined.

Joss grinned. 'Then he wouldn't put it in the map and index at all. Checkmate, Hugo?'

Seven

The next morning I walked over to the rose garden, now preparing for the phoenix shortly to arise from its ashes. I knew Joss wouldn't be there, and it was a good opportunity to study it on the ground. Designs only take one so far, and I needed to see it in my mind's eye and on my own.

Joss had done a good job in preparing this canvas for the forthcoming picture. Not being a gardener with a capital 'G', barren earth had never excited me before with its possibilities, but I was amused to see that Joss had obviously laid strings already to indicate where the sunken part and the steps *might* lie, if he conceded the fight – as he now had. Slowly it began to come alive in my mind. I saw the rose walk under its canopy of ramblers, I saw the completed fountain, the sprawling roses in their stone pots, a cat basking on the sunny steps. Beyond the sunken garden I could see an arbour smothered in pink rambling roses, I even imagined a Fragonard-type swing carrying the Fontenay ladies, surrounded by flowers. Belatedly, I realized with some surprise, that I no longer flinched from the idea of some day having to walk those paths.

There had been women in the family as well as men who dominated the history of the garden, I reflected. Edmund Fontenay had begun it, Charles and St John Fontenay had drawn up *The Book of Roses*, working on their maps and index. It had been Anne, however, owner of Fontenay for thirty years in the late seventeenth century, who had changed it from its formal Tudor knot pattern to provide the long vista of castle ruins to arbour which Joss now wanted to recreate; lawns, paths, and an artificed 'informality' had replaced mathematically precise knots. The famous Abigail, a century later, had created the Hermit's Retreat; and David's great-grandmother, Victoria, had introduced underplanting with cottage garden flowers for continuous colour. And then there had been Jennifer. Had Jennifer changed it, added her own touches? Or had she simply loved it, which was just as important. Now there was me, the one that didn't like roses. I was getting used to the idea of the rose garden existing once more, but that was a far different cry from loving its inmates, as Jennifer had done. I couldn't see that ever happening.

I wondered what Gerard was thinking deep down about our plans. He had been tolerant so far, but what were he and Sarah making of all this emotion spent over a plot of land? They'd find out, I told myself. The obligations of the past, or at least its tentacles, creep up on one with the years. They can support you into the future, or bury you in history. I was determined that, even with two skeletons to contend with, I would not be buried. This was tomorrow's garden, not yesterday's.

Plans had moved on slightly for the sunken area. A small lavender-hedged garden with Gertrude and Edmund's roses and the fountain would be the centrepiece, such as inspired Chaucer. It had been agreed that there would be two more planted roses in the sunken area – one for the gardener who died in the flying bomb incident, and one for Jennifer. Both should be the Peace rose, Joss suggested, golden yellow tinged with pink, and fragrant. The rose, a hybrid tea standard, was born about the time of the flying bomb, so what more suitable tribute?

As I stood there that early September day, some of the trees in the woodlands near the garden were already showing signs of changing colour and the air had the atmosphere of mellow autumn. It was easy to imagine a blaze of colour that this garden would have next summer, and to see how it would harmonize with the gardens around the ruins of the old castle. Joss told me he was dreaming up a pattern of paths and gardens, a universal maze design with the rose garden as its centre. It would be a sort of Fair Rosamond in her bower, he explained. This had thrown me. I couldn't see what he was getting at.

'I thought she was bumped off in a tower in Oxfordshire.'

'Depends which book you read. Some say it was in Kent,

near Folkestone, so maybe it could even have been here. It's a familiar Snow White theme, anyway, the innocent beauty bumped off in the middle of the garden, because the wicked witch – in Rosamond's case, Henry II's wife – found a way to poison her.'

Remembering that conversation, I was brought back to my two skeletons. This couldn't be the garden I was foreseeing until I felt any evil they represented had been purged. In neither case could I be sure that murder was the cause of death, but the probability was quite high. One skeleton I had seen myself, but the other lingered in my mind just as compellingly. It was as if they were demanding their stories be heard, by the very place in which they had been buried. A rose garden of remembrance in which they had no memorial – yet.

I realized I was no longer alone. Joss had come up quietly behind me, making me jump.

'I thought you were ordering rose trees today?' I said, as I got my breath back.

'I was, then I thought I'd come here.'

'Any particular reason?'

'I imagine the same as yours. To meditate on the garden.'

I wasn't prepared to admit to him that this was indeed what had brought me here. His meditation, after all, might be confined to the practical; mine, I was all too conscious, wasn't.

'Should you give the other skeleton a new rose too, Joss? Or just leave the climber in place?'

I spoke unthinkingly, until I saw his startled look. I grinned as I realized I had given control to him – a rare mistake on my part. Still, he accepted it.

'Difficult,' he replied. 'We only have a theory about it. We only know for certain what Jennifer told us, and with the war on and less advanced archaeological methods, that isn't much. Today stratification could have helped establish the time it was buried at least.'

'Surely we could assume now it was between 1787 and 1799?'

'And that the skeleton was the beloved, or not so beloved, of the lord of the manor?'

'Yes.'

'In the absence of any other theory, Mrs Fontenay,' he announced gravely, 'I can accept this thesis.'

'In that case, Mr Foxley, could you explain why he buried her in the rose garden and not the cemetery?'

'Murder still comes to mind, Mrs Fontenay.'

'Then why the rose garden and not the woods? It's the same argument as with Jennifer and Michael Sinclair.'

'Not quite. In Jennifer's case there's a logical reason, because of the flying bomb damage ensuring that's the last place anyone would search again.'

I sighed. 'We're going round in circles. Maybe it isn't possible to establish the truth about either skeleton now.'

'Does it matter?'

I stared at him in astonishment. 'I thought you agreed with me that it did.'

'I agree it would be good to find out what really happened, but essential? No, not if they're remembered. And their secrets may be better left that way. I know you want to be able to ditch this whole project if you can't establish the truth, but you may come to the point when you have to acknowledge it's impossible and decide whether you abandon all the Fontenay ancestors for the sake of two skeletons, one unidentifiable.'

'As you said to me once, there's more to it, isn't there?'

'Perhaps.'

'You know me well enough to tell me.'

'Do I?'

'Yes.' Looking at him I wasn't so sure he thought so, how-ever. He played his cards close to his manly chest, did Joss.

'I'll have a go. Remember the old Chaucer legend?'

'Here we go again. This is the story of my married life.'

'Tough. Chaucer is where it all began unless you care to go back to the Bible and the Rose of Sharon, or Gardens of Allah.'

'Chaucer will do.'

'The narrator of the poem wanted to grab his perfect rose, yes?'

'Agreed.'

'What stopped him achieving this grand object at first?'

'Danger, False-seeming, Jealousy – you name it. These

106

illustrious personages stood around the fountain and tried to deflect him.'

'And what makes you think a 21st-century garden would be any different?'

It took me a second or two to see what he meant – and then I couldn't believe he was serious. Danger? Jealousy? 'Oh come off it, Joss. It's two skeletons in the past we're interested in, not nasty bandits behind bushes coming out to bash us over the head.'

'Your eighteenth-century skeleton might have met a bandit. Jennifer certainly did, and that's only fifty-odd years ago.'

'But how could that be linked to us in today's world? Our dangers, in the west at any rate, usually come by post with big bills and council red tape, not with physical violence – well, not over a rose garden anyway.'

'You mean there's no danger or false-seeming around now? No jealousy? You don't think the past murders were linked by them to each other, or to today?'

'Of course not. How could they be?'

'How could they not be?'

'Easily. Much harder to say *why* they might have been linked. If Jennifer was murdered, it was because she fell in love with another man, and was probably carrying his child. We know that.'

'Do we?'

I lost my temper. '*I* do, even if you don't, Joss.'

'But then you're the one who *knows* there's no jealousy around today guarding this rose garden. I mean this, Anna.'

The casual arm round my shoulders suddenly tightened, and the other one went round my waist. I'm not sure what happened next, except that his lips were on mine and my treacherous body was leaping in, saying, 'More please, *now*.'

'Can I ramble?' he whispered.

I was all too eager, and we rambled happily for some minutes. Until he remarked, 'And suppose Hugo were once again watching us?'

Startled, I looked around. 'There's no one here but us.'

'Jealousy's always present.'

'Not in a paradise garden.'

'You know, Anna, human beings are odd creatures. This garden existed quite happily for centuries, with pink, red, mauve and white roses, but then tales came back from China of yellow roses. Yellow for jealousy in the language of flowers. Had yellow been missed till then or did everyone decide they wanted it just because it was new? So in comes the Parks' Yellow. In comes jealousy, and has never left.'

'Fanciful, Joss,' I said uneasily.

'Is it? What, I wonder, would the blue rose bring with it?'

1944

'Oh, Michael, you don't know how much I've longed for today.' Jennifer sank down beside him in the Hermit's Retreat.

'I'm not exactly the handsome fighter pilot you waved off last October.' He winced as his back stabbed in pain. The Spit hadn't even been shot down in enemy action; he'd been on an uneventful escort op, and had to crash-land on his return after an accident with a bomber taking off. It was the bomber's fault, but the Spit had paid the penalty. That had been over four months ago. His back put paid to any more flying, and his face and arms still bore scars.

'You've done your share,' she said quietly. 'And you're still at West Malling.'

'Flying a desk,' he said bitterly.

'It depends how well it's flown, just like a Spitfire.'

He held her close. 'You make it sound as if I should be glad.'

'I am. And I'm sure Hazel is.'

'I don't think she gives a damn.'

Hastily she changed the subject. 'I'm afraid it's a very early March garden here. Signs of leaves, time for pruning, and all promise. Like your job,' she added craftily.

He laughed at that. Huddled round the paraffin stove, it was warm and cosy, and he began to feel better. 'Well, if we can't sniff roses, tell me what's been happening to your famous skeleton since your last letter about it.'

'Plenty. At long last I've had the report back. I've decided it's probably eighteenth-century and a girl. I've been delving into *The Book of Gertrude's Garden* and the maps and index. My guess is that the girl was Charles Fontenay's mistress. I think he bumped her off and hid her in the rose garden.'

'Does it matter, lovely lady? In the middle of war?'

'I think it does.' Jennifer felt stubborn over this. 'There are stillborn babies recorded in the book, but at last Mary, Charles's wife, produced a son and heir in 1796. Charles would have wanted to keep all signs of a mistress quiet then.'

'Suppose it was just the gardener who killed his shrew-ish wife?'

'And put it where someone might find it? No. I'm sure I'm right. You see, I've been studying the records. There's a rose shape on the map that may have a false number, right where you found the skeleton, and I found that dead rose.'

She proceeded to explain why this was so significant. Michael listened attentively, but all he said was, 'I suppose I can't blame you for taking an interest. After all, I've had time this winter to do some delving into family history on my own account. I've something to tell you.'

'What's that?' Jennifer was agog.

'I don't think I'm a Sinclair after all.'

She stared at him in amazement. 'You mean not a Sinclair at all? Or not a Fontenay-enemy-Sinclair? Well, that's good news if you want to keep in John's good books.'

'I do, believe me I do. I'm angling for a posting here.'

'Now look here,' she teased him, twisting his hair and snuggling up to him in the warmth of the stove, 'don't tantalize me. Firstly you tell me you're not a Sinclair and now you drop this bombshell.'

'Which do you want to hear first!'

'Guess!'

'The posting here. The army has informed us it's looking for new premises for troops to move into. You can make your own assumptions why – and, I'm afraid, where.'

He watched her assimilate this unwelcome news. When the

Allies made their long-awaited assault on occupied France, the obvious place for the build-up of troops would be Kent. Where else? But troops in Fontenay Place would be a major spanner in her running of the vegetable and fruit business she'd set up, and John was most certainly not going to be pleased.

'It's not the men themselves,' Michael told her, 'though they may be barracked nearby, but the army need HQ and Staff Quarters.'

'What does this have to do with you and Fontenay?'

'The army will need a liaison officer with the RAF, and now I'm back, I'm hopeful they'll use me. This seems the next best thing now I'm grounded. The squadron pilots don't need a constant reminder of folks who've crashed, and it's the answer to all sorts of problems.'

'It would be wonderful if you could get the posting.' Jennifer's eyes shone as she hugged him. 'Even John can't complain about your being around then. Now you can tell me the other bit of news.'

'I asked my parents for the Sinclair family files and so on, and I suddenly realized there was no birth certificate for me. I'd never actually needed to see it myself. So I asked Dad and he was a bit cagey.'

Jennifer laughed. 'Did they preempt the wedding day? It's happened before.'

'They never had any more children, so I began to think I might have been adopted. My father admitted as much. So, I'm not a Sinclair.'

'Who were your parents?'

'He doesn't know.'

Jennifer sighed with pleasure. 'That's good. If John asks again, I can tell him that.'

'Has he asked? I thought he didn't care about my wicked Sinclair name.'

'He didn't at first, but then he began to mutter about Sinclairs secretly stealing into Fontenays' lives, and no good would come of it. He dropped it while you were ill, but don't be surprised if it crops up again if you are posted here.'

'Does he know I'm here today?'

'No, I thought it best not to tell him.'

Michael put his arm round her. 'I've something else to tell you, Jennifer. Something I've realized while I've been away.'

'I think I can guess.'

'Is it so obvious? I suppose it is. I'm in love, really and truly.'

She looked at him, her face full of delight. 'What about Hazel?' she asked quietly.

'We'll work it out somehow. Somehow, someday I'll be free to marry again.'

He'd had a long time to think while he'd been recovering, to think about what was important. Hazel had been dutifully attentive while he'd been at home, and William was a delight. At three years old, he was becoming a person in his own right. He was in no doubt however that there was still someone else in her life, and finally she told him so. The reason she had all this time to spare was that the other man had been posted away, heavily involved in high-up discussions about the forthcoming invasion of France. Relief had made him delirious with joy. There was a chance for him after all, and a chance that would mean no dishonour, if Hazel wanted a divorce as much as he.

Later that day I puzzled over what Joss had said. I realized we had been taking a lot for granted, but not so much as to justify his cryptic warnings – presumably that's what it was – that we walked in dangerous times (even if I was prepared to admit the jealousy). For heaven's sake, we were restoring old gardens in the heart of Kent, not delving into virgin jungle territory. Whatever we discovered could have little bearing on today. This was my logical conclusion, but even when Joss left me, his parting words were to 'tread carefully'. After the briefest of pauses, he added, 'The ground in the centre's still very loose where I dug it.'

I'd got the point. He must see Hugo as some kind of threat. Presuming I was the football, this was flattering but hardly borne out by the facts. Two kisses from Joss, one easily repelled approach from Hugo. Hardly a duel at dawn for my fair hand. What else could arouse jealousy? It could only be Fontenay itself, and that was securely in my hands and would then pass to Gerard. No question of that, so as a bride my dowry would be somewhat deficient.

Right on cue, there was a message on my answerphone when I got back to the lodge to ring Hugo. 'I've some news for you,' he informed me, when I did so.

'I hope it's good.'

'I think you'll be fascinated, Anna.'

'What is it?'

'Some of it's about your skeleton and it's arriving this afternoon. May I bring it along tonight?'

'Which skeleton?'

'The eighteenth-century one.'

'Come to supper.' It was the least I could offer, and it would be pleasant. Having cleared the air over the sex issue temporarily, there wouldn't be any problem there. I pondered over inviting Joss too, and decided this might not be such a good idea. Whether I was the subject or not, there was an antagonism between them that contact over a dinner table was not going to help. As it happened, Gerard announced he would be present. He would be leaving shortly and I didn't want to pass the opportunity of an evening with him. Most of them, he spent with Sarah.

I managed to produce a tolerable beef casserole, with a chestnut soufflé to follow, and decided it was time for a celebration. Although the rose garden was taking precedence in my thoughts, most of my actual activity at that time was still at the tea-room and giftshop buildings, which were reaching the stage when the interior and not the exterior was the main concern. They would open in the spring, so I could even start thinking turnover – and whom I could get to cook the delicious goodies that were going to win the hearts, stomachs and purses of our paying public.

We made polite talk during dinner and a bottle of claret; even Gerard was entertainingly chatty. I was therefore pleasantly mellow, though still fairly alert, when we settled down to the grim business of skeletons once more.

112

Hugo produced his coup, in the form of an old book, albeit leather-bound. 'It's a volume of memoirs of life in Cranden in the late eighteenth century by its vicar, published by one of his descendants half a century later. I found a copy in the archives office to browse through, and then managed to buy one over the Internet. I purchased it at enormous expense for Fontenay Place.'

'Send in the bill,' said Gerard grandly.

'I wouldn't dream of it. *My Life* by the Reverend Benedict Lee, the Vicar of Cranden, is mine, all mine.' Hugo grinned.

'What does this old vicar have to say?' I asked.

'It's a sort of personal diary-cum-village history. Maybe he'd been reading too much Pepys. Anyway, I found an entry you would be interested in for 1795.'

He handed me the bookmarked page, which was badly foxed but still readable. 'On 16th June,' I read, 'came to us at our school, Miss Gwendolen Sinclair. I am acquainted with her father, schoolmaster at St George's School in Belhurst near Tunbridge Wells. Miss Sinclair lodges with Mrs Tufton, and seems a good and capable girl.'

Sinclair? and in 1795? Immediately my brain raced ahead. Why hadn't I thought to investigate Sinclairs earlier than Michael?

'Any more?' Gerard demanded.

'There's another entry in early January. "Miss Sinclair left our school today, having confessed her sin. Her father is wise to cast her from him. Let those who share her evil share her pain,"' I continued.

This could surely mean, in eighteenth-century terms, that Miss Sinclair was guilty of fornication or that the girl was pregnant.

'Bless you, Hugo,' I said fervently. 'Just the evidence we needed.' I was indeed grateful, but it was a chilling story. The attitude both of father and vicar was standard for the time, but even so I wondered how they reconciled it with Christian compassion.

'There are two last references.' Hugo handed the book back to me. 'The first is 31st May 1796.'

It read: 'Mistress Ovenden was sent for to the cottage at

Fontenay where Miss Sinclair dwells by courtesy of the lord of our manor.'

The second was for 14th June: 'The child of sin was stillborn, and Miss Sinclair is seen no more, having returned to her family.'

I shut the book, moved by this terrible story. There seemed little doubt now that whether Miss Sinclair was our skeleton or not, the father of her child was Charles Fontenay. Naturally the vicar would be circumspect to say the least, since he held his living by gift of the Fontenays, who were the lords of the manor, and there was a certain sniffiness about the tone of this last entry.

'Hey,' Gerard got into the spirit of the thing, 'those Sinclairs got around. No wonder Dad was always going on about the pestilence walking in darkness.'

'You seem very pleased about it,' Hugo observed. 'As a future lord of the manor do you have your eye on any Sinclair wenches?'

'No. Though that's a point. If I sell up to a rich American I can offer a bit of *droit de seigneur* over the local Sinclairs. That'll pop the price up.'

'Sell?' Hugo looked horrified, much to my amusement. 'Are you planning to?'

'It's always a possibility. Mum knows that. She's easy about it, aren't you?'

'Yes.' I was quite clear. 'My duty to David is to get it in running order for its future. I'd hope, but don't expect you to stay on.'

'But there'd be no Fontenays here,' Hugo said.

'Masses of stately homes no longer have the original families cowering in the attics. It doesn't stop the punters coming.'

'This is Fontenay. It's different. What will happen to the portraits—'

'I'll see you out, Hugo,' I said cheerily, though I was puzzled at the way Hugo was taking this. 'I've no intention of popping my clogs for a while.'

Hugo suddenly smiled. 'Good, if you do outlast me, promise me you'll pop my skeleton in the rose garden.'

'With or without a rose?' I asked.

'You can leave me a blank like the name of Gwendolen Sinclair, assuming that Miss Sinclair did not return to her family, but landed up in a corner of our garden. Amazing the way these Sinclairs keep popping up. First Michael Sinclair, now Gwendolen Sinclair.'

'That's only two.' I noted the 'our'.

'I imagine there are more, don't you?' Something was now making Hugo very happy indeed.

'In the garden, you mean?' I was getting out of my depth. 'Or in the records? Have you found more?'

'I have, as a matter of fact.'

'You *have* been delving.'

'This one didn't take much of a delve. I found out through my chum at Cranhurst Court.'

'Who?' My mind went blank, then cleared. 'Where Joss used to work?'

'Yes.'

'So how does your chum come into it?'

'He met dear Joss's mother one day. She's called Foxley, too. But her full name used to be Foxley-Sinclair. She and Joss's father split up and our Joscelyn took his mother's name when she reverted to it.'

Hugo was watching my face. Gerard burst into laughter. I was trying hard to disguise the shock I felt, as Hugo continued, 'The pestilence that walketh in darkness indeed. Do you think by any chance Joss is what I might call a Fontenay Sinclair?'

115

Eight

'**A**re you all right, Mum?'

I looked up at my son. I'd retired to the sofa with a drink to blot out the effects of Hugo's little coup. If Gerard thought I looked bad, I must look worse than I thought. Somehow I had managed to stumble through the rest of the evening, determined not to reveal to Hugo how much he had shaken me. After all, a small voice from somewhere deep inside reminded me, it might not be true. Unfortunately a louder one told me that it explained a lot about Joss that I hadn't quite grasped before. I felt ring-fenced by Sinclairs, for Hugo had left me the vicar's memoirs to read, and the book lay on the coffee table with its threat of yet more skeletons waiting to be revealed. Thankfully he had just departed for home.

'Don't worry,' I said to the Reverend Benedict. 'You can wait.' Just at the moment there were too many skeletons falling out of closets close at hand for me to worry overmuch about Gwendolen Sinclair.

Unfortunately I must have spoken aloud since Gerard replied blithely:

'I won't. But you look pretty green. What he said about Joss upset you, did it?'

'You could say that. Didn't it shake you?'

'No. I don't fancy him.'

'I *don't* fancy him,' I shrieked, all control gone.

'While you were in the kitchen coping with the pud, Hugo told me he'd narrowly avoided interrupting a touching scene between you and Joss. How touching was it?'

'Gerard—' This was too much. So Hugo had been lurking in the bushes, after all. He seemed to be following me everywhere. Coincidence? Was he jealous, or just concerned I wasn't getting in too deep with a Sinclair?

'All right, Mum. Only trying to lighten you up a bit.'

'Sometimes I feel I'll never be light again. I feel as doomladen as Tennyson's Lady of Shalott.'

'As a kid,' Gerard observed, 'I used to wonder why Her Ladyship called herself after an onion.'

'Because she cried a lot,' I managed to quip.

'That's better. A dim light at the end of the tunnel.'

'It's all very well, Gerard, but wouldn't you be worried in my position? Here I am, trying to keep the home fires of Fontenay burning until you come home to claim your heritage, and now you say you might sell it. I know I said I'd do it anyway, but I was surprised, to say the least, when you threw out that little corker.'

'Ah.' Gerard threw himself into the armchair opposite me. 'Any cocoa going?'

'Cocoa? How quaintly old-fashioned.'

'*Au contraire*. It's an "in" drink at present. Cheaper than booze, too.'

I stirred myself to go out to make cocoa. My stomach was heaving, and I supposed cocoa just might soothe it down a bit. Besides, I realized I needed to think. A mother and son chat was clearly necessary, so when we were ensconced with our cocoa, I asked him to enlighten me on what he had meant, and, slightly to my surprise, he took me seriously.

'To tell the truth, Ma, I haven't a clue what I'll do. All I know is that it looks, to me, like a rocky situation here.'

'I'll make it pay, give me a chance,' I exploded. 'I've shown you the accounts, the overdrafts can be paid back within five years at most.'

'That's not what I meant. You, to coin a phrase, are between a rock and a hard place, namely Master Hugo Brooks and Master Joss Foxley-Sinclair.'

'They don't like each other, it's true, but—'

'And they both like you.'

'For heaven's sake, I can handle that sort of thing. *And* I can tell whether they're after me or fancy a spell as temporary lord of Fontenay Manor.'

'Perhaps you underestimate how much they both want the latter – and that's what they recognize in the other.'

'You're way out,' I said quietly.

'Am I? Ask yourself why Hugo dolls up the conference centre with every Fontenay picture and bit of memorabilia he can scrounge.'

'Sound commercial sense.' Gerard, as usual, had touched a nerve.

'And why Joss feels so strongly about the rose garden that he was prepared to walk off if he didn't get his way,' Gerard continued.

'You've answered it – he was prepared to walk off. So he acknowledged it was in my control not his.'

'But he didn't go. You don't think he contrived to make you see things his way?'

I took a sip of cocoa. It was good staying power against a spinning mind, a mouthful of certainty in what was a very doubtful world indeed. Joss was apparently a Sinclair, so it was too much of a coincidence to imagine he wasn't one of the pestilent Sinclairs. If that added up correctly, then indeed I had to ask myself what he was doing here. What kind of stake did he think he had in the rose garden? Hitherto I had put it down to his gardening integrity; that my ideas for the garden had interfered with his great vision, so that like all great artists he had preferred to walk off into the sunset rather than accept compromise. His being a Sinclair put a vastly different complexion on it. I could see now that his behaviour had all been in line with his assumption that he had some kind of right to have a say in the rose garden over and above his job as gardener.

Everything in me cried out to reject this thesis, but I couldn't think straight enough to do it. All I could think of was that he'd kissed me and what kind of contribution to rational argument was that? A wave of nausea came over me, and I put my mug down unsteadily on the table – just as Gerard observed, 'After all, as I said, you're not too old to have another kid, are you?'

'Not on my own, I can't.'

'If one of them obliged, I meant.'

118

'Don't be so ridiculous, Gerard.' I was even past being annoyed by this time.

'Is it so ridiculous? If I died without issue, as they say, that kid would inherit, even though he wouldn't be a Fontenay. I don't remember anything in Dad's will about the heir *having* to be a Fontenay.'

'Aren't you getting just a wee bit fanciful?'

'If you study the history of the Fontenays, I think you'll find that that's fairly modest in the drama stakes.'

All that night I lay half awake, half dreaming – or rather nightmaring. Monstrous grinning Hugos and Josses closed in around me, while I tore my way through smirking rose bushes and my boots sunk into heavy clay soil, with the occasional doodlebug aiming straight for me. It was one of those nights when one wakes up with relief that all the problems ahead can't possibly be as bad as the ones you left behind in the night. Was I right, or was I wrong?

By the time I'd had breakfast, the steam was beginning to rise again within me, until I realized I'd go off pop if I didn't work some of it off. I laid aside my working clothes and put some 'boss' type clothes on: smart trousers, smart sweater and jacket. It made me feel better, if nothing else, and I marched forth in search of Joss.

Inevitably I went to the rose garden first. It was odds-on he'd be there, and I had to crush an instant desire to bawl him out in *my* garden – as well as one to burst into tears and throw myself in his arms. By the time I arrived, I'd calmed down, but I still hadn't decided what to do.

The garden was changing daily. I was taken aback to see that in the short time since I'd last been here the fountain had appeared in the sunken garden, and the wall surrounding its water outflow was complete. It looked so natural there, even without the flowing water, that it was easy to imagine it with flowers climbing over its walls, and the two roses flanking it. It unnerved me even more, however, for it seemed a foundation stone for the emergence of the new garden. There was no going back now. The rose garden would happen, and what lay between Joss and myself was an irrelevance.

I could see Joss's back towards me; he was squatting down

119

marking out the rose walk in the main garden, peering at the plans. For some reason this brought all my anger to the surface again; how dared he look so innocent when he knew full well he was a snake in the grass.

'Joss!' I called more sharply than I intended.

He leapt up. 'Anna? What can I do for you?' he added, having obviously caught sight of my face.

'Or for yourself.' I plunged right in. To blazes with being cool, calm and collected.

He looked puzzled. 'What do you mean?'

'Hugo says your real name is Foxley-*Sinclair* – is that right?'

'Wrong.' Joss looked stirred but hardly shaken as he strolled up to me. 'Legally, I'm Joss Foxley. My mother changed her name after the divorce. My father is the Sinclair, and before you ask, yes, we do come from the famous feuding family. Nevertheless, I wasn't aware you needed a family tree provided on my CV.' He looked amused, damn him.

'You didn't think it was any business of mine that you were a *Sinclair*?' I yelled at him. 'Come off it. What about all the fuss there's been about the Sinclairs and Fontenays?'

'There wasn't any when I arrived, if you recall.'

'Oh yeah? So it was entirely coincidence that you came here for a job.'

'No.'

'You seem very cool about it.' I felt like a matador prowling round a bull trying to figure out a way to get at it.

'I was interested, I admit. My mother told me something about a feud, so I looked up all the history about the place before I came. Anything wrong in that?'

I fumed. It sounded so reasonable. Then suddenly my brain cleared, and I put my finger on the flaw in the argument. 'You didn't,' I asked sweetly, 'even think it relevant to mention your ancestry when we found that Jennifer was in love with Michael Sinclair and that he probably murdered her?'

His face changed, and he looked very upset. 'I think we'd better talk, Anna.'

'You bet we'd better talk,' I said fiercely. 'Here, *now*.' He had stepped so near to me that I involuntarily took a step backwards. He saw it.

'Anna, I can't talk here, not in the rose garden.'

'Here, *now*,' I repeated.

'No, come over to the cottage.' This was a tumbledown wreck tucked out of sight behind the old ruins, one room of which Joss had turned into a working base. It was very lonely.

'No way. We can go to the bar at Fontenay Place.'

'No.'

Unwillingly I conceded this was not a good idea, but I didn't want to go to the lodge where Gerard was prowling nor to be in a remote cottage, closed in with Joss by four walls. I told myself this was stupid, that I could listen to my own mind anywhere, and so I agreed reluctantly. Belatedly, I wondered if this were the very cottage where Gwendolen had lived while she had her baby. The Fontenay estate used to be larger than it is now, and a great many cottages, even in Cranden, were originally owned by Fontenay. Most were sold off after the last war. This one, however, was so remote that it could well have been the one Charles Fontenay selected.

My mind was whirling as I accompanied Joss in silence along the footpaths to the far side of the ruins, over to the cottage, which he'd equipped, if not with heating, at least with thermos-flasks of coffee and biscuits. I bit into one fiercely as though it might work off my anger.

I sat down on the canvas chair and carefully balanced my coffee cup in the space provided. He lounged against the workbench so that he loomed over me, perhaps deliberately.

'Tell me what you're worried my reasons might be for working here – apart from my job.'

'I don't know, but I want to.'

'Simple curiosity isn't enough to satisfy you?'

'No. If that were all, you'd have told me about being a Sinclair. Instead you rope in Sarah with her connection to Jennifer – that wasn't a coincidence either, as you admitted.'

'What should I have said? That Michael Sinclair was my grandfather?'

'Your *grandfather*?' I was thrown completely. I'd never

121

even thought that the relationship might be so close. 'Don't you think that might have been relevant? All this time, you had the story at your fingertips. You were involved *yourself*.'

'So I left it to you to find out what you could. You notice I didn't play much of an active role, save to set you on track with Sarah.'

'*Why*?'

'Because I didn't know the full story either and—'

'But he was your grandfather, for heaven's sake.'

'If you'll calm down and stop interrupting me, Anna, I'll explain why I couldn't tell you.'

'Make it good,' I muttered vengefully.

'My parents split up when I was eight, and my mother changed my name as well as hers to Foxley. Just to spite my father. He's William Sinclair and Michael Sinclair's only son. He was born in 1940 to Michael and his wife Hazel. My mother moved to Cornwall, and I didn't see much of my father for yonks, not till I was a student. The person I did see frequently was my grandfather, Michael, simply because he lived not far away at that time – in Devon – and he'd always been fond of my mother and vice versa. So I knew about the Fontenays, and of course the rose garden.'

Of course. 'And about Jennifer?'

'No. Everything Gramps told me was way in the past. He never talked about anything much later than the mid-nineteenth century. All he told me was that there was a Sinclair legend that every so often to get their revenge for the supposed Sinclair misdeeds, the Fontenays snatched a Sinclair who disappeared for ever.'

I gazed at him. 'You expect me to believe this rubbish? That Michael didn't tell you anything about Jennifer – though I suppose if he murdered her he's hardly likely to have done so.'

Joss flushed angrily. 'This is my grandfather you're talking about. He's no murderer.'

'How can you *know* that?' Then I realized the import of what he had said. 'You said he *is*, Joss. Slip of the tongue?'

'No. My grandfather is still alive.'

The hut seemed very lonely. 'Alive?' I whispered. I'd

thought about the possibility of this being the case, but now it was brought home to me in earnest. 'Michael Sinclair alive, and you didn't even mention it?'

'There wasn't any point, Anna. He won't talk. I was pretty upset when Sarah revealed what her family thinking was on who murdered Jennifer, so I went to see him. He lives in Sussex now. Gramps wouldn't discuss the subject, or even talk about the rose garden. He just said it was a long time ago, and time heals even the biggest wounds sufficiently to get through life. He wouldn't even talk about his days in the RAF, let alone at Fontenay. I did check into his record though, and found that he was based at West Malling from April 1943 and had a crash later that year. It must have been serious because there was no more active flying and he was posted to Fontenay in the spring of '44 as RAF liaison officer for the army there. In August, after West Malling was closed so far as wartime flying was concerned, he went to Biggin Hill.'

I battled with the hundreds of questions that hurled themselves at me, wondering which to alight on, and came down on the heart of it. 'But how can you be so sure, Joss, that he isn't connected with the murder?'

'I can't. Who could be? But he's eighty-three, Anna, and I won't hound him. There's no *proof* Jennifer was even murdered, though it seems likely in the circumstances. But there's no evidence on what happened after she left her sister's that night, or that Gramps was with her.'

I wasn't going to give up that easily. 'Did he look surprised when you told him the skeleton was found in the rose garden? After all, if he didn't murder her, then it would have been a shock to him to know what had happened, and that she wasn't killed by the bomb after all.'

Joss was white-faced. 'Anna, I *know* he's not a murderer.'

'Case not proven, Joss.' I hesitated. 'Could I meet him?'

'Absolutely not. I won't have him bothered. He wants to forget the past and that's that.'

How could I fight that, except by stealth behind his back – and I wouldn't stoop to doing that. 'So where does that leave you and me, Joss?'

'Where we were.'

'Not quite.' I rose to my feet with what I hoped was dignity. 'I still don't know why you came here in the first place.'

'I came because of the rose garden. I've told you how I feel about roses. The idea of a rebirth of this garden was irresistible. The reason I stayed, though, was because of you *and* the rose garden. Believe me?'

Down came the fog of war again. The warnings, Gerard, Hugo – 'No.' I turned round to leave, partly as I regretted my instant reply, partly because there were tears in my eyes.

'So I'll have to leave.'

I spun round. '*No!*'

And then I was in his arms again, and he was kissing me, as though he wasn't going to let go.

'Anna,' he kept repeating in between long kisses, kissing me as I hadn't been kissed – or touched – for many a long year. Somewhere, sometime, I heard him whisper, 'It's all right now that you know about the Sinclairs.'

I was in no doubt about what he meant, but I couldn't have asked him anyway. That was the last thing I heard apart from words of love, for the rivers of feeling trembling up and down my body became a raging torrent, crowding all else out. I realized that we were lying on the couch, that I was uncomfortable because it was too short, and that it was heaven. Somehow most of our clothes seemed to have disappeared, the golden sunlight danced in through the window and my heart and body danced with it.

'I love you, Anna.'

'I'm years older than you,' I managed to force out.

'Case dismissed,' was muttered against my lips as I felt him against me, and hungrily fitted myself to his body. Then at last he was inside, and it was roses, roses all the way, with never a thorn on the horizon.

1944

'Jennifer? Where are you going?'

'I have to get back to cook John's supper, Michael.'

She stirred in his arms on the arbour seat. It was early April now, and in two months or less the garden would be a mass of bloom.

'Stay a few minutes longer.'

'You know what might happen if I do.'

'Sweet.' He stroked her hair.

'I can't do it, Michael. It would be for all the wrong reasons and you know it.'

'Yes.' He swung his legs to the ground and let go of her. 'I'll go and wrestle a rose bush or two to the floor to work it off. In fact, I ought to be getting back to the desk. After all, I'll be coming back for my posting here in a couple of weeks. Just good timing for the garden. All the blooms on the way and none of the hard work.'

'Ever heard of weeds?' Jennifer said dryly. 'Not to mention there'll be tough work on the farm on offer in between desk stints.'

'I'll get the troops on that.'

'John will love that. Me in command of a platoon of troops. He'll be out with his spy glass every minute of the day. Poor John. He'd be so much happier if he just relaxed and trusted in me.'

'I feel much the same about Hazel. Listen, Jennifer, while you're trotting around with your pruning shears, I'm going to tell you something.'

'Good.'

'You may not think so.'

'About Gwendolen Sinclair?' Jennifer had told him about the Vicar of Cranden's memoirs, and that she was now quite sure that the mysterious rose and a misleading map reference indicated the burial ground of Gwendolen Sinclair.

'No, about me. You remember I said I was adopted.'

Jennifer nodded.

'It's more complicated than that. My father finally confessed that I *was* his blood son, but that my mother isn't my real mother. My real mother had died in the flu epidemic of 1919, only a month or two after I was born, and Louise, Dad's wife, agreed to bring me up.'

'Oh Michael.' Jennifer was horrified. 'Does that upset you?'

'Yes and no. It makes me feel uneasy. Louise is my mother to me, yet I feel she's being taken away and replaced by a question mark.'

'Wouldn't your father tell you any more?'

'He simply said her name was Beatrice Rose, and that she was a girl he met during the last years of the Great War and that they intended to get married, but she died before they could do so. So here I am, a true-blue Sinclair again, walking pestilentially in the darkness. I feel that just about sums me up, too.'

'It doesn't make much difference, Michael,' Jennifer consoled him. 'You're back where you were before, and John doesn't seem to care whether you're a naughty Sinclair or not.' That still seemed odd to her since he was beginning to spend most of his free time poring over family history.

'I didn't mind when I came here, but now knowing so much more about the history, I feel as though I really am sneaking in.'

'That's ridiculous. You're merely visiting us and taking an interest in the garden. The fact we keep it secret from John is merely because he's so absurdly jealous, nothing to do with Sinclairs.'

'I suppose you're right. It keeps me away from West Malling, anyway. God, it's hard, Jennifer.'

'It's only fair to Hazel and the baby to try, Michael, and then see what happens, and how she feels. War changes things, distorts emotions and values. Soon with luck, when the Allies invade France, this war will be over, and everything and everyone will return to normal. The vegetable gardens can go back to being the Fontenay gardens again, I'll probably go back to being a lady of the manor and you—'

'Will go back to civil life. Yes, I know that. It's going to be damned dull after the RAF. I might even stay in if they want me.' His earlier euphoria about the chance of splitting up from Hazel had evaporated. Jennifer had made him see that William had to come first – if Hazel agreed to give up this other chap and stick with him instead. Ten to one she'd refuse, he thought on his optimistic days. Maybe she'd even leave William with him. On less happy days, he realized the odds were far lower.

'Will the RAF . . .' Jennifer hesitated.

'Take me because of my back? Why not? They'll have desks to fill after the war just as they do now. And if they don't . . .'

'What will you do then?'

Michael shrugged. 'Who knows? Perhaps I'll become a gardener.'

I needed to be on my own while my heart and body simmered down – if that were possible. I couldn't go back to the lodge in case I ran into Gerard, so I went instead to 'supervise' the builders, who promptly made it clear they could cope better without me. I didn't even feel I would be capable in charge of a car, so I walked around the castle ruins. I wandered up to the two transplanted roses, which had now caught their breath and both the red and the white bush were beginning to produce some splendid red hips. 'It's all right,' I assured them. 'You're safe from me now.' In my idiocy, I even thought those waving hips looked grateful, as they inclined their heads in the breeze. Why had I ever feared them? At least I could be alone there. Joss had an appointment at a garden nursery, and had had to leave. I had a lunch with Hugo booked, but I needed to calm down first.

Joss was all around me – I could still feel him, still hear his loving words. It had been a damn silly thing to do, I told myself. I wasn't even on the Pill, he wasn't prepared – but I failed to care very much. At the back of my mind I could hear his 'I love you, Anna', and I couldn't even remember everything I'd said to him – but it wasn't exactly restrained. Somehow, however, this morning had made me feel a part of Fontenay instead of an outsider trying to cope with its problems, even though it had taken a Sinclair to do it. Now I was part of its history, in my own mind at least. I was locked in – just the situation Gerard had warned me against.

I told myself that in this respect nothing had changed, even though I knew that 'nothing' excluded the shimmers of happiness radiating through me. After half an hour, I walked back to the lodge, changed clothes, tried to ignore the tell-tale flush in my cheeks, and sallied forth to meet Hugo.

'You're late,' he remarked when I ran him to earth in the bar.

'Sorry, I've been in the rose garden.'

'Ah. Inspecting Mr Foxley-Sinclair? I'd love to have been present at that meeting.'

Glad you weren't, I said to myself. 'Yes.'

'Who won the fight?'

Who indeed? 'There was no fight, but I won it.'

'Are you going to tell me what happened?'

I lost patience. 'No, Hugo, I am not – any more than I report to Joss what you and I talk about.'

'Fair enough. Watch it though.'

'Watch *what*?' I was beginning to get very tired of being warned to be careful about imaginary dangers.

'Joss may pretend to be objective about Fontenay, but he's not. He's berserk about the feud, *and* about Fontenays. I should know. He pores over those paintings and everything else he can lay his hands on, whenever he gets a chance to nip in here. He's a historical fanatic. And not just the historical side either. He fancies himself as the Sinclair that finally makes it to the top of the Fontenay tree, for a takeover, if you ask me.'

I didn't, and resented the implication that the embrace he had apparently overseen was simply a move on Joss's part towards a different end. Nevertheless, some of the rose of the day clouded over.

Nine

That evening I was alone for Gerard had gone out for the evening – with Sarah, I presumed. I'd warmed to Sarah on further acquaintance, after I realized that her laid-back manner was as skin-deep as Gerard's. And what business was it of mine anyway if Gerard liked her? He would be off to university very shortly, and she, too. If there was anything serious between them it would have to stand the test of separation. I doubted whether it would. We were cut off here at Fontenay, and the village of Cranden doesn't offer much in the way of entertainment, nor can Tunbridge Wells match the variety of bright lights in London – or of York, which was where Gerard was headed. It was natural enough that he and Sarah should turn to each other at present.

I was relieved that Gerard wasn't with me, and that he had his mind on his own affairs, for I doubted my ability to keep a calm façade. I felt as though the transformation that had just hit my life was proclaiming itself loud and clear from the housetops, but it was something I preferred to keep to myself if I could. Firstly, it gave me a warm inner glow, a secret to hug to myself and mull over. Secondly, I knew that when I felt calmer I had to think through what Gerard had said and then what Hugo had said. Conversely I had to consider what Joss and Gerard had implied about Hugo.

It was frustrating and I hoped unnecessary. All I had wanted to do was to create a Fontenay that could be a paying concern, not for my own but for David's sake. Nevertheless here I was in the middle of a web that, if it existed at all, was invisible, but in which I was caught. Was Joss the spider in the middle? At the moment, he most certainly was, and I most willingly trapped. Or was the spider Hugo? Or could it be merely my own imagination, conjured into being through loneliness and too much indoctrination into Fontenay tradition?

I couldn't even remember how Joss and I had parted (apart from with great satisfaction and happiness). Had we talked about where this was taking us? Had we said – surely not – that this must not happen again? I remember seeing his back as he strolled away. I fancied the back looked happier, and that was certainly my imagination. I didn't know what he wanted of us, or even what I wanted. All I knew was that in front of me, after two years in the forest, there stretched a path to the sunlight, which I proposed to take. It might be a yellow brick road beset with dangers on all sides, but it led somewhere I wanted to be. What was the next step, however? Ridiculously I didn't know. I felt like a teenager again – should I invite him over, should I seek him out, would he seek me out? A hundred scenarios clashed in my head.

And then it dawned on me that I was taking a lot for granted. What about this Gemma woman? I still couldn't be absolutely sure. Joss could well be married. An over-powering need to know gripped me. I wanted to know right *now*. I half rose from my chair, and then kicked myself for stupidity. It was half past seven, for heaven's sake, nearly dark. Joss would have left for home hours ago. Without telling me? Ridiculously, I was indignant, and had to laugh at myself to get things in perspective. I needed to try at least to maintain a cautious objectivity, though I had little confidence I'd manage it. Restraining myself from wander-ing out just to see if he were still around, I threw myself once more into Fontenay history. I picked up the Reverend Benedict's memoirs, so that I could return the book to Hugo tomorrow.

I skipped through it idly. Eighteenth-century vicars were not known for their overall diligence; many of them were absentee, more eager to collect tithes than souls, and more interested in the venal side of life than spiritual guidance. There were no Mothers' Unions and church bazaars then.

There seemed to be a lot of squire-grovelling in his entries, and I wasn't sure I took to the Reverend Benedict. I turned to the pages where Gwendolen Sinclair appeared (Hugo had stuck bookmarks in for me):

> I am honoured by the visit Mr Fontenay paid to me this morning. I enquired after Mrs Fontenay's health (it being said she is with child and poorly with it), and was told she was in excellent spirits. Mrs Fontenay has been unable to pay her usual charitable calls in Cranden for some weeks. I observed that, after leaving the vicarage, Mr Fontenay visited our school where I am told the new assistant Miss Sinclair was greatly pleased to see him. She is a most amiable young lady, and I trust will not be swayed by the honour of Mr Fontenay's interest.

It was dated 2nd October 1795, roughly three months before the disappearance of Miss Sinclair from Cranden to the cottage on the Fontenay estate. I turned to the entry for the following 10th January to reread the passage about that confessed sin. I supposed that if the Reverend Benedict admitted the girl was amiable she must indeed have been an innocent, and so the more I read between the lines about the subsequent vanishing from the cottage the less I liked it. It seemed quite clear that she had been placed there by Charles, but what his poor wife thought about this, goodness only knows. Perhaps she didn't even know, if she was pregnant herself at the time. Intrigued, I put Hugo's bookmarks aside and read on to see if there was anything he had missed. Rather to my surprise, there was:

> Great Tom [the biggest bell in the church peal] and his fellows rang today as Mrs Fontenay, who has led a secluded life from illness for the past few months, was delivered of a fine boy, an heir to Fontenay.

The date was 11th June 1796. I knew where I was now, since the Fontenay family tree was imprinted on my brain. This must be St John Fontenay, who lived from 1796 to 1862.

Partly out of interest, and partly to keep my thoughts away from Joss, I read on. The Reverend Benedict might not have been much of a spiritual adviser, but he was a great one for social detail. Later in June 1796:

> Mr Goderic Fontenay, I hear, is to be wed, he having left our little community some two weeks ago. His future wife is the former Miss Elizabeth Sayles, of the well-known Oxfordshire family. She is indeed a fortunate lady. Mr Goderic's amiable character, seriousness of purpose and noble appearance will make him a most admirable husband. We had hoped to see him as godfather at the baptism of little St John Fontenay, but, being indisposed he was unable to be with us to his great regret. Mr Goderic sent me the most charming letter to apologize for his absence.

No more about Gwendolen Sinclair in the memoirs, and to me it seemed probable that her disappearance from the cottage was due to death rather than her return to her family. What had happened to the stillborn child, I wondered? Was it buried in the garden with its mother to avoid scandal? That might have proved risky. A gardener might have come across them at any moment. And scandal would spread quickly through the village midwife. Surely the twitchy nose of the Reverend Benedict would have made it his business to convey the news by innuendo? Perhaps he did, and perhaps Gwendolen really did return to her family. Somehow, however, I could not believe she did so.

I found one more entry, of direct interest:

> Mr Charles Fontenay paid me the honour of providing the means to repair the roof of the church and a splendid pulpit from which I can preach of the sin that lies amongst us. He has given a most gracious gift to our Lord who in His mercy looks down upon us all.

So there was my answer. Surely it had to imply that the roof was paid for with conscience money, in return for silence about Gwendolen Sinclair? I could never reach the whole truth now with any certainty; these tantalizing clues were all there were.

I had become quite absorbed in the vicar's memoirs by this time. I decided that had he lived a century or more earlier, he might well have been another Vicar of Bray, changing religions as the political tide dictated. Nor were the problems of village life very different to those of today:

> Mrs Kettle gave voice to her feelings over who might claim the privilege of embroidering the altar cloth, much to the distress of Mrs White, who had already begun upon the work. I was obliged to choose between them, and following the example of King Solomon chose both, the cloths to be used alternately.

The door bell rang as I was deep in the problem of Farmer Wills, whose tithes were late once more. The Reverend had been aggrieved: 'The vicar deserves his daily bread whether times be hard or no.' I sprang up, wondering who on earth it could be at this time of night. Hugo perhaps, who sometimes called in if he stayed late at an after-conference drinks gathering.

I went to the door crossly, annoyed at the interruption. It wasn't Hugo, however. It was Joss. My face must have shown my pleasure, and I forgot all about maintaining a cautious objectivity.

'Come in,' I glowed.

1944

'I remember in the first war my mother complained that there was nothing to put in a pie but vegetables and now here we are again,' John grunted. 'Different name, that's all. Lord Woolton's pie. A fatless piecrust, I ask you. My father would turn in his grave if he were asked to eat this.'

'It tastes very good, Mr Fontenay,' Michael said politely, then grinned as John laughed out loud.

'No need to lie, Michael. Anything that tastes good must come from Jennifer's home-grown veg. Isn't that right, Jen?'

'I do my best,' Jennifer answered demurely. 'At least we've got some early broad beans to help out.' She was wary, for she had been surprised when John suggested that they invite Michael to dinner. It was unlike him to be so sociable, but she was pleased that he made the effort. It made things easier, for she need no longer worry about being overheard or spied on if John gave his official approval to Michael's visits. After all, it was he who had invited Michael to Fontenay in the first place. There had been a rumpus when John was told the army was requisitioning Fontenay, and John had only been pacified when they got permission to stay on at Fontenay by moving into the lodge. Jennifer had avoided pointing out the obvious – it was her essential presence to look after the market garden in Fontenay that had ensured this was granted. There was another rumpus when he found out that Michael was being posted here, but not so fierce a one as Jennifer had expected. John was so deeply involved in the moving arrangements that he didn't have the energy to fight on both fronts. The army and Michael had arrived two weeks ago, and so far all had gone reasonably smoothly. Or perhaps she hadn't noticed – it was hard battling in the antiquated kitchen, at which Mrs Pink had taken one look and decided it was a convenient time to retire to her sister's in the village.

'How's that skeleton hunt of yours going, Michael?' John asked. 'Jennifer tells me that you've been helping her go through the family tree and so forth. Can't think what the interest in old bones could be, but it takes your mind off things, I suppose.'

'That's right, sir. I like delving into the past. It's a privilege to be here at Fontenay, and there have been plenty of wars fought around here. So it seems to me its history is all part of today. Soon this war will be history too.'

'As well as us,' John laughed. 'Whose did you decide the skeleton was?'

'We think – it's only supposition,' Jennifer said quickly, 'that there was a Gwendolen Sinclair in the village at that time who seems to have disgraced herself in some way, presumably with one of the Fontenays, and was given a cottage on the grounds. I found an old book in the library. It might explain why the skeleton was buried in the rose garden – and why it had no name.'

John snorted. 'A Fontenay by-blow, eh? By a Sinclair.'

Jennifer noticed John glance at Michael, and suddenly felt uneasy. She knew that expression. He'd switched back into his father's world, the world that cursed every Sinclair who ever lived. But perhaps she was wrong, for when he spoke he was the old John again. 'You know, Michael, all my life I've had the Sinclair–Fontenay feud pushed down my throat. My father indoctrinated me, almost as a condition of letting me take Fontenay over, though with only two sisters, one of whom was dead and the other in Australia, there wasn't a lot of choice. My mother, too. She was as bad as father. The women of the family usually are, if not worse, eh, Jennifer?'

'Oh, yes, John,' Jennifer smiled. 'Take me for instance.' It was going to be a happy evening after all. She must have imagined that sudden chill.

'You're one of the Sinclairs who've dogged us all these years, aren't you? Jennifer told me about that.'

'I am, sir, but in the middle of this war it doesn't seem very important.'

'It's important, but I agree it ought to rest a while. After all, you're living in our home, aren't you? The Sinclairs move into Fontenay at last, and we've been consigned to the dog kennel.'

'John,' Jennifer protested, turning it into a laugh. 'You know this is a very superior kennel. It has a cold water tap, after all.' She hastened to change the subject. 'I didn't know you had two sisters, John.'

'One died in an asylum very young. Not a thing we boast about. My father didn't anyway.'

'That's terrible,' Jennifer exclaimed.

John shrugged. 'Not that unusual. I was in the war in the Far East and didn't get back until late 1919. By then she was gone. Seven years later Esther went to Australia. You can see why my mother got possessive about me and Fontenay and so forth.'

'Yes,' Jennifer replied seriously, 'I can. It must have been hard for her.'

Adelaide had been a tough old bird, and fiercely protective of her beloved son. She was convinced – naturally – that Jennifer was by no means good enough for John, and the relationship between them had been difficult for the first couple of years, even though Adelaide lived in the lodge. Then Adelaide had fallen ill, and it was a different matter. She had even grown quite fond of Jennifer until she died two years ago. A truce had developed, first into a working relationship and then into reluctant fondness. Jennifer missed her. She loved John, but the house and responsibilities were vast, especially in wartime and with virtually no staff. It had whittled down to poor Mrs Pink, and now she had gone too. Seeing what few amenities the lodge had to offer, Jennifer could hardly blame her.

'Since my father was so paranoic about the Sinclairs,' John continued, 'you can understand why it seems strange to find you moving into the house while we're condemned to this place. Talking about a pestilence walking in darkness. Only joking, of course, Michael,' he laughed. 'You're doing a grand job for the country.'

'I don't feel like a pestilence, sir, and we'll be gone as soon as the war's over.'

Jennifer could see that all this artificial banter was beginning to irritate Michael and she could hardly blame him.

'And the gardens,' John went on, regardless of Michael's comment, 'you're rose crazy too, I understand.'

'Yes, sir. It's a fine Fontenay tradition, and I'm glad it's being kept up.'

'Don't see the attraction myself. Sentimental twaddle. Still, the older I get the more maudlin I become. Perhaps I'll even get round to my father's views about the Sinclairs. I have to confess that when I invited you to the house that first time I had an inkling you were one of those Sinclairs. Something you'd said, can't remember now.'

'I may have told you about my father, sir. James Sinclair.'

'James Sinclair, that's it. That rang the old family bell.'

Jennifer looked from one to the other as they chatted. The mood had lightened now to her relief. It was the war, they were all on edge, waiting for the invasion, which must come this summer.

'Lunch?'

The voice in my ear made me jump. I'd been miles away, once more studying the portraits in Fontenay Place. Joss was bringing the approved plans for the Hermit's Retreat tomorrow, since winter was approaching and the builders wanted to get it finished before it set in. This had concentrated my mind wonderfully on its contents and I decided to make an early start on organizing copies of the portraits. The final selection now had to be made. The Three As, as I'd mentally termed them, obviously had to be there, Arabella, Abigail and Anne, as did Robert Fontenay, Gerard and – I presumed – Charles, loth as I was to include a murderer. Innocent till proved guilty, I told myself, but failed to be convinced. And of course Gertrude and Edmund.

I also fancied Timothy, born 1670, who held the record for the greatest number of mistresses (according to David) and his wife Polly, who seemed easily the most beautiful of the Fontenay women. I wonder what a psychologist would make of *that* particular marriage.

I spun round to find Hugo behind me.

'No, thanks. Well, perhaps a quick one.' Self-interest won. I could ask him to organize the photography and prints.

We sat in the bar, while they produced our sandwiches – the cook did rather good ones.

'How's the garden growing?' he asked then.

'Still ordering roses. Sometime I'll have to give some thought to the question of beginning a new *Book of Gertrude's Garden*.'

'What will you call it? Volume II?'

I laughed. 'Hardly. I don't know. I'll have to think.'

'I'll give you a hand if you like. I'm rather good at calligraphy, and I know an illustrator or two.'

'Thanks. The final choice of candidates is still under discussion.'

'Maybe another opinion would help.'

'Maybe it would at that.' I seemed to be accepting rather a lot of help from him, and on this question I felt reluctant. It was for me and Joss, my heart told me. My British sense of fair play told me Hugo had as much right as Joss to be consulted. Accordingly I went on to tell him about the plans for the Hermit's Retreat, that they were almost ready, and what roughly they were.

'Sounds expensive,' he commented.

I pulled a face. 'Don't talk about it.'

'Perhaps we should. Perhaps I – the company that is – could sponsor it.'

Hope shot through me as if I'd just checked the bottom of Pandora's Box. 'Really? Joss or I could bring the plans up tomorrow.'

'How about you?'

'Done.'

All the same, grateful though I was, there'd be no long evening sessions, I decided. 'And there's what to do about the skeletons,' I added, determined to *really* play fair.

'In what way? I thought you'd decided, melodramatic soul that you are, that both of them were murdered, one by Michael Sinclair, and the other by Charles Fontenay.'

'Those aren't facts, they're theses.'

'So what makes them complete?'

'The story behind them.'

'My dear Anna,' Hugo sighed. 'How on earth do you prove these theses?'

'I don't know, but I shall. I could put them in the Hermit's Retreat perhaps as a special exhibit, but I'm not sure about it. It would make a visitor attraction, yet Jennifer seems too close to home to treat that way.'

'And is Master Joss aiding you in this? Is his family going to get a mention?'

I hesitated – and was lost, because Hugo continued, 'Don't bother to answer. I can read your face, Anna. Joss is a descendant of Michael, isn't he?'

'Well, yes.'

'It figures.'

'What does?'

'The way he sneaked into Fontenay by the side door, just as Michael Sinclair did sixty years ago.'

'It's not like that.' It was a weak reply, but looked at from Hugo's viewpoint – *any* outsider's come to that – it was just like that.

I, however, knew it wasn't – didn't I?

'This is playing truant,' I mocked Joss. I forgot about my sudden doubts as soon as I saw him again.

'Buying rose trees is hardly that.'

'But we're not buying them. We're sitting in a pub by a river on a lovely autumn day.' As if to emphasize my point a golden leaf fluttered down on to the table.

He stretched out his hand and took mine. How can a hand be rough and soft at the same time? I don't know, but Joss's was.

'Do you mind, Anna?'

'Not in the least. It seems right, somehow.'

'I need to ask you. You know about my grandfather now. What difference is it going to make? Can we just go ahead with the garden as we planned?'

I thought about this. 'Yes,' I agreed finally. 'Let's go ahead. This is the garden of the future, you're right about that. And if I want to continue delving into the past on Gwendolen, I shall. So far as Michael Sinclair is concerned, however, I won't do anything about contacting him unless I have your permission. OK?'

'Very OK.' Joss's finger ran up and down my hand till the nerves cried out for him and the shandy slid down my throat like honey. Past over, future begins.

What we'd agreed sounded good, which was a relief. Joss produced the plans of the Hermit's Retreat, plus a sketch of the envisaged final result. Any hermit who lived here would have to be immune to frostbite, I thought. The windows had no glass, only a lattice of wood, and the entire structure was of wood and thatch. The floor – with thought given to visitors – was of crazed stone. What delighted me was that there was a second storey, not as large as the first but with steps each end

139

to provide an in and out flow. The perfect place for special exhibits.

'Like it?'

'Yes, but it needs heating and glass for exhibits.'

'The cold voice of realism. I knew you'd say that.'

'My purse says it.' I'd keep the news about Hugo for a while. 'I can't afford new exhibits every year because the frost and damp have got them.'

'So be it.' He folded up the drawings. 'I hope the purse is still open for roses – we need to order some hybrid perpetuals for the nineteenth-century Fontenays.'

The perfect opportunity to tell him about Hugo's offer. Rather reluctantly he agreed it was generous and handed me the plans. We then made our way to the nursery, and spent a happy hour arguing amicably over the catalogues and the roses on offer. We agreed on a Sidonie, a Jean Rosenkrantz, a Paul's Early Blush, and a Clio, and then moved on to hybrid teas, where I fell in love with a yellow Lady Forteviot. Joss vetoed it on the grounds it didn't fit anybody. I countermanded it, since I was paying, and said I'd find someone suitable later. We glared mutinously at each other, and then agreed over a pink flora and the lovely semi-double white Adelaide d'Orléans for ramblers to cover the rose walk dividing the centuries.

When I got home late that afternoon, I was highly satisfied (on all counts, though I won't go into details). I even surprised myself over my enthusiasm over the roses. Perhaps I would, after all, turn into another Jennifer. Only then did I realize that there was just one more line of enquiry that I hadn't followed up over Michael Sinclair. It had been growing subconsciously in my mind for some time and in the bliss of the emerging relationship with Joss I had ignored its niggle. I had given my word to Joss, however, and couldn't go back on it. Unless – it occurred to me – I followed the letter of the law. I had only promised not to contact Michael Sinclair. There was one avenue that was not closed, and even though it was cheating in spirit I guiltily knew I was going to follow through. There were things puzzling me that only she could answer, so I was going to ring Deborah this very evening.

'Anna, good to hear you, darling.' Her strong voice whistled down the line, and I chattered about Fontenay, of the changes there and of the rose garden. This must have come as quite a surprise to her, since she was well aware of my former feelings about it.

'Hugo keeping you in order, is he?' she asked when I drew breath.

'Actually no, Joss is.'

A pause. 'Isn't he the gardener?'

'Yes. But he's also Michael Sinclair's grandson.' I could almost hear the silence that followed, and finally I could hold out no longer. 'Deborah, you said you met Michael Sinclair at West Malling.'

A pause. 'That's right.'

'Where did you meet John Fontenay?'

Another pause. Then: 'Don't go there, Anna.'

But I did. Of course I did. I was going to throw all I'd got into this one.

'Did you know that Michael Sinclair is still alive?'

I regretted it immediately. I liked Deborah, and even over telephone lines you can tell when you've upset someone. 'No,' she replied. 'I didn't know that. Does it matter?'

Deborah has great social skills. She didn't hang up, she didn't yell at me to mind my own business, she simply switched topics to something completely different. By the time we had finished discussing the entrance prices, and what kind of cakes we should sell, the awkwardness might never have been.

But I still had no explanation for my niggle.

1793

'Goderic, I will walk with you if I may.' Charles tried to suppress the anger inside him. He must move gently, when everything in him shouted out to vent his fury on this most terrible of monsters. The grounds of Fontenay were mellow in the golden light of autumn, yet they brought him no peace this year. He could not even find happiness in his roses. Such beauty only served to remind him of the ugliness of man himself, as exemplified in his own brother.

'By all means, brother. These are your gardens after all.'

'I have spoken with Miss Sinclair again.'

'I trust speaking is all you did, brother. I should not like to think you might betray Mary. Especially now you tell me she is with child.'

Charles flushed angrily. 'You, *you* to speak so. You to mock me. How could you behave so despicably towards Miss Sinclair, Goderic?'

'You are easy to mock, Charles.'

'I did not mean that, as you know full well. I meant, how could you seduce Miss Sinclair?'

'*Seduce*?' The elegant eyebrows rose. 'Dear Charles, what strong words. Do you imply I have misbehaved towards her, or simply that I have told her how fair a maiden she is?'

'Would that I could believe she still is a maiden.'

'So that you could do as I have done, Charles?'

'So it is true.' Charles gave a moan. 'Goderic, you are betrothed to Elizabeth. Would you surrender all that life offers you with her?'

'Good gracious no. Miss Sinclair, however, is all too willing. She understands the situation perfectly, and sees herself as bringing solace into my life until I can be wed to my true love.'

'You lie, sir. She believes in you, she trusts you.'

'I fear you are too easily misled, Charles. She is a Sinclair after all, and you know how father instilled in us that the Sinclairs are snakes that inveigle us trusting Fontenays into their wicked toils. Alas, she has done so, I admit, and not myself alone judging by your interest.'

'You will look after her, Goderic,' Charles cried in agony. 'You will take care. She comes of respectable family, and cannot be abandoned.'

Goderic laughed. 'Dear Charles, what an old woman you are at times. If I do not care for her, I see someone at my side who undoubtedly will.'

Ten

For the next few days, I buried myself in catalogues and notes from *The Book of Roses*. I hauled out learned tomes on roses and costume books, throwing myself into the research necessary to create the exhibition for the Hermit's Retreat. Thanks to Hugo's generosity, the wooden building itself was now under way, plans had gone through like clockwork, and the builders were heavily leaned on to complete the main structure, excluding the thatch, before winter. Hugo had held out strongly for Kentish peg tiles for practicality – and expense, but in the end had agreed that mock Hermit's Retreats deserved the full treatment. The thatching would be done in early spring, with a temporary covering over the building for the winter.

The Fontenay pictures and biographies, together with a replica of the relevant page from *The Book of Gertrude's Garden*, would be in the larger ground floor room, but I was still wavering about the eaved upper room. Should it be devoted to the skeletons, which still seemed to me distasteful, or a Tudor room for Gertrude and Edmund, and the history of roses in Britain?

The further I immersed myself in it, the more vivid grew the pictures of the Fontenays over the centuries. There were families who had obviously struggled for an heir, like Charles and Mary, and others that were overflowing with fertility, such as their son St John and his son George in the nineteenth century. I discovered that the garden had not always been confined to the families of the Fontenay in possession at the time. Sometimes other members crept in – Goderic for example, though more often they were children. I had decided to copy out the tribute to each family member in the book, then leave a page blank in my notes to record what was known about them from other sources. Some remained an enigma, with nothing yet known save the tribute. It was tantalizing to try to puzzle out whether each tribute was the *whole* truth, or indeed any truth at all. For all I knew there were omissions in the family tree as well as in *The Book of Gertrude's Garden*. Black sheep of the family might have been totally ignored. I toyed again with the idea that the eighteenth-century skeleton was such a black sheep, or a 'Mrs Rochester' hidden in the attic, but dismissed the idea. My money was still on the Sinclair link.

All in all, it was an absorbing task, and somehow Joss had become part of it in my mind. It wasn't that he was present every evening – far from it, alas, but that he *seemed* to be present. In three days' time Gerard would be going back to university, and I realized Joss probably thought I needed the time for mother–son bonding. Far from it. Gerard had taken to spending most of his time with Sarah and immediately her working day was over – I noted the times – he would disappear from the house.

This particular evening, a Wednesday I recall, Joss wanted to discuss the improvement of the gardens by the castle ruins, so we took a stroll there in the autumn sunset. The air was heavy with the peace of a fruitful year's end and in the golden light, the flowers looked happily set to bloom for ever. It was hard to think that there were perhaps only six weeks to go before the first frosts might arrive. In fact the first inkling of winter chill came that very evening out of the blue of the day.

As we strolled back, however, we had no hint of it, and our arms were entwined round each other's waists. It was hardly an erotic scene, but as we arrived at the lodge still earnestly discussing nothing in particular, it could have left Hugo in little doubt that our relationship had progressed, to put it in formal terms. For – of course – there he was again, waiting on the doorstep for me, his car parked nearby.

He didn't blink an eyelid, but he could hardly have missed the implication. Joss kept his arm right where it had been. Hugo had brought back the copy of the rough plan I had made for the interior of the Hermit's Retreat. I asked him in, but he declined. It was all very urbane, yet something about the encounter, probably in my imagination, disturbed me. We made an appointment for the morrow in the tea-room, and off he drove.

'What did he think of it?' Joss asked after Hugo had gone, and I had poured us both a glass of wine.

'He didn't say. He's scribbled a few notes on the plan, and I'll find out the rest tomorrow probably. About the Hermit's Retreat, that is. I doubt if he'll let fly on the subject of you and me.'

'I'm sure you'll get the hidden message that the gardener's not good enough for you,' Joss joked. 'Hugo most certainly won't want to see a Sinclair insinuating himself into the Fontenay stronghold.'

'I'm not a Fontenay.'

'Your son is.'

'You're not romantically involved with my son.'

'True, but it'll confirm his worst fears that I have dastardly plans to marry you.'

'Do you? Or are you married already?' The words slipped out quite naturally and were answered in the same vein.

'Yes and no. I leave you to guess in which order I answer your questions.'

'Well, thank *you*.' A warm glow that had nothing to do with the red wine slid all over me. No matter the order of the answering, it pushed me onto a plateau from which I was, temporarily at least, lord of all I surveyed.

'Anna,' he laid his hand on my arm, 'you'll take care, won't you?'

'Of what?' I knew quite well, but I was defensive.

'Hugo Brooks.'

Here we go again, I thought. 'You mean because you and I aren't exactly platonic towards each other.'

'Partly and beyond that.'

'Are we by any chance,' I asked patiently, 'back to the "Hugo wants to marry me for Fontenay"?' I was taking the bull by the horns, but the bull answered very soberly.

'Yes. With Fontenay the major factor.'

I stared at him. Joss had never been quite so outspoken about Hugo before, and the gloves seemed to be coming off with a vengeance. I felt a perverse loyalty to Hugo. He'd done nothing to suggest that at all. On the contrary, for years he'd done his best to help me (and Fontenay, it was true). 'Rather melodramatic, aren't you?'

'I want you to keep your eyes open.'

'And what do you think is going to happen, Joss? Do you honestly think I'm suddenly going to leap into his arms after yours?'

'No.'

'Then what, for heaven's sake?'

'If I knew – if I could even guess – I'd tell you, but I can't. It's just that his passion for Fontenay seems excessive. Take that row over the formal gardens. He was involved beyond what the situation called for.'

'Possibly the reason you can't be more specific is that there's nothing to tell.'

And there we left it. Twilight was falling on the golden evening skies.

By the morning, my intangible fears seemed absurd, and had vanished completely when I went to meet Hugo first at the future tea-rooms, and then back to the warmth of Fontenay Place. He did not comment on the previous evening, and I gradually let my defensive hackles lie at rest.

We discussed how we could arrange the finances of the tea-rooms, and agreed that if we did some of the catering for his conferences at the house, this would help our trading position. This reminded me that I had been dragging my feet over setting up the necessary company to trade with, and we talked about lawyers, contracts, and Articles of Association for a while.

Then he asked, 'Did you look at my comments on your plans last night, or were you too busy?'

I ignored the implication. 'Yes, I did.'

'And do you agree about the upper floor? That it should be about the two skeletons? It would be a hell of a draw.'

'The jury's out still.' Of course, Joss and I never got round to discussing it the evening before, and after he'd gone I'd had other matters on my mind – particularly Hugo himself. 'Until,' I continued, 'I've got to the bottom of both mysteries to the best of my ability.'

Hugo groaned. 'That might take for ever. 'There's no harm in a bit of mystery. Why not caption them: Thought to be the skeleton of the adulterous wife of etc or thought to be the mistress of Charles Fontenay. What's wrong with that?'

'Would you understand if I said that I'm too close to them now to want to defame their memories unless I'm sure?'

He looked at me very gently. 'Understand? Of course I do. But I don't agree. You'll never know any more than you do now about either of them.'

'Then I won't base the room on the skeletons.' I had a brainwave to deflect him. 'How about another mystery?'

'Try me,' he said resignedly.

'Come and look at the family tree again.'

He looked startled, obviously wondering what new bee I had in my genealogical bonnet, but accompanied me through to the entrance hall.

The place was buzzing with conferences; Fontenay could take one large conference and two smaller ones at a time, and all three were going strong today and beginning to spill into the stairways and entrance hall for lunch.

'Look at this.' I planted my finger on the glass in the bottom left-hand corner. 'David's grandfather Edward was the last to work on this tree. Right?'

'Agreed.'

'According to this, he and Adelaide had two children, Esther, the daughter born in 1905, who wiped the Fontenay dust off her feet and went out to Australia, and John himself born in 1897, neither of whom is in *The Book of Gertrude's Garden*.'

'Naturally not. John was still alive when the last entry was made, and so probably was Esther, so they would not be in the book.'

'Agreed. However, if you look at the tree closely . . . here –' I jabbed again – 'you'll see that there's more distance than there should be between John and Esther's names. And if you look even more closely you'll see that there's another very short vertical line between them, so short it's almost a blob.'

Hugo peered at it closely. 'Mapping pan error,' he said finally.

'And underneath that is the coloured drawing of the Fontenay coat of arms, which could have been added at any time.'

'Coincidence.'

'Suppose it wasn't. Suppose there was another child, who died young, long before John and presumably Esther.'

'There'd have been a rose for him or her,' Hugo pointed out.

'Not if the child were still alive now.'

'She isn't.'

'How on earth do you know?' I stared at him in amazement.

'David mentioned her.'

'He never did to me.' Odd, very odd.

'Nothing much to tell. She died quite young.'

'Then,' I said softly, 'why wasn't there a rose for her?'

'I've no idea.'

'If there were some mystery about her –'

'You'll never get anywhere with ifs, Anna. Edward probably didn't want to upset his wife by a prominent reminder of her death on the family tree, and they were too upset to plant a rose.'

'I hadn't thought of that.' I felt deflated.

'Your chum Joss got you going on this latest Fontenay whodunnit, didn't he?'

I steeled myself. 'No. Believe it or not, I have a mind of my own.'

'Which he's successfully taking over.'

Hugo was grinning, but bearing in mind Joss's warning last night I decided to play warily.

'Nonsense, Hugo.' I managed a casual laugh. 'It is possible for us flibbertigibbet females not to be bowled over when a man comes in sight.'

'Do be careful, Anna. I'm fond of you, you know that. I don't like to see you heading straight for danger, and I'm beginning to realize why you didn't want to sack the man.'

'He's a gardener, Hugo, and a very good one. That's why I – and initially you – didn't want to sack him. Anything else is my business.'

'And Gerard's.'

'Now look here—' My dander was distinctly on the rise.

'No, you look, Anna, that's all I ask. Look *very* carefully before you jump – whether it's into bed or into Fontenay. I don't want you to say that you weren't warned.'

'Oh, I've been warned all right,' I retorted grimly. 'One might say too much.'

'You don't think it's a mite strange that a descendant of Michael Sinclair comes marching along into Fontenay?'

'There are all sorts of reasons. The rose garden is one of them.'

'You're an innocent, Anna, just like all the Fontenays over the centuries. We rule, we're okay, no one would want to take advantage of us, and even the Sinclairs are good at heart.'

That did it. 'Hugo, keep out of my affairs, is that clear enough for you? I know you want the best for Fontenay, fine, but don't assume you know the best for me. We're strictly business, you and I. We are also friends, and that's where it stops. OK?'

Hugo didn't look put out. He merely shrugged. 'He's fooled you, Anna, he has indeed. I hope to God you don't suffer too much, you and Gerard.'

1795

'I'm sorry indeed to disturb you, Mr Fontenay – Charles.'

Gwendolen Sinclair entered the Hermit's Retreat hesitantly, drawing her heavy cape around her. 'Your gardener said I might find you here.'

Charles leapt to his feet from the armchair where he had peacefully been reading *The Times*. Even in December the solitude of the rose garden had its attractions. 'It is no disturbance, Gwendolen. I am delighted to see you. You have news of the school to bring me?' These formal words belied his racing heart.

'Might we walk in the garden? I should like that very much.'

He was surprised, but willingly accompanied her.

The garden was almost barren at this time of year, but it still

149

retained a beauty and promise of its own. Some China roses flowered even in this climate through to late autumn or winter with ease, but to him this was not important. Far better to see the perfect bloom for a month, and to treasure its perfume in one's mind until it bloomed again. Far better to have loved Gwendolen, even from afar, than never to have met her.

'Charles, you once said I might come to you if I was troubled.'

'I did, and I meant it. I am distressed to learn that anything concerns you.' What had Goderic done? Terrible thoughts flashed through Charles's mind.

They walked past the fountain in the centre of the garden, and Charles was reminded of Chaucer's poem where Danger, False-seeming, and Jealousy lurked even in the loveliness of the walled garden, and he waited to hear what ailed Gwendolen.

'I am,' her voice faltered, 'with child.'

He had expected it, he had dreaded it, and now it had come true.

'With child?' he repeated helplessly. He had known there could only have been one end to this charade of Goderic's, and yet had pushed the thought away, making no plans as to what could be done to help her.

He took her hands in his. 'My dear Gwendolen, my brother—'

'Is the father.'

Charles stood for a moment in shock. To hear the words spoken put an end to any lingering hope that this nightmare might go away.

'Have you spoken to him?' he asked gently.

'Yes,' she whispered, flushing red.

'He will wed you?' Charles hoped against hope.

'He,' Gwendolen swallowed, 'he will not do so. I was mistaken in him, Charles, and – oh, what shall I do?' Her cry was heart-rending.

'I will speak to Goderic,' Charles assured her quietly.

'No. I would not wed him if he does not wish it.'

'By heaven, Gwendolen, he shall wish it. I am head of the Fontenay family, and he will not dare refuse.'

'But I would not wed him. I see now that he is not the man

I thought him. He –' she went on with great effort – 'offered to give me money. There is a woman he knows of—'

'You shall not do it,' Charles commanded in horror. 'Never. You understand? It is too dangerous. Now tell me. What of your family, Gwendolen?'

'My father will not allow me to remain with them. My uncle would, but I cannot bring such disgrace to them.'

Charles put his arm round her, unable to hold back. The time for restraint and etiquette was past. 'My poor dear girl.' He thought quickly. 'There is a cottage in our grounds, quiet, secluded. You may live there.'

'But your wife – no, it is impossible. I thought to go abroad.'

'My wife is also expecting a child. I shall speak to the midwife and find someone to tend you.' He thought rapidly, his mind clearing now. He remembered Mistress Ovenden, the widow of his late gardener. She was in dire straits, and he – as was only natural – had been assisting her. She would welcome such work, and would not betray his – or Gwendolen's – confidence.

'At the school,' he continued gently, 'it can be given out that you have left Cranden to return to your family since your mother is ill. We must guard your reputation.' The world dealt harshly with unwed girls of respectable family. But there was a chance that this scheme might work. The cottage was a long way from Cranden. Only Mary need know. Her own pregnancy was progressing well. She must sleep apart from him for the child's sake, she explained, and he agreed. She had her own rooms now, for nothing must endanger the coming child. And Goderic – he would talk to him, by heaven he would.

'You are scared, Gwendolen?' he asked tenderly.

'Yes, sir.'

'Do not be. You are safe with me.'

Her eyes filled with tears. 'Thank you.'

Charles looked at her, the girl he loved so much, and who would never be his. Even in the depths of winter in her ugly black cape, her face was beautiful, for in it innocence had conquered over her terrible experience. Yet his beautiful rose had been corrupted by Goderic. Charles cursed his brother.

It was his responsibility, and he must be made to see it. Why should Gwendolen suffer alone? He took the girl in his arms in deep compassion. 'Dear Gwendolen,' he murmured. 'Dear rose.'

What, he forced himself to wonder, would have happened had it been he whom Gwendolen loved, and if there had been no Goderic? Would he have betrayed Mary and done as Goderic? No, he did not think so. Did one have to pluck the rose in order to enjoy it? The temptation would have been there, but with God's help he would have resisted it. He had reward enough in Mary's coming child, and that made him all the more determined that his beloved Gwendolen should have everything he could give her.

He could not know that Mary was once again watching in hatred from the garden entrance. One needed spies when Sinclairs sought to steal what rightfully belonged to the Fontenays, and she had her own loyal spy.

'Have you no shame, Goderic?' Charles asked quietly.

'Very little, brother.' He didn't even lay down his newspaper.

'Then employ what little you have in Miss Sinclair's interests.'

'Ah. I see she has fled to you even sooner than I expected, Charles. You are a fool. You see an angel, where there is only a trollop. Because she claims to love roses, because she is fair and lovely, and because she is with child, you believe me a devil and her an angel. Dear brother, there are few angels walking this earth today.'

'But Gwendolen is one of them,' Charles replied steadily. He trusted his own judgement, he knew Goderic and he knew Miss Sinclair. He would not be swayed. 'I have offered her the cottage near the old castle.'

Goderic stared at him. 'You are a bigger fool than I thought, brother.' He threw back his head and laughed. 'It will be assumed by everyone that it is you who got her with child.'

'You will be here and you will tend her.'

'Dear brother, unfortunately not. My darling Elizabeth has returned early from Italy unable to bear life without me. The

152

wedding will be in the summer and I am summoned to be at her side until then.'

'You intend to leave now?' Charles was aghast.

'I thought you would be pleased. You have much to occupy you with the approaching birth of the new heir. *If* Mary bears a son of course. Otherwise I shall return in due course to claim my inheritance.'

'You really intend to abandon Gwendolen?'

'Such a pity, such – as you consider – a little angel, but she knew of my betrothal all the time.'

'And was told that you would break it.'

'Did I say that? I have no recollection. I believe she is bamming you, Charles.'

Charles stared at him coldly. 'You leave me no option, Goderic. If you insist on leaving, I shall reveal the parentage of Gwendolen's child to Miss Sayles and her parents.'

Goderic was shaken at last. 'You would never do so. You hate me. You cannot wait for me to leave. Would you jeopardize that?'

'For Miss Sinclair's sake, I would.'

Goderic stared at him. 'I do believe you mean it, Charles,' he replied slowly.

'You will stay then.'

'Until the birth.'

'My dear, there is something distasteful I have to tell you.' Charles had come to see Mary immediately to explain. He sensed that she was distrustful of his emotions for Gwendolen, and had decided to explain the situation to her fully.

'Indeed?' She looked up, puzzled.

'You will recall Miss Sinclair whom we met at Bath, and whom you observed now has a position in our Cranden school.'

'I do.' Mary's head was bent over her work.

'I regret to tell you that that position was arranged for her by Goderic and that she is now with child,' – Mary's head shot up – 'by him.'

'Goderic?' she echoed strangely.

'He misled her into believing that his betrothal would be broken, which is why she agreed to leave home to come to

Cranden. Now he has told her he is unwilling to marry her. I have therefore offered her a cottage on our estate until we can sort out her future.'

'You have *what*? My dear Mr Fontenay, how can this be?'

'This is Goderic's child. The family owes her the help that Goderic denies her.'

'Of course,' Mary said, with an obvious effort. 'It is *Goderic's* child. We must do what we must.' She smiled at Charles, but there was little warmth in her eyes.

I tried with difficulty to get my mind round solicitors and limited companies, but it was hard. It was also, I reminded myself, urgent for the big bills would start arriving shortly and I needed the company set up. If I was not careful, however, I would become a mere punchball in the battle between Hugo and Joss, and that was preoccupying me more than logistics. But battle for what? I still didn't know. Joss had laughingly talked of marriage – or had he? I was torn in two. Half of my mind was bound up now in Joss and the rose garden, a quarter with Hugo, and the rest prosaically jaunting around with tea-rooms and business. Somewhere lost in the middle were Gerard and myself.

By daylight the idea of anything seriously wrong seemed ridiculous, by evening doubts had flooded back. Unless Joss came, that is, which dispelled all thinking at all, as we laughed and joked. It was like the old myth of Cupid and Psyche. By night it was all delight, by day she wasn't even allowed to look at his face. It wasn't quite that way with Joss, of course, for I did quite a lot of looking, but the two worlds seemed entirely separate.

Tomorrow, Saturday, Gerard was going up to university, so it was hardly surprising that there was no sign of him today. The affair with Sarah seemed to be hotting up, for Joss had told me that Gerard was following her around like a lovesick puppy.

'Like me,' he added amiably.

'You – a lovesick puppy? Convince me,' I jeered.

'Right now?'

As we were in the middle of a muddy, barren rose garden, and not alone there, I declined the offer – with a rain check.

'Did Hugo warn you off me?' Joss asked casually.

'He did.'

'Are you warned?'

'No.'

'Good.'

With the fountain installed, three men were busy on creating the steps. The paths would be next. It was beginning to take shape, and the first consignment of roses had already been delivered. In fact, two were already laid in place, Gertrude's damask and Edmund's white alba, in the soon to be lavender-hedged small garden by the fountain.

'I tried to get Jennifer's Peace rose, and the gardener's, but I'm having trouble. They may have to wait till spring, but we can get these in,' Joss said. 'Shall we have a ceremonial planting? The ground's fertilized and ready.'

'Can we?' My eyes lit up. 'And before Gerard leaves. I reckon he'd like to be here.'

'After lunch?'

'If I can find him.'

'Try the barn over by the eastern boundary. That's where he and Sarah hang out.'

'I thought she was supposed to be *working* for us.'

'She is, but I gave her a few hours off since Gerard's going off.'

'Very thoughtful – non-conjugal visits for staff.' I grappled with the image of Gerard locked in Sarah's bonny arms. One can assume that one's offspring are indulging in sexual romps, but evidence can still come as a shock.

In the event they both turned up for lunch. They seemed a bit subdued, but I took this to be through lovers' partings, and it was only when we were walking back to the rose garden I realized Gerard was limping.

'I had a fall,' he said when I asked. 'It's okay. I'm fine.'

I quickly forgot it in the excitement of the tree-planting ceremony. Joss had even brought Hugo along in a rare spirit of co-operation.

Edmund and Gertrude's roses lay puddling, as Joss put it, in

155

a tub full of very wet mud, and by the time we got there Joss had already dug the holes in the agreed places.

'Here.' Joss handed the shrub rose to me. 'The red damask, Gertrude's rose.'

'Gerard, you're the Fontenay,' I said, handing it to him. 'You do it.'

He refused the honour, so I planted it myself under directions from Joss about pressing the soil all around the roots and where the budding union should be.

'I name this rose,' I said seriously, 'Gertrude's rose. May she be remembered for ever in this garden of tomorrow.'

'Hear, hear!' Sarah clapped vigorously, giggling slightly. I suppose if I were her age I'd have giggled too. Gerard decided he'd back me after all, so he took over the planting of Sir Edmund's rose.

'Mind you,' he observed, 'I'm not sure the old fellow would have liked a Sinclair in the garden.'

'Why not?' Joss asked mildly. 'For all you know he was the best of chums with the Sinclairs.'

'I don't think so. I did a spot of research a few weeks ago to get in the mood for working again. Old Edmund hated the Sinclairs like poison. Something to do with Gertie.'

'Don't,' I said forcefully, 'tell me. I've quite enough mysteries already.'

'Gerard can look it up at his university library,' Hugo joked. 'After all, Edmund's son was called Gerard. It gives you a stake in it. Maybe you'll change your mind about selling the place.'

'Could be,' Gerard said non-committally. He finished loosening the earth round the top of Edmund's rose. 'There you are,' he muttered to the bushes. 'Edmund and Gertrude, where it all started. And may it all *finish*.' This was an aside to Sarah, but I overheard it and was puzzled.

That evening Joss left Gerard and me to our last evening, and so I asked him what he meant by that last remark. It was a casual question, so I wasn't prepared for the answer.

'You really want to know?'

'I do.'

'I said I had a fall, right?'

'Yes. I'm sorry I didn't ask you more about it.'

156

'I'm okay,' he cut in, 'but only by luck. The floor gave way on the top level where we usually go. I went straight through it, and Sarah damned near joined me.'

'But –' I was aghast as I racked my brains – 'that's at least a twenty-five-foot drop. It's a high barn.'

'Too right. Fortunately I didn't go all the way down, I managed to hang on at the angle of the steps, and Sarah, not being able to haul me up, rushed down and piled so much straw beneath me I could make the drop. I rolled off unfortunately, hence the limp.'

'Gerard! I'll have that floor looked at immediately.'

'I gave it a look myself, Ma. We've been up there a few times now, and it was as sound as a bell. I'd swear to that. Suddenly it isn't.'

'Okay, so old floors . . .' I stopped and began again. 'Are you suggesting it wasn't an accident, Gerard?'

'Maybe I'm imagining things, but I don't think it was. It all split too quickly, too completely. There's probably no proof. But if I'm right, things here are more serious than I thought. You'll take care, Mum, won't you? Not that they'll want you out of the way. Only me.'

I seemed to be groping in thick fog. 'What are you getting at?'

'I'm getting at the fact that someone might want a clear path to you and Fontenay – without my being around. I can tell you, I'm out of here, pronto, and I'm not going near any steep cliffs either.'

'Hugo?' I asked in dread.

'Maybe. Or your famous Joss.'

'No!'

Gerard shrugged. 'I'm serious, Mum. Don't get too close to *either* of these geezers.'

Eleven

The next day I watched Gerard climb into Sarah's dad's people carrier with relief. In this case it wasn't so much people who were being transported as a mountain of luggage for university. There was no way I could have stowed it into my Peugeot and I was grateful to Sarah for the offer. Whether her father was equally grateful, I'm not sure, but he seemed resigned to such requests from his daughter. In any case, Gerard was now safe. He was away from Fontenay. It was only then I could face examining what had happened to him and what he had implied about its cause.

By day, it was easy to pooh-pooh the idea. Here I was living in the twenty-first century, not caught up in a history book tale of greed and violence. I even forced myself to go to the barn to inspect the damage. I was proud of the way I related the story casually to Hugo and to Joss, dismissing it as an accident, but nevertheless I decided I'd get the builders in to repair it straightaway. Not that the accident or otherwise would be repeated, but I wanted to ask the builder, one Mike Simmonds, what his opinion was. I even managed to make myself sound fairly normal in talking to him.

'What did happen here, do you think?'

He looked at me as though I were out of my mind. 'It just gave way, Mrs Fontenay. Boards get rotten, no heating, plenty of damp, no one keeping an eye on them.'

I picked up one of the smashed boards, thinking of all the corny ancient fiction I used to read, wondering if a sign of deliberate cutting would reveal itself to me.

'It seems strange that they hadn't shown any signs of doing so earlier.'

'Maybe.' Mike nodded his head sagely. 'You can never tell though. It's what's going on *inside* those little planks that makes the difference.'

Very impressive. I looked at the said planks, but they kept their inner thoughts to themselves. A jury would dismiss the case straightaway. And yet, but for good fortune, Gerard could have been killed. With nothing looking strange to me, I couldn't pursue the subject. Nor did I want to. I walked out into the sunshine again, leaving Mike to his work, and resolved to leave the physical record, if any, behind me.

That was by day, however. At night my mind churned over what was going on inside those boards, and more to the point inside Hugo's or – I forced myself to acknowledge – Joss's minds. Fancifully I saw myself fighting my way past Chaucer's Danger, False-seeming, Jealousy and anything else you care to name. The drawback was that suddenly my perfect rose no longer seemed within my grasp. Things don't happen like that.

Joss had obviously noted some change in me in the days that followed Gerard's departure. At least, I assumed this was the reason he stayed away. He must have picked up some innuendo when I was telling him about the accident, much as I'd tried to keep my account neutral. I was even grateful about his keeping away. I was busy having nightmares of more floorboards being eaten away in York by unseen seething little creatures inside them, until Gerard, my son, my only child, came crashing down to his death.

Oddly enough, it was Sarah Dodds who got me through this stage. She dropped in after returning from York to report on Gerard's safe installation. Needless to say, Gerard had been too busy to ring himself.

'Come in. Have a coffee.'

'Thanks.' She removed her boots and wandered round the lodge, quite at home, while I made coffee.

I had to go carefully. After all, I was her boss but she reported to Joss and knew Hugo. I couldn't count on her objectiveness. Nevertheless, she had been with Gerard in the barn, and I could ask her more about it.

'I dunno how it happened,' she answered. 'Maybe Gerry's

got too much of a bee in his bonnet about Hugo and Joss fighting over you and Fontenay. For all he says about selling up, I reckon Gerry rather fancies being lord of the manor – that's why this bee's flown in.'

'I don't agree with his bee,' I said shortly, not fully at ease with being thrown in at the deep end.

She glanced at me, a knowing look on her face. 'He could be wrong,' she announced diplomatically. 'He told me he announced he might sell up and then, whoops, he has an accident like that.'

'I don't see that Gerard's death, or lack of it, would make any difference to the situation over Fontenay.'

She looked at me as though I were dumb, and maybe I was. 'If he sells up, Fontenay is out of the family, right? Perhaps you'd sell up too, if he'd been killed.'

'Then someone else would buy it.' Even Hugo could buy it, if not by himself then with a conglomerate, I supposed. 'And that would put paid to Gerard's idea that his possible murderer is after me for the estate.'

'Not really,' Sarah murmured vaguely, and the discussion ended with her bright: 'Still, they're both pussy cats, aren't they?'

'Who?'

'Mr High and Mighty Hugo and Joss of course. Better look out though. The cat family have painful claws.'

I didn't know whether Sarah was producing all this from her own mind or whether it was Gerard speaking through her. It didn't matter, because I suddenly crystallized on what she meant. If it were Fontenay itself that was the prize, the future of Fontenay would be up for grabs if Gerard died. Married to me, the grabbing would be that much easier. And the next step would be . . . I decided to stop right there.

'Let's take the coffee into the conservatory.' I picked up the tray and Sarah docilely followed me.

I was getting used to her laid-back manner now, and apart from the sex, I could see what Gerard liked in her. There was a sharp mind, and maybe even a heart, well hidden, there. 'Are you going up to see Gerard in York?' I asked.

'Nah. I'll wait till the Christmas vac. I'm working.'

'In a bar?' What other evening work was there.

'No. My college work. Starts in a week's time. I'm doing a three-year course in architectural landscaping.'

I was losing it. Of course I knew about the course. Gerard had told me she would still be based at home though, and I knew she was still going to do part-time work for Joss. I asked her more about the course, and eventually, inevitably, the subject came back to Joss.

'Joss is a good teacher, met him at Cranhurst Court when we were both working there. He suggested I came here for work incidentally, not because of the Aunt Jen connection. I told him about her and the Fontenays after he suggested it, and being a Sinclair, he was mighty interested.'

'Did you know about the feud?'

'Yeah – and he told me right away he was Michael Sinclair's grandson.'

'Didn't you think that odd since your family thinks Michael Sinclair murdered your aunt?' I was grappling with a feeling that I'd been cocooned in a web of ignorance about Fontenay, the very thing I was here to preserve. How could there have been so many gaps in the stories David told me, although he was avid about family history?

'Sins of the fathers and all that. I didn't hold it against Joss, how could I? Anyway, he says his grandfather didn't do it.'

'Then who did?'

'The husband most like. Usually is. Jealousy,' she pronounced, worldly-wise.

'You're forgetting something. Jennifer was pregnant, and her husband was desperate for an heir to Fontenay. Even, I suspect, if it was someone else's child.'

'Dunno,' was all she replied, indicating the subject was closed.

'What do you think of the plans for Fontenay?' I asked, obligingly changing the subject.

'Not bad. Mind you, this history stuff is all right to draw the punters in, but you can get too involved in it. Like Hugo, mad about all his blessed portraits and bits and bobs. When you start believing it matters, it takes you over. History's okay in its place, but you've got to keep it there.'

With this profound thought, Sarah finished her coffee and departed.

Was that the answer, I wondered, after she'd gone? Had David isolated Fontenay into the past, preserving it in a glass cage for all to see and none to touch? Or had it been his father who had done that, and passed it as a legacy to an unquestioning son? But David wasn't unquestioning, so that couldn't be the answer.

For the first time since his death I tried to look at David objectively, not as how he had appeared to me, his wife. Had I always seen him in the role I first met him: admiring student to all-knowing lecturer? No, I decided, but even so as his wife I had a far from objective viewpoint. I conjured up his image, shopping in Tesco's, halfway through a curry in the local Indian restaurant, walking in Greenwich park, straight-faced and earnest but with a devilish sense of humour. Yet that never seemed to apply where the Fontenays were concerned. Was there an inconsistency there? Had he deliberately not delved too far into the Sinclair feud, and accepted hook, line and sinker everything he'd been told?

With relief I thought I could see an escape route (for me). David had left Fontenay when he was ten years old. In his eyes, it was paradise, not a millstone, and paradise had to be passed on to Gerard. In his mind there was nothing to query; he had no skeleton thrust under his nose as had I. Everything at Fontenay was on hold while his family was absent. His father had died when he was fifteen, and after that he would have had only his mother Deborah to remind him of the Fontenay heritage.

Deborah . . . whose message on Fontenay's past to me had been 'Don't go there'. What, I wondered, had her message to David been?

1944

'I can't tell you how grateful I am, Mrs Pink.' Jennifer began to relax in the primitive lodge kitchen, as the sainted Polly Pink,

162

her lined face grimly set to do the best she could, put on her well-worn apron with the pink roses on it, and tied the strings round her ample waist. Jennifer couldn't believe her luck when she bumped into her in Cranden and found out that Mrs Pink was as anxious to leave retirement as Jennifer was to have her back at Fontenay. Until Adelaide had died in 1942, she had clung fiercely to her old ways, and they'd even had to battle to put in a boiler to heat water for her. The old stone sink and range still ruled supreme here though.

Nothing would change until after the war, but if anyone had doubted that the invasion of France was close at hand, they didn't now. Nevertheless there were curious signs. Firstly, although there were many soldiers around, both at Fontenay and in Cranden, there didn't seem to be sufficient for an invasion. Surely all the troops in Britain would be gathered here for the invasion? There were lots of rumours, but little hard fact. The camps were well away from the villages, and though tanks were seen, they were hardly covering every spare inch. It was rumoured that the US General Patton was here, but not a great number of Yankee soldiers. Still, the airfields were as busy as always, for though Michael had moved into Fontenay Place, he seemed to spend more time at West Malling than here. More and more airfields had been built in the country, more and more police were around to push civilians back from blocking roads where convoys might pass and the local shops had been given sealed containers with emergency rations designed to last 'over a period'.

'How about potato piglets, Mrs F?' Polly demanded.

'Not again.' Jennifer sighed. 'I'll check the carrots. Maybe there'll be some ready.' Whoever it was had said that English cookery needed a Society for the Prevention of Cruelty to Vegetables was off the mark now. Without her vegetables, it would be potato piglets every day (and often just with the potatoes and sausages, if the cabbage wasn't available).

She remembered with pleasure that she'd be seeing Michael today. He'd been back to West Malling for a day or two. He'd come to see her while she was planting sprouts, pushed a strand of her dark hair back under its snood, and told her he'd be back to see the early roses on 1st June. He whispered he had

163

something he wanted to talk about. So had she. She longed to tell him she was almost sure that she was pregnant now. She was filled with great joy, even though it made work tiring. There was something to work for now though, a Fontenay that could continue the line.

She still had not told John – and that meant not telling Michael. She would not do so until she was certain. She could withstand the pressure till then, for luckily John had taken a fancy to Deborah, the Waaf driver at Fontenay. She was a nice girl, outspoken and lively, and Jennifer liked her too.

In the afternoon, Jennifer left the vegetable grounds and walked over to the rose garden, looking forward to this moment in her haven.

As she walked in, she could see Michael lolling on the arbour seat, eyes closed against the sun. He seemed to sense her approach, she drew quite close to him and the blue eyes flew open. And the worry lines came back.

'I can't tell you how good it is to get away, Jen. I'd do something stupid if it wasn't for you. You keep me in order.'

'I thought you fighter lads didn't want to be kept in order.' Jennifer sat down beside him, her arm around him, watching the bees on the rambling pink roses.

'I'm not a fighter lad any longer. Remember?' Michael laughed. 'Don't look so horrified, Jennifer. You haven't upset me. I don't care any longer. If I can do my bit behind a desk that's as good as in the air, even if I don't enjoy it so much. There's another side to life now.'

'Your son?' Jennifer reminded him.

Michael sighed. 'You know, Jen, I think about him a lot, but I see him so little now that he's growing up without me. I'm just a visitor, and I have to say – don't be shocked – that much as I love him, he seems Hazel's kid but not mine. I don't mean I'm not the father. Of course I am, but he doesn't *feel* part of me.'

'After the war—' Jennifer began. It was an oft-repeated and perhaps meaningless phrase about some paradise that would probably never come.

'You know very well where I want to be after the war, and it's not with Hazel.'

164

'You have responsibilities to her.'

'Don't remind me, Jennifer. Not today. Not here. It's all going to start, you know.'

'The big one?'

'Oh yes. I'm going back to West Malling again tomorrow for a few days – but don't make any connection, will you?' He grinned, so Jennifer knew the invasion was going to be very soon indeed.

'Will you be back?' She didn't know what she would do without Michael here. He was part of her life now, though she knew it could not go on that way.

'I'll be back.'

Jennifer relaxed. That probably meant Fontenay would be his base after the invasion had begun.

'What do you think John will make of my being here?' he continued.

'I don't know. Oh, Michael, he's beginning to behave very oddly. He's been poring over family records, muttering about the Sinclairs and goodness knows what dark secrets.'

'He's not still on about my being a dastardly Sinclair out to capture you?'

'No. I think it might be something else.' Jennifer hesitated. Should she tell him this? It was after all a Fontenay concern, and it seemed a betrayal to be telling a Sinclair. Then she pulled herself together. They were in the middle of a war, when the past was buried very deep, and the glories even of this rose garden might soon be overwhelmed by its horrors.

'He's been to see Uncle Alfred, his father's brother,' she explained. 'He's a fair age now, but he's still as sharp as a button. Alfred's fairly sure that there's more than John thought to the story of the elder sister I mentioned to you, whom he had always believed died while he was still away at the war in a lunatic asylum. Apparently she wasn't mad at all. She had got herself pregnant, and being unmarried, the family did as was all too often the case; they clapped her up in an asylum and mother and child were dead within a year.'

Michael whistled. 'Some story.'

'When John returned, he naturally believed what he was told. This new slant has made quite an impression on him.

165

He's blaming himself for not being there to help. He adored her, he told me.'

Michael grimaced. 'Yet more family secrets, eh?'

'It's a ghastly story.' Jennifer shuddered. 'I suggested to John that we planted a rose bush for her, and for once he liked the idea. We're going to have a ceremony soon, when we can get the rose he's chosen. A white Mrs Herbert Stevens tea rose – if we can get one. It's very hardy, which appeals to him.'

'That's a nice idea – typical of you, my love.'

'In a way,' Jennifer said thoughtfully, 'it would be like the noisette I planted for Gwendolen Sinclair. Only I won't tell John that.'

It was Michael's turn to shiver. 'I wish you hadn't mentioned her.'

'Why?' Jennifer was startled.

'Would you think me crazy if I said it was like death entering paradise? I can't stand the thought that something dreadful happened here, something that resulted in a skeleton. This has seemed to me the last stronghold against the war and evil, and now we know death came here, too.'

'We *don't* know that, Michael. If she was killed, it could have been anywhere on the estate, and the body buried here later.'

'No.' Michael hesitated. 'I'm not given to fancies, Jennifer. But weird things happen in war, especially to pilots. Maybe it's the heightened sense of awareness, up in the sky, the adrenalin at full peak, surrounded by the beauty of blue skies, and then comes the hun out of the sun, as they used to say in the last war. Death strikes and all that beauty is tarnished. It makes me wary of too much beauty up there, as I'm always looking around for its companion.' Michael stared at the roses cascading, the peaceful sight before him. 'You know, some of the chaps' dogs howl, when their master doesn't return from an op. I feel like this about this garden. It's *too* beautiful. It's waiting for something, sensing something – and its name is death.'

Jennifer put her arm around him. 'Fight it, Michael. This garden *is* an escape, a tiny walled-in piece of paradise for you to call your own.'

'There is no escape,' Michael replied soberly. 'The serpent has to be faced – and first it has to be recognized.'

I knew Joss was taking a long weekend off, so I had a temporary respite in thinking out whether my feelings towards him had changed after what had happened to Gerard. It was unfair if so, since there was no proof of any deliberate tampering at all. As Sarah implied, history was smothering me, blotting out the glorious future that had seemed to exist only a few days ago. The Tweedledee of history was having a great big battle with the Tweedledum of the future, and it was going on right inside me, with Anna Fontenay undecided as to where she should send the cavalry.

In fact, the respite went on for over a month. There had to be a reckoning, I finally decided. I couldn't continue like this, not knowing why Joss stayed away from me, on the personal level at least. It had been weeks now since we had spoken personally. If I wanted to see him, I had to seek him out, we would discuss work amicably and then he would have another appointment and leave. The rose garden, I knew, was taking shape. Joss was spending a lot of his time there. At first I was relieved, because it meant I didn't have to struggle to seem normal, but then the tension began to tell. Hugo seemed just the same as usual, and I even went out with him on the odd occasion, just to prove I could. With both of them, however, the insidious voice of the serpent whispered: *Was it you? Was it you tried to kill my son?*

I had the sense to realize I was letting things get on top of me, and also that I had to sort it out before Gerard returned for Christmas. So where better to face Joss than in the rose garden? I stiffened my resolve, put on my anorak, dug my hands deep in my pockets and marched forth. I needed to see it, I told myself. I had been deserting the actual garden, by making the excuse that I needed to work on the exhibition for the Hermit's Retreat. Goodness knows, this was true enough.

The garden looked so familiar as I walked up to the iron gate, and I could see Joss working inside.

'Hi,' I called brightly, as I entered.

For a moment his head was still, as was his foot on the fork, then he deliberately finished, firming the rose bush in place before he straightened up. He said not a word.

'How are you getting on?' I asked.

He waved an arm. 'See for yourself.'

I saw. Probably I couldn't quite match the vision his mind must have dreamed up in all its clarity, but it was near enough. I could see the beds, edged with lavender, the barren twigs of the bush and standard roses which next summer would be in glorious leaf and flower. I could see the wooden pergolas over the rose walk. I could see the fountain flanked by its two roses, one red, one white. I could see where gillyflowers, foxgloves and love-in-a-mist would add their rainbow glories where they were to be used as underplanting. I could see the shallow steps down to the fountain where huge stone urns would bear cascading roses.

Then the all too familiar feeling of claustrophobia returned. Could I really bear all those roses? At the moment they were vulnerable, all but bare twigs and tender roots. But next spring, they would come to life, turning into an army of thorns and impenetrable bushes, preparing their assault on eyes, nose and mind.

'So what next?' was my second inspired question.

'It's nearly finished, and over to you to complete the Hermit's Retreat. I'll go back to my work on the formal gardens – if you still want me to?'

'Still want—' I echoed stupidly.

'Still want me working here. I've done most of what I came for.'

This was a declaration of war, or so it seemed to me. If I had anything else in mind, I had to make it known now.

'*Have* you finished?' I asked. 'Haven't you just piled soil on two incomplete stories?'

'We'll not get any further with either of them, and you know that, Jennif—'

Jennifer? I stared at him, and he had the grace to laugh. 'Sorry, old age is getting to me. Anna, I mean. Anna.'

'I wonder if you did,' I whipped back, thanking fortune for

such a windfall. 'If it's on your mind so much as that, it most certainly isn't finished. Joss, there's *still* one route we could take. Or I, if you prefer.'

'No. I won't let you talk to my grandfather.'

'And Deborah,' I countered, 'has warned me off. Forbidden ground. Do not enter here.'

We stared at each other, he and I. We who had lain in each other's arms as the year's garden harvest blessed us. He and I who had loved just as Jennifer and Michael had done, just as Gwendolen and Charles.

I took a step towards him. 'Joss . . .' I saw in his eyes the look that must have so often been in mine recently: Do not touch me. 'Come to me, Joss,' I said. I meant emotionally, but he perversely took it to mean physically.

'No. I don't want to get mud all over the paths.'

'Can you blame me, Joss?'

'For wondering whether there's a ha'p'orth of difference between me and Hugo Brooks? Oh, yes, oddly enough I can, Anna.'

'That's not true,' I began, then stopped. I *had* wondered that and there was no hiding it. Despite my endeavours, it must have been written all over me from that moment Gerard told me about his fall. 'Gerard could have been killed, Joss. It shook me. Is that so odd?'

'And is it still shaking you?'

'Not now we're talking about it.' It was an awkward, stupid thing to say, since it laid openly on the table the fog of doubt that had beset me in the last weeks. I did my best. 'Tell me, Joss, do *you* think Gerard's fall was natural?'

'I've no idea. If it was, I find the idea that I had anything to do with it somewhat offputting in someone to whom I've made love. If it wasn't, I can't see why the hell you look at me as though I'm a serial killer.'

I made a mistake. My God, did I make a mistake. I tried to make a joke of it. How stupid can you get. 'Am I next in line then?'

Have you ever watched love fly out of the window? I did just then, but you can't take words back just like that. 'Help me, Joss, help me,' I gibbered in terror. 'I don't want to lose you. And remember you kept from me the fact that you were a Sinclair. You have to make a leap of faith now, just as I did then.'

He considered this. 'I'll go on working here. I've taken a fancy to it.' His voice was cold, dispassionate. 'Besides, I like to see things through. I don't want to leave barren earth. I want to see it leaf up.'

It won't with Joss and me, I thought in despair. Not now our very roots have been attacked. I tried once more, tried with the last weapon I had: the rose garden itself.

'This is the *new* garden, Joss. Don't you think maybe it's still poisoned, that we have to get the poison out of the garden before we can enjoy its fruits?'

He laughed at me, though not too unkindly. 'Come off it, Anna. Don't get melodramatic. This is a garden just like any other. It's not special. All that's important is what we are doing to it *now*.'

'You didn't believe that when you began work on it.'

'No, I thought . . .' He shrugged. 'But I do now. It's earth, that's all, and what we plant in it is what will come up. Nothing more, nothing less. Skeletons don't bear fruit.'

'Then we've changed positions. That was my thinking at first. Something new, all planted by ourselves. Now I've changed. Something terrible happened here, Joss. I'm sure of it. I don't mean just the flying bomb, but what happened before and around it. They say ghosts leave their imprint on the scene of violence that caused their death. In this enclosed garden whatever happened is still here.'

He slammed down the fork. 'Roses, Anna, that's all. And that's the crux for you, isn't it? Have you ever asked yourself whether it's not the roses that are the problem, but the demands of life? You thought you had that all nicely walled in by your love for David, but when he died you were on your own. A few rough winds shook the darling buds of May. So it was the roses to blame, skeletons to blame, anything, anything that could stand between you and getting on with life.'

'It's not . . .' I stammered in shock. 'I took on Fontenay. I fell in love with you.'

'But you took the first chance that presented itself to wriggle

170

out of trusting in me. One foot in the rose garden, one foot out. What do you want? Thornless roses?'

If he'd shouted, it would have been easier. But he didn't, so I had to do my best, and that couldn't be by accepting everything he said.

'Don't you think you're in a walled garden too, Joss? You're devoured by this place. Come out, meet me halfway, *please*.'

'Anna, I've tried. You fought me once and we survived it, but not this battle.'

'Then I will fight it alone, Joss,' I said steadily. 'If you think this is just earth, then you've lost the ideal you started out with. I think it's the skeletons that have done that to you, as well as to me. If you won't help me find out the truth. I'll do it myself.'

'And what then? Suppose you do find out the true stories? Will it make any difference?'

'I hope so.'

'It won't to me. You can come to tell me you've discovered everything, but why should that take away from me the memory of your face when you thought I'd tried to murder your son?'

I was drowning in this nightmare. He was right, he was wrong. 'Can you honestly say that all feeling between us is dead, Joss? I don't think you'd be so bitter if it were.'

'Let's describe it as deeply bruised and still in shock.' At least he was looking amused.

'I'll make a deal with you, Joss. By the time this garden blooms again, I'll have laid those ghosts to rest, and any private ones you claim I have. There'll be new life in the garden and you – we – can believe in ourselves again.'

I thought for a moment he was going to reject this as ridiculous nonsense. But he bent down and patted the earth by Gertrude's rose.

'I'm not sure if this will take or not. If it does—'

'No, that's not fair,' I protested, seeing my battle half won. 'You said roses had nothing to do with it.'

'I'll give it some more peat.' He looked at my indignant face. 'And maybe some frost-proofing.'

171

Twelve

Everything, it seemed to me, was waiting for spring. Fontenay itself was waiting. The rose garden would lie dormant, until the bushes that Joss had planted came into leaf. And I, too, was waiting; nothing had been resolved, I could see nothing that would take me forward – or these ghosts away. I had four to five months to put my life in order, and Fontenay with it. November was almost out, soon the Christmas season would be upon me, and the problem of where Gerard should stay. It was stupid, but grown son or not, this exercised me more than anything. Gerard had said something on the telephone about spending Christmas with Sarah's family, which seemed a good idea to me, in view of the atmosphere – and possible threat – at Fontenay. The next problem was what to do with myself. Fortunately Sarah's grandmother turned up trumps: Amelia invited me, too.

It wasn't how I had envisaged spending Christmas in the rosy glow of my affair with Joss, but it would get me away from Fontenay. There was one minor but irritating problem connected with Joss. In this fallow period what should I do about a Christmas present for him? In the end I found a copy of the original edition of Eleanour Sinclair Rohde's *The Story of the Garden*, which I knew he didn't possess. I told myself it at least made a bridge of friendship between a Fontenay and a Sinclair, and could be construed either as a loving or as an employer's present.

Meanwhile I devoted myself to the Hermit's Retreat exhibition. Hugo had now given me the copies of the relevant portraits, I had copies of some applicable photographs, and I was busy working on camera-ready copy for the biographies to be printed on suitably flower-ornamented boards.

While I was preparing it, an idea came to me. I realized that apart from the portraits I had never fully been through the Fontenay memorabilia stored at the house. Hitherto I had relied on Hugo's knowledge of it to provide the answers to any questions I might have. David had kept the good stuff here, together with his father's photograph album, from which I had extracted a photo of his father and one of his grandparents.

I was suddenly and belatedly curious as to what the rest of the family archives consisted of. I could have kicked myself for falling into the trap that Hugo would no doubt encourage: that the memorabilia were under Hugo's control and that he and no one else could go through them.

Rubbish! I was the ultimate owner, and I was going to consult them.

I had a faint memory that there was an inventory somewhere, and went through the bundle of legal papers to do with Fontenay Place with some excitement. David was meticulous in his record-keeping, and had drawn up the inventory donkey's years ago, so I had never bothered to check it. It was rechecked by the solicitors each time a new lease was signed – and as this would happen in the spring of next year, I decided I would take over the task this time. And *now*.

I found it attached to the old lease, and ran my eye through it. The bulk of it was household account books, and a few bundles of letters, each dated, and named. There were also one or two diaries, the odd manuscript recipe book – someday I could look at those with a view to publishing a Fontenay cookbook to sell in the new gift shop. To my surprise the family bible was included – odd, why hadn't David kept that?

Obviously Hugo would have been through the archive. Clues to Jennifer and Michael Sinclair, however, would surely have been in David's collection. Or would they? Had his father industriously combed any reference to them out? Ah well, at least I was clear-headed now. Ten to one there'd be nothing either in David's small collection or in the Fontenay Place archive, but I was going to till this earth very thoroughly. No stone would lie unturned.

I decided to have another look through David's family photograph album. I had skipped through it earlier, merely to discover whether there were any photos of Jennifer – forlorn hope – and to extract the photos I had needed. I'd then abandoned it as a source of information. It might be worth a second go, and at the very least would set me on the road for delving deeper into the archives. This album went back to the 1920s, when John was a young man, and of course it was full of photographs of the then middle-aged Adelaide and Edward. It was begun too late to include photographs of the mystery daughter. I suppose I had hoped that Adelaide or John might have slipped one in, but there was nothing. There weren't even any of Esther, whereas I'd have thought there would have been at least one perhaps sent from Australia, with a couple of babies on her lap. I was sure David had said she had married.

There were pictures of John and Deborah's wedding, in strictly utilitarian clothes, as they were taken in 1947 when rationing was still severe, and a couple of Deborah in Waaf's uniform, outside what looked suspiciously like Fontenay Place. Odd. Nothing labelled Michael Sinclair, but I had hardly expected it. There were one or two of groups of soldiers in the Fontenay grounds, and a figure in RAF uniform too, but I had no means of knowing if this was Michael Sinclair. All the major doors to the truth were firmly locked. Deborah, alive, but warning me off. Michael Sinclair alive – and unreachable.

All the more reason not to be frustrated more than necessary, I decided, so I spoke to Hugo casually when I next saw him, and told him I'd like to look through the memorabilia and I'd check the inventory myself at the same time.

He glanced at me. 'Sure. Tell me what you want to know, and I'll get it out for you.'

'No problem. I'll see all the papers wherever they are, and in whatever order. No fuss.' I smiled to show how lightly I was taking this.

'They're all packed away,' he answered doubtfully. 'I'll think about it.'

I was astounded. 'What do you mean, *think* about it? I want to check the inventory. I could do it in the spring, when we sign the new lease, but I'd prefer to do it now.'

'Fontenay Place is leased to me. All I have to do is produce the items one by one, not give you free entry.'

He couldn't be serious, and obviously he wasn't because he then grinned. 'Give me a day or two till I get the worst of the Christmas parties off my slate, and then we'll talk again.'

I realized I'd unexpectedly put my foot on boggy ground. Hugo was making it clear who was in the driving seat at Fontenay Place. It made me all the more obstinate, and I went home to re-read the lease. I was horrified to find that there was no provision for access to the memorabilia either by family or outside historians – and made an instant note that the new lease would carry just such a clause. In fact, I might go farther, and exclude the archive from the list, on the excuse that the memorabilia were all part of the Fontenay heritage that I needed to exploit. Nevertheless this sub-text clash sent not only prickles of resentment up my spine, but a definite antenna that was crying out: 'Marshy ground. Wear big wellingtons.'

In fact, the spat all passed away peacefully. I only had to wait a couple of days, before Hugo rang me to suggest lunch and a journey through the inventory together. The lunch was highly enjoyable – and so in a way was the inventory check. Some of the trunks were in the attic rooms, and we climbed up amid the beams to inspect their contents. Picking them up, book by book, bundle by bundle, I could see it could be a long job to go through them individually. One of these days, I told myself, they would make a splendid book of how the house was run from Tudor times through to the present day. But not now. The letters and diaries might be more fruitful for my immediate purpose, and I selected some of the apparently more relevant, at first appearance.

'Can I borrow these?'

Hugo made a face. 'I'm responsible for them. Why not go through them in the library?'

I agreed, reluctantly, that this was a fair compromise, and he read my expression correctly. 'They go with Fontenay Place, Anna. That's in the lease.'

I debated whether to mention the delicate question of the next lease, and suddenly realized this could be why he'd mentioned the legalities. It could be he was trying to draw me out, to give him a lever for withdrawing all access until the new lease was signed. Ridiculous, I told myself, but all the same, I decided not to push my present luck.

'The library would be fine, Hugo.'

I took what interested me, and followed him down to the library – which still possessed a few fine bound volumes from earlier centuries. One of them was the family bible, and I eagerly flicked open the flyleaf on which the births and deaths of family members were recorded. This bible had begun its life in the early nineteenth century, and the last entries were for Edward and Adelaide's children. My eye went straight to it. There was one thick black line, expunging an entry. John was there, born in 1897, Esther's birth was recorded in 1905, but between them was confirmation of the family tree. David had had two aunts, the second born sometime between 1897 and 1905.

Why? I wondered. Just because of the pain of her early death? Surely not. This line implied disgrace. I peered at it, fancying I could make out the name. It eluded me at first, for the December light was fading fast. I took the bible to the window and slanted it against the light. Thick though the paper was and heavy the ink, I could just make out the faint outlines of the letters. An initial B – quite a long name – and then another shorter one, definitely beginning with an R – such as Rose for instance. And perhaps Barbara – or Beatrice.

1944

'How are things, old chap?' John asked Michael.

He had his jovial expression on, Jennifer saw, which meant that he was anything but jovial inside. Her heart sank. Things had been so much easier recently, partly, she had to admit, because Michael had been away for a few days. John seemed to be more relaxed, even though he spent much of his time with his beloved family memorabilia. Surely June, even at such a critical time in the war, deserved more than that. The D-Day

176

landings had taken place, and there was general optimism, even though the fighting was fierce and the outcome uncertain. A step forward had nevertheless been taken; Jennifer sensed the atmosphere had relaxed in the Fontenay Place HQ and that spread itself down to the lodge. Nothing much seemed to have changed in Kent, however, and the local opinion was that the preparations here were to fool the Germans that another invasion force might yet land in the Pas de Calais from Kent. They knew now that the true invasion forces had sailed from the south coast for Normandy. Whatever was left in Kent must therefore be either reserves or – people were beginning to whisper – dummy war material to fool the Germans.

Michael had come back yesterday, D-Day plus 6 – and Jennifer was both delighted and concerned, wondering if he too would notice the change in John. Michael's head was so full of romance and happiness, he probably wouldn't notice it. Deborah had seen John's mood alter, and she, like Jennifer, had tried to warn Michael, who merely laughed it off. She was relieved that Deborah was here with them this evening as a calming influence.

'Fine, sir,' Michael replied to John's cheery greeting. 'Wish I was over there too, in France.'

'I'm sure you do,' John replied heartily, but that look came over his face again. He had once again invited Michael to dinner himself – another bad sign, in Jennifer's opinion. What could he be hoping for? To see some tangible signs of love between Michael and herself? To torture himself further? Despite all her denials, he was increasingly suspicious.

She had tried her hardest to make this a very special dinner, to celebrate D-Day, she told them. The English Garden pie, and dandelion salad with beetroot, were delicious, and she'd even found a few strawberries to go with the Poor Knight's pudding.

Despite this, she commented ruefully, 'We're going to be so healthy when this war is over.' She hunted for one of the few pieces of meat she'd managed to put in the pie. For John a dinner wasn't a dinner without meat.

'We are now,' Deborah replied cheerfully. 'It's very good of you to entertain us, Mrs Fontenay.'

The goodness was all on Deborah's side, Jennifer thought. John liked her and her presence might deflect any flaring animosity between John and Michael.

'Call me Jennifer.' She smiled at the girl. She felt positively ancient at twenty-nine, beside Deborah who couldn't be more than twenty.

'We love living at Fontenay Place,' Deborah continued, smiling in acknowledgement. 'Mr Fontenay has been telling me all about your family history.'

'Has he indeed?' Jennifer laughed. 'Well, he certainly knows a lot about it. The fount of all knowledge in that respect.'

'And that rose garden, too. I don't wonder you love it, Jennifer. Squadron Leader Sinclair has told me about that.'

A quick glance of surprise from John, Jennifer noticed, probably at Deborah's formality. Michael was, after all, her superior officer and they were in public.

'Would you like me to take you round it one day? I'll show you where the skeleton was,' Jennifer offered.

'The one you think is a wicked Sinclair?' Deborah laughed.

'That's me,' Michael grinned. 'The black sheep of the family, the pestilence that walketh in darkness. I reckon that's what the chaps in the squadron call me behind my back, too.'

Michael could only be about twenty-five, Jennifer thought. It was hard to remember the weight of responsibility on his shoulders.

'Jennifer's been telling me all about the Vicar of Cranden's revelations about Miss Gwendolen. Perhaps you're even descended from this Gwendolen Sinclair's baby, Michael,' John joked. 'What do you think of that?'

'It's possible, sir. I don't know much about our background. I seldom see my father, and my mother naturally isn't interested in Sinclair history.'

Instantly Jennifer saw John's mood change. He scowled. 'Your mother? Which one?'

For a moment the awfulness of the question – and the shock – didn't sink in. Then she saw Michael freeze, and cast a questioning look at her, and to her horror she realized he was blaming her, accusing her of betraying him to John!

'Jennifer?' he asked slowly.

Deborah leapt in to smooth the appalled silence, but John drowned her voice by saying loudly, 'You needn't blame Jennifer for this, Michael. I've been doing a bit of detective work.'

'Into Sinclair history?' Michael looked furious.

'Only when it affects the Fontenays, young man.'

'And mine does? How, might I ask?'

'You mean you don't know who your mother really was?'

Michael went white: 'If, sir, you are really interested—'

'You mean if it's my business,' John interrupted. 'It is indeed – go on.'

'My real mother died in the flu epidemic in 1919. Her name was Miss Beatrice Rose. So far as I know, she was not married to my father. Is that what you wish to know?'

John laughed harshly, but there was no humour in his voice. 'Certainly Beatrice Rose was her name. Beatrice Rose *Fontenay*. Who died in a lunatic asylum giving birth to her bastard.'

Jennifer stared at the plate in front of her, nausea welling up inside her. 'I didn't know, Michael, I didn't know,' she choked out.

'That's right, Jen.' John turned malevolent eyes on her. 'You comfort him. Blasted Sinclairs everywhere, taking over the blasted estate, the blasted house, *my* house, *my* wife—'

Deborah cried out, as Michael scraped his chair back, and stood up, eyes blazing. 'You insult Jennifer, sir, and you insult me. If you have any proof of what you are saying, it would have been better had you told me privately. And does my parentage matter anyway?'

Deborah was now in tears, and Jennifer hurried round to take her from the room, and persuade Michael to leave, too. The last thing she heard was John hurling his reply after them:

'You tell me, Sinclair, you tell me. You're my nephew, aren't you? That's why you came sneaking in here. Walking in darkness, you bastard, striking by night.'

179

When she returned, much later, John was sleeping peacefully as she crept into the bed beside him. In the morning, he had forgotten the incident completely.

'Beatrice Rose.' I read those words for the night of 2nd June 1944 in John Fontenay's diary. Hugo had at last left me alone to read through the material I had gathered. Just that, nothing more. As the days passed, however, Beatrice's name occurred more and more. Even D-Day was dismissed with a mere 'They've landed'. It was as though he were obsessed with his sister's name and then I came to it. For 12th June 1944 the entry read: 'Beatrice Fontenay, harlot, mother of Michael Sinclair, Adulterer and Snake'. The 'Snake' was underscored several times, the work of someone in deep mental turmoil.

I stared at it, trying to take it in, wondering whether it was even true. After all, it would have made John Michael's uncle – and Jennifer his aunt-in-law. Had that precipitated the final row between Michael and Jennifer? Perhaps, especially if Jennifer were pregnant by him. There would be no incest involved, but the shock would nevertheless have been extreme for both Jennifer and Michael – let alone John. There were no more references to her that I could see. The following day's entry recorded a matter-of-fact: 'Adolf's secret weapons at last. 4 pilotless aircraft bombs fell.' After that, the diary was restricted to war news, until it ended with Thursday 13th July, the day of the Fontenay flying bomb, marked merely with a black cross. Nothing more.

'I brought you this.'

I spun round to see Joss behind me, looking way out of place in his jeans and anorak in the Fontenay library. 'I was told this was where I'd find you.' His voice was neutral, it implied nothing, but I read into it that he thought I had traitorously fled to Hugo, having forsaken Joss. It made me defensive, until I realized that this represented a considerable climb-down by Joss too, since he had opted to stay out of my researches.

'What is it?' I tried to sound neutral too, but all I managed was a croak.

'My grandfather sent me some family papers.'

'I think I can guess what's in them, Joss. Michael Sinclair was John Fontenay's nephew, wasn't he? The son of Beatrice Fontenay.'

Joss was completely taken aback. He couldn't have managed to fake that. 'Say that again?'

'Come on, you must know what's in this material you've brought.' I was uncertain now.

'I do, and it's not that.'

Stunned, I had no option but to show him the diary, which he quickly read. He was frowning, obviously absorbing its implications.

'My grandfather never said a word about that, I promise you, Anna. John Fontenay must have been hallucinating when he wrote this.'

'I don't think so. Look at the family bible where her name's been erased. The story fits all too well.'

'She could have slept with anyone. John Fontenay had a bee in his bonnet about my grandfather, that's for sure.'

'And if he hadn't? If it's true?'

Amusement began to creep into Joss's face. 'Then I've got Fontenay blood as well as Sinclair in me. Maybe I'm the true owner of Fontenay.'

'Not unless your great-grandmother was married to Michael's father.'

'Interesting problem, isn't it? Not that it affects anything legally, because Beatrice would never have inherited, even if she were older than John.'

'She wasn't. She was older than Esther, but younger than John.'

'Still, if Beatrice was married to her Sinclair and anything happened to Gerard, then I'd be right in the firing line, depending on how your husband's will was worded. Not to mention *your* will. So be very careful indeed, Anna. And look after your son. I trust you don't still think I may have evil intentions, but I wouldn't mention this new information to anyone else. I'd hate to be next on the removal man's list.' He laughed. 'I speak metaphorically, of course,' he added.

'Of course,' I replied stonily. 'Then what have you brought me, if not information on Beatrice Rose?'

'Some of the missing bones in the skeleton of Gwendolen Sinclair.'

He had been quoting from *The Importance of Being Earnest*, I remembered after he had gone, having dumped his material on the table. Important? It seemed to me that the more earnest I got, the more the truth eluded me.

1796

Mary Fontenay, at her own wish confined to her two rooms, picked up her self-imposed task, to record for posterity the story of these troubled times. It amused her greatly, as it had for many months now, since the day she had told Charles she was with child. Since then Charles had paid her every attention that she could wish for – except for one: his love. He reserved that for the whore. Charles thought she had not known about his secret rendezvous in the Hermit's Retreat, and in the rose garden. A cottage on the estate indeed. Did he think her a fool to believe his story that it was Goderic who got the whore with child? Goderic was the only person who ever understood her, and realized what she was enduring from Charles.

Goderic too was bitter. He was prevented from leaving to marry Elizabeth until after Miss Sinclair had produced her bastard in order to maintain the fiction, he explained.

'You know the reason, Mary, as well as I,' Goderic had said.

Indeed she did. It was to cover the fact that a child was to be born to the girl. Remote though the cottage was, there would be talk on the estate, and perhaps in the village too, so Charles needed an alibi. He needed there to be uncertainty as to whose the child was. If Goderic left before the child was born who would doubt but that it was Charles's own, and he with his pompous pride in the Fontenay name – in his own position as lord of the manor – could not have borne that. So Goderic had been made the scapegoat. He was dependent on Charles for money and was being forced to remain here, so that it should be thought that the coming child should be his and not Charles's.

Charles's hypocrisy had enraged her; she kept a smiling, contented face to him, for after all, was she not carrying his child? The laughter came after he had nightly left her at her request for his own solitary bed – or for the whore's bed. She did not care. It was enough that he did not claim her own.

She looked up as Goderic knocked and entered. 'Good-day, Mary.' He sat down opposite her, elegantly lounging in the large leather chair. 'It is a fair one, is it not?'

'It seems so from my window. How delighted I shall be when the child comes, and I may leave this room again.'

'Indeed, yes. An heir to Fontenay. I hope I am here to see him born.'

'You plan to leave? I had thought—'

'As soon as brother Charles's bastard is born,' he explained, 'I may go.'

She inclined her head. 'I shall be sorry to lose you. Charles tells me the child is due late in May, a little over a month away. So there is little time left.'

'And I shall be sorry to leave you, dear Mary. We shall meet at my wedding, however.' Goderic paused for a moment or two. 'The date of my leaving however is not yet fixed. I could perhaps stay longer.'

She looked up in surprise. 'How long?'

'Until your own child is born, Mary. Early in June.'

She smiled. 'Charles would like that.'

'And so would you, Mary. Another witness to Charles's discomfiture.' Goderic studied his polished fingernails.

She looked at him warily. 'What do you mean by that, Goderic?'

'There is no child, is there, Mary? This has all been a charade, to thwart Charles for his pursuit of Miss Sinclair.'

Her face went white with combined fear and rage. 'No. You are wrong,' she shrieked.

183

'I am not. Do not worry, Mary. I consider it a most excellent scheme. I long to be present while Charles is so mocked. He will have a bastard by his mistress, but no true heir.'

'You will not tell him,' she shrieked in alarm. 'I will tell him myself. How did you know?'

'Your pretty little kitchenmaid who burns the monthly signs that—'

'You seduced her!'

'What a thing to say, Mary. We Fontenays are above reproach. You know that.'

'If I did not know Charles to be so hypocritical, I might think that you—'

'But he is, Mary, and I am not. What is your plan, how will you inform Charles of the missing child? Or shall it be a stillbirth?'

'I shall tell him there is no child. That in my desire to please him, I imagined the whole thing,' she replied sullenly.

'You risk much, Mary. He could put you away for less.'

'I would make his liaison with Gwendolen Sinclair known to all.'

'You underrate Charles,' Goderic said seriously. 'I have a better plan. Better that Miss Sinclair disappear and her child with her. Best of all, that they be dead at the hands of an unknown marauder. The shock of that, I suggest, might cause you to miscarry.'

She looked at him sharply with hunger in her eyes. 'Murder,' she whispered, thinking carefully. Why not? Was death not the biblical revenge for adulterers? The girl was a whore. Then doubt again: 'But why would you do this – just for me?'

'For you and for myself. Miss Sinclair has long claws. She is determined upon revenge upon me, for, alas, it was me she preferred to Charles, but was rejected. I was but recently betrothed. Then she threatened to tell Elizabeth that the child was mine. I fear she is so crazed she might yet do so, thrusting the child in my Elizabeth's face.'

'But murder, Goderic.' Already Mary was seeing the sense

of what he said, though there was one doubt. 'The whore, yes, but the child? It would be a mortal sin.'

'Dear Mary, I have a plan.'

I looked eagerly at the material that Joss had brought me. The most interesting item was a diary written by Thomas Sinclair in the mid-nineteenth century. He was obviously the family historian of his day, for he had been excited at finding some letters from Gwendolen Sinclair to her uncle, Joshua, who had expressed concern about her predicament and pleaded for her to go to live with him. He quoted one of them, the last perhaps:

> Dear Charles has been so good to me, and myself so undeserving. He takes it upon himself to do all he can to save me from prying eyes. Goderic also comes to see me each week, so tender that I can hardly believe that he has betrayed me so vilely. But he has, and I pity the woman he marries. I liked Miss Sayles greatly, and to think of the life she will lead with him – what terrors we women face. I would rather be unwed to Goderic than wed. And yet . . .

To my horror, I realized we – or rather I – had been mistaken all along. It had been Goderic, not Charles, whom Gwendolen loved, and Charles who had tried to help her. Or was that a bluff to conceal the truth? Somehow I could not believe that, although my faith in my powers of deducing truth from my historical research had just taken a nosedive. Who then had taken the last terrible step to rid the Fontenays of the threat they might have thought Gwendolen posed to them? Goderic, anxious to marry Miss Sayles, or Charles, keen to preserve the Fontenay reputation?

The next offering from Thomas's pen was an extract from his diary of 1882 which someone – Michael, I wondered? – had carefully copied:

Tonight I attended Mr Henry Irving's and Miss Ellen Terry's *Romeo and Juliet* at the Lyceum Theatre. Not, in my opinion, their best work, but it set me to wonder in my study of the Sinclair family whether the feud of the Capulets and Montagues would in reality be so solved by the death of their children. Would this not deepen the rift, each blaming the other? I fear the sad history of the Fontenays and Sinclairs suggests that each subsequent contact merely widens the gulf, despite the rose garden at Fontenay which from its very beginning, with the red rose and the white, should have brought peace.

Just what did that mean? I stared at it in bewilderment, then gave up and went to bed. I was beginning to feel like a certain Dr Foster from Gloucester who in an old children's tale trod in a puddle so deep he fell through to Australia.

Thirteen

The next evening, instead of fearing the empty hours ahead, as so often in these Jossless days, I returned with relish to his treasure trove. To my astonishment, the best find of all awaited me: Mary Fontenay's diary. It was a complete shock, even though I had seen a reference to diaries of 1795 and 1796 in Thomas Sinclair's meticulous inventory of his own hoard. I could hardly have dared to hope to find a Fontenay diary amongst the Sinclair papers, and in my eagerness to fill in the missing pieces of the story, I did not devote much time to wondering how this could be. Perhaps I had some vague notion that Thomas Sinclair had wormed his way into the Fontenay affections in the nineteenth century, and whipped this piece of memorabilia.

The diary proved to be scrappy and spasmodic, unfortunately, with references to unexplained events. 'Goderic came', for example, heavily underlined. What did that mean? That she was having or had an affair with him? It was all very odd for a woman confined to her room waiting for the birth of a child she had desired for so long. I speculated on this Goderic, especially since it was clear now that it was he and not Charles who was the father of Gwendolen's baby. Was it possible he'd even fathered Mary's child? Were these odd visits to Mary playing a role in the drama that I was following up? Pure disinterested brother-in-law affection for Mary didn't sound likely from a man who had so abandoned Gwendolen.

I read on through the diary with its mentions of 'the day fast approaching', and then a triumphant 'The deed is done' some pages further on entered for June the eleventh. It seemed a weird way to refer to the birth of one's precious child, but what else could it mean? Where was the 'Yesterday I was delivered of a fine baby boy'? Not to be found. In fact, apart from an entry for July the nineteenth recording the baptism of St John Fontenay, the diary came to an end with the birth. Was she too busy to continue it? I knew from the family tree that Mary had died a mere three years after the birth of St John, but it seemed strange that she had not felt the need to communicate her thoughts to paper again. Unless of course she had begun new volumes of diaries, which were yet to be found. There was none amongst Thomas's papers, however.

I went up to my office, once an attic, and brought down her portrait. I remembered it clearly because the entry in *The Book of Gertrude's Garden* had been so curt; merely her dates were recorded, and 'wife to Charles Fontenay'. When I first read it, it had seemed to me that with the ghastly Charles as a husband she had deserved her place in the garden, and to be remembered more kindly. I had gone to some pains to include her in the Hermit's Retreat exhibition for that very reason. I studied the picture. If one took away the enormous stylish hat and bouffant hair, I was left with a plainish sharp-featured woman who stared into some world of her own. She wasn't looking into the artist's eyes, for sure. She had the kind of face which had come to terms with life, in the need to co-exist with husband, house and children. What would she be today? Fifty years ago a suburban housewife. Now? A middle manager, I decided. Or perhaps not, for there was no initiative there, no spark of life. What there was spoke of a limpet-like determination in her own interests, and not in those of others. Was it she who had chosen the pose, or the artist? Had he intentionally caught a sense of reluctance to share her space with anyone? Was she in fact saying 'You shall not know what I am'? Was she False-seeming herself, preventing me from getting to the truth?

I laughed at myself, deciding I was getting too way-out and that a photographic copy of a portrait might well lie.

All the same, I was curious enough to walk up to Fontenay

188

Place next morning and study the picture itself. I was vindicated. The photograph had been a good one, and the portrait itself, if anything, emphasized the traits I'd observed.

'*Yes,*' I said to the picture in triumph. 'I've got your measure, lady.'

'Anna?' Hugo's voice boomed out just behind me. It was hardly surprising that he should find me here since the Fontenay entrance hall not only has the reception desk, but is the crossway point for all human traffic moving anywhere within the house. It is one of my private dislikes about it. As a home, Fontenay Place must have seemed to have this all-seeing eye in the midst of it, surrounded by rooms over two storeys opening onto it, with their occupants appearing and disappearing like jack-in-the-boxes. Excellent for French farce, but not so good for everyday living.

'What on earth are you doing here?' he asked me.

'Meeting the ancestors,' I told him cheerfully. 'What else? It's my constant routine.'

'This good lady?' He came to stand at my side. 'Ah, the mysterious Mary.'

'So you think there's something odd about her, too?'

'Try putting her in a modern frame, with a modern hair style, and think whether you'd give her a job.'

I laughed. 'Just what I was doing in fact. And the answer is that I don't think I'd have her in the tea-room. She'd turn the milk sour. Do you know when this was painted?'

'Of course. 1798.'

'Two years after her son was born. She doesn't look the happier for it.'

'It's hard to tell,' Hugo said fairly. 'Just as for the early photographs, people had to sit still for a considerable time, and it's hard to do that with a grin on your face. Besides, remember the artist's personality comes through the face, too.'

'You mean the jury's out on Mary Fontenay?'

'She may have had a lot to put up with.'

'You're all charity, Hugo.'

'I know. Aren't I just wonderful?' He put an arm round my waist and gave me a quick hug. I felt good – but not quite good

189

enough to respond. I treated it for what it was, a friendly wave. I needed it.

1796

'Goderic!'

Charles's strangled voice made Goderic look up, and for once his urbane brother looked taken aback at the look on his brother's face.

'A message was sent.' Charles managed to speak coherently. 'I sent a *message,* did you not receive it?'

'Not I.'

'You lie, Goderic. It was to say your son had been born. Gwendolen needs you at her side. You have not visited her, or even sent word.'

'I am sure you fulfilled my paternal role perfectly, Charles.' Goderic yawned. 'Perhaps you practise for your own imminent child.'

'You are a disgrace to the Fontenay name.' Charles was aware he sounded ineffectual, and that pomposity replaced the words that would not form themselves.

Goderic laughed out loud. 'What name is that, brother? It is a family like any other, full of adulterers, thieves, dishonest brokers, self-seeking ambitious rogues – and harlots.'

'Of which you are one.'

'A harlot? Oh, come, Charles, hardly.'

'You jest, you *jest* – when your son . . .' Charles could not speak. He was close to tears.

'A son. I am fortunate indeed,' Goderic mused. 'More fortunate than you, Charles.'

There was a mist of both rage and grief before Charles's eyes. He thought of Gwendolen's sweet face contorted with pain, the joy as she saw her son, and the disappointment she tried to hide when he and not Goderic had walked through the door to see her son. Quickly he had told her that the red damask roses he brought her were from Goderic. She had smiled, but he knew she was not convinced. And she was right. He had picked them himself, sad that there was no white musk in the garden. But this damask, too, was beautiful in its simplicity, each rose as perfect as Gwendolen herself. 'Rough winds do shake the darling buds of May,' he had thought as he gathered them. Early roses, for a child born on the last day of that month. No rough winds should touch Gwendolen, nor her child, he vowed.

'Will you go to her now?' Charles pleaded with Goderic.

'I will not, Charles. I'm so demn'd bored, I'll take a turn with the horse. Besides someone needs to be here to comfort Mary.'

'Mary? Why does she need comfort?' What was this, some new trick of Goderic's?

'The news of Gwendolen's babe must have reached her perhaps. How do you think she feels, the father of her coming child more intent on his whore's whelp. She cannot be otherwise convinced, I'm afraid.'

'You may leave *my* son out of this discussion.'

'You're very sure he'll be a son,' Goderic sneered.

'Or daughter,' Charles amended quickly. 'And Goderic, if you do not intend to visit Gwendolen, you shall leave Fontenay this very day.'

'I think not. I shall stay till your son is born, Charles.'

Why was the fellow smirking? He seemed almost to be gloating. Charles knew that look on Goderic's face well. It meant he had discovered something that would distress Charles, and was waiting for the 'best moment' to tell him. It enraged him and he could control himself no longer.

'If you do not go to see Gwendolen, Goderic,' Charles shouted, 'I shall tell Elizabeth what kind of a man she proposes to marry.'

'Has it occurred to you she knows already?'

'No, Goderic. If you imply by that either that you have seduced Elizabeth or that you have confessed your sins to her, I do not believe it. You would not risk your future so. You are a schemer, brother. You make no rash moves.'

Goderic stood quite still. 'You may yet have need of me, Charles.' Each word was spat out now, like a serpent's tongue issuing forth. 'Tell me, what does my darling Gwendolen propose to do with her son? Will he be brought up on the estate as your bastard?'

'If she wishes it, yes. But I would not have her open to public affront, when she is far superior to either you or me. I prefer she accept her uncle's offer to dwell with him.'

'He would make a splendid friend to your son.'

'Perhaps.'

'But what if there is *no* son, Charles.' The words shot forth venomously.

'Daughter, then.'

'Or daughter either?'

What was the fellow getting at? 'Another stillbirth? I pray to God that it will not be so,' Charles replied quietly. 'But if it is, then next time He may be merciful.'

Goderic laughed at him. 'No, Charles, do you not realize there *is* no child? Poor Mary is so insulted by your behaviour she pays you out in kind with deception. The child that grows so large within her is but cushions and padding.'

The words did not make sense at first. And then they did with full terrible force. The room seemed to be spinning round him. He was choking, about to vomit. Impossible, impossible – or was it? 'You lie, Goderic,' he managed to croak.

'Why does she keep to her room? And do not believe it an illness of her mind or body like Queen Mary Tudor. She planned this jest.'

Goderic's face with its mockery and hate swelled in Charles's distorted vision to monstrous size, as it spewed forth peals of mocking laughter.

'Jest? I will kill you if this is so, Goderic. You put this idea in her mind. She would not have thought of it. She is not so clever, so wicked.' How did he put the words together to sound so rational when all around him lay a dark chaos?

'You underestimate your wife, Charles.' Goderic shook with mocking laughter.

Charles tried to clutch at reason, swirling though it was in a fog of blinding terrors. Could it be true? He thought of Mary's dislike of being touched, her reluctance to share any intimacies, the midwife she had chosen against his advice, the secretive smile on her face that he might have mistaken for contentment.

'Just think, Charles, just *think*,' Goderic's hiss followed him as he half walked, half stumbled out of the room, 'how useful Gwendolen's son might be if you act quickly.'

He had to see Mary. He had to know, and know *now*. But first Charles knew he must deal with Goderic. He might need him yet, to help with Gwendolen. 'In two weeks, Goderic, you leave my house. Kindly make your arrangements.'

'Oh, I will, Charles, you may be sure of that.'

Charles did not even hear him. Reason told him he should wait and consider this awful charge from all angles. But he could not. He must know *now*. Unsteadily he made his way to Mary's chamber, propping himself against the door frame for strength as he knocked. The familiar 'Pray enter' and the familiar face would greet him politely as they had done so often before. This time they paved the way to a terrible and unfamiliar world.

He knew he must school himself to take this gently, despite the turmoil inside him. It might yet be a trick of Goderic's, trying to instil a miscarriage at this late date, by inciting Charles to shock Mary by his violence.

'Charles? How pleasant to see you.'

Mary looked so ordinary as she lay on the day-bed sewing, that it was hard to believe in anything being amiss. Surely his child must lie within her? It was merely Goderic's mischief. Hope began to rise in him, and he felt calmer.

'Mary, I must talk with you.' He sat in the armchair facing her. 'How are you feeling?'

'A little tired, Charles. It is not long now. A week perhaps, Mrs Parsons tells me.'

Charles disliked the midwife, and was glad that he had arranged for Mrs Ovenden to attend Gwendolen. Either Mary lied or Mrs Parsons was bound in the conspiracy with her.

'I have news for you, my dear. I regret that Goderic will be leaving us very shortly. He is trying to make mischief between us, Mary, and that I will not have.'

'Over Miss Sinclair, Charles? I recall you told me he was the father of her son.'

'You have heard then.' Charles's heart sank. The child had been born only twelve hours ago, and he had been at pains to preserve secrecy. She could only have heard from Goderic.

Mary replied quickly – too quickly. 'I hear much. I must have sources of information to make my day lively. I am determined to bear this son for you, Charles, which is why I have sacrificed myself to endure this solitude.'

'We shall love this child, Mary.' It cost Charles dearly to speak these loving words before he knew that they were deserved.

Everything in him fought not to believe Goderic's monstrous story, and looking at her face it was easy to do so. Yet he had to be sure. 'My dear, Goderic slanders you with a terrible tale. I do not wish you to distress yourself, however. May I feel our child? I shall be gentle.'

'No, Charles, it would not be proper. You will see it when God pleases.'

'When *I* please,' he insisted.

'No, Charles.' She shrank back as he rose from his chair, and he sat down once more, with heavy heart.

'Goderic lies to me, Mary. He says there is no child.'

Her face changed so terribly he could hardly believe this was his wife of ten years. 'He says *that*?'

'It is not true, I know.' Charles fought down the panic inside him.

'It *is* true, you fool,' she shrieked at him, swinging her legs to the floor. 'He swore he would not speak. He has betrayed me. Look,' she grew hysterical as she stood up, pulling up her gown and petticoats to reveal taped in cushions. The sight was grotesque, riveting his eyes, sending vomit into his mouth.

Mary burst into tears, not of grief but of anger. 'It was *my* secret, and he has spoiled it.'

'Why, Mary, *why*?' Charles moaned. 'Have I been such a bad husband?'

'Bad husband? You keep your whore in style on our estate. She bears your son. Well, this is your son, too.' Hysterically she tore off a cushion and threw it at him, catching him full in the face. 'Here, take him.'

'You are overwrought, Mary.' Charles realized he was

suddenly icy cold, in complete command of himself again. 'I will call our doctor to tend you, and this time you *will* see him. I shall return to discuss this further, and meanwhile you are to say nothing to *anyone*, you understand. You shall not see Goderic. You shall not leave these rooms. Replace the cushions until I decide what to do. You shall be attended by –' he thought rapidly – 'our housekeeper, Mistress Pye.'

'I do not like her.'

'Your wants, Mary, are no longer of interest to me. Your future shall be dictated by me.'

For the next week Charles considered Goderic's mocking suggestion of one child for another. He needed an heir and he would never touch his legal wife again. Yet what would the child's loss mean for Gwendolen? He had seen the love in her eyes as she held him in her arms. Far better she take him to her uncle's home, with the fiction of her being a young widow. How could he even suggest that she hand him over to a madwoman's care? It was out of the question.

At the end of that week, on his daily visit to Gwendolen, Charles told her that she should accept her uncle's offer. Sad at heart, he returned to Fontenay Place, and shut himself in his library. Gwendolen would never surrender her child, and he would never ask her to do so. The tears ran down his face, for the loss of his love, for Gwendolen – and for himself.

Goderic smiled tenderly into Gwendolen's eyes, as he caressed the baby. 'How could you think I had deserted you, my love? Charles is so ridiculously jealous of the love between us that he has only just told me of the birth. I came at once.'

'I knew you would come, Goderic.' Gwendolen spoke calmly, though not as passionately as Goderic might have wished. 'Is he not a fine child? I thought to call him St John.'

'A bonny lad, as bonny as his mother. He deserves the best in life.'

'He does. We shall live with my uncle. He is prepared to welcome us. You need not fear I shall be a burden, Goderic.'

'Is that wise, Gwendolen? With your uncle he will be brought up as a tradesman; he is the son of a Fontenay after all.'

'And of a Sinclair, Goderic, who sees no harm in honest trade.'

'But would St John agree with you? Should he not have the chance of a fine education and the status of gentleman?'

Doubt entered her eyes, as he kissed her gently on the cheek. 'We differ as to the meaning of gentleman, Goderic. You mean you would rear him yourself.' Her hands reached for the baby.

'No. But yesterday poor Mary lost her child. A stillbirth. Charles aches to take St John to rear as his own, and Mary is willing.'

Gwendolen's face went white. '*Charles?* But he has said nothing of this to me, and he suggested I go to my uncle.'

'Of course. He is an honourable man, and thinks only of you. But he is consumed with grief at the loss of his own child. Would you not do this for him, and for St John? Charles has done much for you. I promised I would speak to you for him, for he does not dare.'

Gwendolen began to weep. Goderic waited patiently, holding her hand, and eventually she said, 'For Charles, and Charles alone.'

'Splendid.' Goderic patted her briskly. 'Bring the baby to the rose garden at eight tomorrow evening, so Charles may take him in secret. You are strong enough? It is not far to walk.'

'Yes.' Tears still blinded her eyes. 'And you? Shall you be there?'

'My love, Charles wishes me to leave the next day. But I shall be there in the rose garden too, to say farewell.'

The best of times, the worst of times, as Charles Dickens once said. He wasn't thinking about Christmas, of course, but I was. As it drew nearer, I found myself thinking of Christmases past, with David and Gerard. Sometimes Deborah had been there, before she remarried, and sometimes my parents or various aunts or uncles on my side of the family. Typical family Christmases, part happy, part bickering, hardly ever memorable in themselves, but collectively one warm whole.

My father died a year or two before David, and my mother, who was in her late thirties when I was born, is in a retirement home in Surrey, where she lives, quite happily I think, in the past. Sometimes she recognizes me, occasionally with the wrong name, and sometimes she thinks I'm one of the staff. I'd spent last Christmas with her, and it was painfully obvious that my presence made no difference, and so since then my regular visits have been at times to suit me, rather than the calendar. Gerard, too, was increasingly doing his own thing. This year, for the first time in my life, I realized I was the spare rib, and not the human centre of the Christmas universe. Only a few weeks ago, I'd thought lovingly of a completely different scenario.

Hugo had obviously twigged that things between Joss and myself were not the same, but he did me the courtesy of not mentioning it. He did mention Christmas, but as an open-ended deal. He explained that his only close relations were in the north of Scotland, and that this year he was invited to friends for Christmas Day. Would I and Gerard by any chance be free for Boxing Day? We could go on a jolly Boxing Day walk, followed by lunch at his place. It seemed a reasonable idea but in case Gerard bowed out and Hugo thought lunch might stretch on till evening and night, I invented a fictitious date for the evening.

I tried not to think about Joss, but in the end was forced to do so. I was stuck with his Christmas present, and how to get it to him without deliberately seeking him out was a problem. He solved it himself by coming along to the lodge one evening.

Gerard, back from York, invited him in, with all the charm of the Fontenays, but he could hardly keep the grin off his face as he did so. 'Joss is here to see you, Mum.'

'Hi,' I greeted him with an attempt at cheerful casualness. 'What can I do for you? Drink?'

'I'll get them,' Gerard obligingly said, thus committing Joss and myself to a twosome, and an elongated one at that.

Joss sat down at the table, strewn with a mixture of Christmas cards and biographies for the Hermit's Retreat.

'I brought you a present,' he announced.

A present? Leap of heart. Down, girl. I looked politely interested.

197

'I'm not sure if you'll like it,' he continued. 'I do. I needed to explain that it may look a bit loaded since I'm a Sinclair.'

'What is it, a shot gun?' I joked half-heartedly, hoping even he could not take offence at this weak attempt at humour.

'Wait and see.'

It was a splendid opportunity to 'suddenly' recall I had one for him, and I casually handed it over – along with his salary cheque. I don't know what point I thought I was making by doing this, but it helped me to distance the deal.

'How have you been getting on with the formal garden?'

'Working on the hedges and edging. December isn't a good month for fancy work.' He paused. 'I did plant a last rose. I hope you don't mind.'

'Whose?'

'For Beatrice.' He saw my face. 'You don't look pleased.'

'I'm only displeased at myself,' I answered honestly. 'I never thought about it. Anyway, you're hardly trespassing on my preserve – you're a Sinclair, after all, and she's your great-grandmother. What did you plant?'

'A hybrid tea, Golden Dawn. Applicable, I thought.'

'Because of her death?'

'That – and other things,' he answered blandly. 'Mind you, I don't expect dawn to leap into flower straight away.'

'Enough of gardening talk,' said Gerard coming in with the drinks, which was just as well. I might otherwise have thrown myself into Joss's arms, and announced that our own golden dawn could recommence this very moment. As it was, it was back to the inevitable.

'What are you doing at Christmas, Joss?' Gerard asked.

'Visiting relations,' he said. 'I'm doing the visiting, not them.'

'Not,' I asked airily, 'your grandfather by any chance?'

'Since you ask, yes – and the answer's still no.'

Gerard looked from one to the other. 'Anything I should know here?'

'Nothing,' I answered.

'Good.' Gerard proceeded to chat happily about university; you'd have thought he was the first person ever to have been to one, and already I sensed he was living emotionally in a different world. Christmas, I realized, would be his tribute to the past in the way of entertaining parents, but New Year's Eve was a different matter. Sure enough, he described the rave-up he'd be going to somewhere in London.

'What about Sarah?' I asked.

'She might come, she might not. Why do you care all of a sudden?'

'The common sisterhood,' I replied with dignity.

'Suborning my staff,' Joss said idly.

'Mum's staff,' Gerard replied to my horror.

There was a very nasty moment until Joss took the edge off by joking, 'Sure. I stand in between them to make sure the work's done.'

'I must get down to finding out how the estate's run one of these days,' I joked back. 'We fluffy-haired ladies find such matters hard to grasp.'

'You're better at that than cooking,' Gerard pointed out. 'These mince pies are foul.'

And, thoroughly satisfied with the joint slanging match, we drank a reasonably friendly toast to the festive season.

Christmas Day at Amelia Wilson's home was enjoyable, and I drove home with Gerard (rather to my surprise) quite contented. I had my luxury to look forward to – Joss's present, and I opened it in the privacy of my room sometime after midnight. It was the size and firmness of a picture – and so it proved, though it wasn't framed. I stared at it, for it was beautiful. I worked out it was a copy – painted by some modern obviously talented artist and calligrapher, of a Blake poem. It was called *The Sick Rose*.

> O Rose, thou art sick!
> The invisible worm
> That flies in the night,
> In the howling storm:
>
> Has found out thy bed
> Of crimson joy:

And his dark secret love
Does thy life destroy.

I read it, looked at its beautifully executed roseleaf borders, and the sick rose itself, and wondered why the words 'crimson joy' rang a bell. It took some time, as I stared at the lovely painting before me, and then at last I tracked the bell down. It was the rose chosen for Goderic in *The Book of Gertrude's Garden*. He was the invisible worm, his the dark secret love that destroyed Gwendolen Sinclair. The clue had been there all the time. Goderic, I now knew, had died in 1836; his entry in the book followed that of his brother, and was in the same script. It had not been Charles, but his son St John who allotted this rose and damning indictment of his uncle, Goderic, on his death. No wonder his dates in the book had merely recorded 'departed 1796' and not when he'd actually died. I realized there were tears in my eyes. Did I weep for Gwendolen, for Jennifer, or for myself?

Boxing Day proved surprisingly enjoyable. Somehow I expected Hugo's home to be a miniature version of Fontenay Place, but his tastes at home obviously lay in more modern art and furniture. It was a cold, but sunny day, and we duly went for our walk, returning to mulled wine, cold platters and cheese. Gerard had volunteered to be the driver so I was able to relax with Hugo's excellent wine.

'How's university? Are you heading the union yet?' Hugo asked him idly.

'Good and no are the answers. I'm waiting to be discovered.'

'David would have liked to know that.'

'Yes, except I'm reading languages and not Fontenay history. That would have been the only degree he would think worth doing. There aren't many courses in it, unfortunately. Why don't you run one?'

Hugo was amused. 'You flatter me. I am a mere custodian, as Anna will tell you. Now, when you inherit—'

'I'll be sixty-odd at least. I'm not worrying about it now.'

'Unless I make it all over to you now,' I chipped in, half serious.

'Mum, don't terrify me.'

'I thought you wanted to give Gerard his freedom for a while,' Hugo commented.

'I do. Don't worry, Gerard, you're safe for a few years yet. But if the bug bites you hard, you could always come to me on bended knee and plead for the keys of Fontenay.'

'I promise I'll do that.'

When we came home – in time for my fictitious engagement – I asked Gerard if he had deliberately engineered that conversation.

He shrugged. 'Just a whim. The more these geezers know that Fontenay is ours the better it seems to me, since both of them seem to behave as if they had some permanent stake in it. And I haven't forgotten that my coincidental accident came at the time I was shouting the odds about possibly selling Fontenay. I'd hate to think one of them would go so far as to engineer a sudden end for me, but I'd also hate to have another one.'

'That's contradictory.' In my befuddled state I tried to think it out. Since my talk with Sarah and my falling out with Joss, I'd tried not to dwell on this problem, if problem it was. 'You might be in danger – if we're talking wild – whether we keep Fontenay in the family *or* if we sell it. Why should selling make a difference? It would be a long way off.'

'Dunno.' Gerard thought about it. 'Control maybe. If one of them married you—'

'Here we go again.'

'If that happened, and if you in your obstinacy made Fontenay over to me then, and *if* I sold – well, Fontenay would have gone.'

'You can't live a life by ifs.'

'No, but they make good lamp posts. Anyway, keep your car locked up, won't you? We don't want to find the brakes won't work either for me – or *you*.'

'Locked up? A bit difficult here.' Perhaps, I found myself thinking, I would turf the stuff out of the disused barn nearby and put a lock on the door. Then I realized I was already accepting Gerard's thesis, and that *did* make me uneasy.

'Both these geezers, Gerard? That's what you said.'

'I know you fancy Joss, but you fancied Hugo once, too.'

'I fancy it's none of your business.'

'Unfortunately, Mum, since that accident it is.'

I thought of Chaucer's garden; I thought of his long poem written centuries ago, about the troubles of a man struggling to attain his ideal love, only to be blocked at each turn. Every obstacle had to be overcome. And, worst of them all, was jealousy, which in the end, although he attained his desire, triumphed. I thought of Mary's jealousy of Gwendolen Sinclair, and John Fontenay's of Michael Sinclair. And then I thought of what I possessed: Fontenay itself. Was this the perfect rose that Jealousy coveted?

Fourteen

1944

'Darling.' Jennifer found John in the lodge garden. Enclosed as it was by hedges and bushes from the rest of the estate, he seemed to use it more and more as a retreat, devoting his time to reading the newspaper or simply staring into space. Before the war he had worked as a freelance journalist, but now he seemed to have given up, and the only money coming into them was what she earned on the spare produce they produced in the grounds, and the small income from the money his father had left to them.

What could she say? Are you feeling better? No words seemed appropriate to express the concern she felt. John had often been irrational before, but this latest outburst was out of all proportion to its predecessors. In the month that had passed since then, he had never referred to the incident, and though at first she was convinced all memory of it had left, she sensed now that it might be returning. If so, she made up her mind that she must tackle him about it, get him to see a doctor.

'I think all this –' she gestured vaguely at the Fontenay estate – 'may be getting too much for you.'

John looked at her with tired eyes: 'I went over the top that night Sinclair came to dinner, is that what you're trying to say?'

'Yes.'

He stared at her in silence, and she could not understand him. What was he thinking? Always before, she thought she had known the inner man, but now he seemed a stranger. At least he was quieter and seemed anxious to make amends.

'Was your discovery about your sister so very bad?' she asked gently. 'It was a long time ago and I know you were

203

very fond of her, but did you not even suspect that's what might have happened? Your parents, as you know yourself, were very strict, very so-called high-principled, for it can't have been so uncommon even in those days for illegitimate children to be born. Was it such a shock to you? Did you have no idea?'

'I believed what Father told me,' he replied dully. 'Beatrice had become mentally deranged and had to go – voluntarily they said – into an asylum. Maybe – oh – Jen, maybe that wasn't true either. Maybe they forced her. They said she died a year later from the flu. Now I find that all along it was a Sinclair seduced her.' He hissed the last words out.

'Perhaps she loved him.' Jennifer thought of a girl long ago who loved where her heart took her, and not what family history dictated.

'As you love Michael Sinclair.'

Jennifer froze. He had said the words quite naturally as though it were an understood fact between them. 'You're wrong, John, completely wrong.' It sounded weak even to her.

He sniggered. 'Can you blame me? Straight after finding out that Beatrice had been seduced by a Sinclair – I think of it that way, she could never have demeaned herself otherwise – I find you cavorting in the rose garden day after day with another Sinclair.'

'*Cavorting*?' she echoed. 'Oh, John, for heaven's sake. You can't really believe I'm in love with him. He's a mere boy.'

'A damned good-looking one. And to think I was fool enough to invite him into my house. War made all things equal, I thought, bloody fool that I was.'

Jennifer hesitated. Was this the time? Yes, she would risk it. 'John, I've been wanting to tell you something. I wasn't sure but now I am. The doctor confirmed it today. I'm pregnant again, darling.'

She waited for the delight to spread over his face, but she waited in vain.

He gazed at her as though he could not understand what she was saying.

'It's happened at last – it must be all the physical activity in the fields that's shaken my insides up,' she managed to give a light laugh. 'I'm going to have our baby, it's due just after Christmas.'

'Our baby,' he repeated as though the words did not make sense to him.

'As we always wanted. Somehow I know this one's going to be safe. That's another reason I waited before telling you.'

'As you say, all the physical activity.' John had a grin on his face, but it didn't reach his eyes. Maybe he hadn't taken it in. He must have done, however, because he said all the right things. 'We'll have to look after you, Jen. You take it easy. Give the potatoes a rest, and let those blinking roses fend for themselves for a while. You mustn't take any chances. It's wonderful news.'

'I only did it for the free orange juice,' she laughed, relieved now.

Again, he seemed puzzled, but then he answered: 'Yes, of course, you'll have to apply for that. Might as well get it straightaway as an expectant mum.'

He was speaking normally now, thank goodness, and that decided her that she could still go out as planned.

'I'm going to see Elsie this afternoon,' she called. 'I can get the bus there. I'll be rather late back – it's Amelia's birthday. I'll take a torch, but I expect I'll be back by dark.' She didn't think it politic to mention that Michael said he might be able to pick her up in a staff car.

Jennifer enjoyed the afternoon, as always. Elsie's garden, even though growing onions not flowers, was a peaceful retreat, and it was a delight to see her niece. It was hard to think she was already seven. Right from her toddler days Jennifer had a special rapport with Amelia. She took after her mother in her direct no-nonsense attitude to life, with a big dash of her father's fanciful dream world. Poor mite. Not much in the way of birthday presents around nowadays, but Jennifer had managed to get a dolls' house made for her plus some Enid Blyton books which always went down well.

Since the flying bomb attacks had begun in June, going out was always risky – but then so was staying at home. Rumours had been rife for some time about Hitler's secret weapons, but since nothing had happened, people had ceased to fear them – especially after the D-Day landings had been so successful. Michael had told her that they were carrying out a lot of operations in support of bombers on the coast of France earlier this year, but Jennifer had assumed this must be in connection with the coming invasion. It was obvious now that they weren't, and that they were trying to eliminate the threat of the secret weapons. They hadn't succeeded however because the doodlebugs, as they were already becoming known in Kent, had replaced the bombers in their terrible threat. The fighter squadrons were sent up now in an effort to intercept them before they fell, a completely different task than a dogfight between two aircraft.

Jennifer shivered. There hadn't been many yet, but no one was in any doubt that there would be, and those that had fallen had caused many casualties and much damage. Two weeks ago, over twenty children at a nursery not far from Elsie's village had been killed in a devastating attack. The fearsome thing was that you could tell if this bomb had your name on it. The noise of the doodlebug's motor would cut out and the sudden silence would mean that you perhaps had only seconds to live for the bomb was falling right where you were.

Afternoons like this were wonderful, Jennifer thought, for they took your mind off the menace that came by both day and night. Kentish children were used to the way of life war imposed because they had known nothing else, it was only the adults that sighed for past times.

Everyone was in good form this afternoon at Amelia's party, and Jennifer stayed later than she intended. After all, Michael wasn't sure what time he'd be passing and had arranged to see if she were at the bus stop when he came by.

'I should be going,' Jennifer said reluctantly. 'The last bus will be along shortly.'

She made her farewells and walked out into the twilight, so still and perfumed it was hard to believe that there could be evil around. She was completely happy. Inside her was the baby she had wanted for so long, the afternoon had been pleasant, and with the army in France there was hope of the war's end. There was a long queue at the bus stop, and she glanced at her watch. Five minutes to go before the bus came. She chatted with the women around her for a few minutes, then to her delight she saw Michael's car. He was driving himself for once, and trying to ignore the envious looks of the waiting queue she climbed in beside him.

'Am I glad to see you. That bus is going to be late. I can tell it in my bones,' she said happily.

'Good afternoon was it?'

'Lovely.' She told him all about it, and he drove slowly through the twilight towards Cranden. Then it was his turn. He'd been talking to his father on the telephone, and got the whole story of James Sinclair and Beatrice Fontenay, and he related it to her.

'And I've got an apology to make, Jen.'

'What's that?'

'That diary you lent me – Mary Fontenay's. I took it to West Malling to read and left it there. I'm going back next week – I'll bring it then.'

Jennifer made a face. 'Do. If John finds out I've sneaked out a bit of Fontenay history and given it to a Sinclair, I'll be for it.'

'Next week. I promise.' Then he added awkwardly: 'I have something else to tell you, Jennifer. I ought to warn you.'

'What?'

'There are reports of a doodlebug having fallen somewhere in the Cranden area. I've no idea where. It just came in to the station news.'

Her stomach seemed gripped in a vice. 'Fontenay? The house?'

'Probably not,' Michael said firmly. 'There's a lot of space around Cranden. I've no idea where it is.'

Even as he spoke came the noise of an engine overhead with which they were becoming familiar. It sounded like a motorcycle, but no motorcycle brought such death and destruction with it. Michael fell silent, both of them wondering whether it would continue or cut out? It continued on its way, the roar decreasing, but just as Jennifer began to relax she heard it stop altogether. It was so sudden there was no doubt what it was.

'That could be back where we've come from.' She tried to sound matter-of-fact, but her heart was thumping. 'Suppose it's near Elsie?'

'It could be anywhere,' Michael said as the dull thud of an explosion reached their ears. 'Do you want to go back?'

Jennifer agonized over what to do. On to Fontenay or back. 'No. Go on. I must see whether John's all right. I'll telephone Elsie as soon as I get in.'

It was dark now, and Michael was driving to the limit of what was possible in the blackout. Even so, the journey seemed to take forever. Finally, to take her mind away from grim possibilities of what she might find at Fontenay, she decided to talk to Michael.

'I gave John some news today.'

'Good news?'

'Very – I hope. For me, too. I'm sure I'm pregnant, Michael.'

'Oh, that's terrific, Jen. Well done.' A pause. 'Sure he won't think it's mine?'

Jennifer's heart jumped, all her repressed fears coming back to the surface. 'Of course not. He did joke about our being in love and sessions in the rose garden, but there's nothing new in that.'

Even in the darkness she could see how appalled Michael looked, despite her reassurance.

'John's not well, Jennifer. Suppose he is convincing himself I'm the father. Suppose he tells—'

'Michael?' Jennifer was surprised, and then uneasy. 'Look I'm a married woman. We get pregnant. Why should he believe the child is not his? Even your wife wouldn't believe a thing like that with no proof.'

'Thousands of men have slept with married women before,' Michael pointed out.

'But not me, not you. Oh, Michael. I thought I'd done the right thing in telling him such good news.'

'How long since the baby began, Jennifer?'

'Two to three months.'

'John may be working out that that's about the time I returned to Fontenay. I don't like it, Jennifer.'

208

'Why are you so afraid?' It seemed to Jennifer that suddenly she knew neither of the men to whom she was closest.

Michael forced a laugh. 'He may beat me up.'

'Seriously, Michael.'

'Very well. You of all people, Jen, know I want nothing more than to be free at the end of the war – free of Hazel, anyway. Not William. There's every chance Hazel is going to go off with that bloke I told you about, in which case, since he's richer than me, she'll undoubtedly want me to divorce her. The last thing I'd want is for her to have grounds for mental cruelty or whatever, i.e., that I'd been fathering married women's children, so that she could divorce *me*. That way I'd stand no chance of keeping William. See?' He laid his hand on hers.

'Yes, I do. Oh, Michael, I'm sorry. I hadn't thought of it that way. But I'm still sure you're worrying unnecessarily, though I agree we should give up meeting in the rose garden for a while. But I know John better than you. He uses me as a worrybag to get rid of his worst fears on. It means nothing.'

Michael didn't reply, and she said no more. When he next spoke it was to say, 'There's Fontenay now. I can see the outline of the roof. Still there. All okay.'

Spring was on the horizon, the Hermit's Retreat was due to be thatched in three weeks' time and would then be ready for its exhibition pieces. The problem was that I wasn't. I had come to the end of *The Book of Gertrude's Garden* and needed to complete the ground floor exhibits with photographs of those Fontenays who had missed out. I could produce pictures of David, of course, and of John. There was no decent one of Deborah, however, nor of Jennifer. For the latter I decided I would tackle Sarah's grandmother, Amelia.

'I've got a wedding pic,' she announced when I spoke to her on the phone. 'Quite a good one.'

'That would do splendidly. I'll copy it and return it.'

'What are you going to do about her story in your Hermit's Retreat?'

This of course was the real problem. I still hadn't decided what the top storey in the exhibition should hold. This would take too long to explain to Amelia, so I opted for simplicity.

'Died in a flying bomb accident seems safest.'

'What if you prove she was murdered?'

This, of course, was the dilemma, whether Jennifer went on the ground floor or in a tourist attraction skeleton exhibit on the first floor. I liked that idea less and less. How could I say outright she was murdered by whomever, when whatever proof I had could hardly be tested in a court of law. And this made me face another question. Was it for the public record that I was trying to sort out this story, or for myself and Joss? And when I had discovered what it was, how much of it could I relate? Especially with Michael Sinclair still alive. Did I even mention the skeletons? I hadn't made my mind up.

'Do you still think Michael Sinclair murdered her?' Amelia continued cheerfully.

'I don't know. Perhaps she really was killed in the bomb blast,' I prevaricated.

'So why didn't they find her body when they searched the wreckage? Sorry, I still think the villain's Michael Sinclair. That's why he won't talk to you now.'

Rashly I had told her at Christmas about his still being alive.

'Guilt,' she added sagely, 'that's why.'

We finished the conversation amicably and I put the phone down. If only I could meet Michael Sinclair, just once, I thought. I knew it was impossible, even if I and Joss did get back on loving terms again. It would have to remain a question mark in my mind for ever.

And yet my own words to Joss rang in my ears: 'By the time this garden blooms again, I'll have laid these ghosts to rest.' And 'these ghosts' included my own.

It was three months to rose time. Not only had I not laid any ghosts to rest, but Gerard's words about Joss and Hugo also had to be laid to rest if I was to make good my commitment to Joss.

Now that Gerard had so firmly planted the idea of danger in my mind, I found I was watching every single move and looking for every nuance in what Joss and Hugo did and said. Hugo had taken to coming round most evenings, and I welcomed the company with Gerard in York. Bit by bit, he reverted to his practice of a goodnight kiss. It took me back at first, especially when I thought about Gerard's accident. There was no proof I told myself, and a goodnight kiss was no problem. Or was it?

'Tell me, Anna,' Hugo asked me one day, out of the blue, 'do you think I'm gay?'

'No.' It was an inadequate reply to a question that shook me and mystified me. Of course I didn't. He'd been married, and took women out on a regular basis. Including me. It wasn't proof, but it was a pretty good indication.

'Ah. I wondered why you were keeping your distance, that's all. Not reconciled with our gardener yet?'

'None of your business, Hugo.' Perhaps even goodnight kisses betrayed more than I thought.

'I believe it is, Anna.'

Here we go again, I thought, but I decided I'd go with the swim – providing it was paddling distance only.

He took me in his arms, very gently, and it felt reasonably good. He kissed me, and that felt reasonably good too. His hands moved over my body, until I could feel their warmth through the T-shirt, and over my breasts – and then he moved in for the kill – I was enjoying it (reasonably) and had it not been for the image of Joss's indignant face I might well have gone further and removed the 'reasonably'. As it was, I extricated myself promptly.

'Sorry, Hugo.'

'So am I,' he sighed. 'Joss, is it?'

'No, it's Anna. Until I get Fontenay up and running—'

'It's not that,' he interrupted. 'What you're trying to say is that we're just good friends, is that it? For ever and ever.'

'Yes.'

'Pity. We'd have made a good team. I take it the lease will still go through?'

I blinked at the sudden change and he laughed his socks off. 'Thought that would get you. Just testing your womanly pride. Sometimes, Anna, you're a cold fish.'

And sometimes Hugo, I thought, but I did not say it, you are a pompous ass. Something seemed to have got settled between us, however, and I was glad about that. The way was now clear for the new lease – with whatever clauses I decided to put in. If – just if – Gerard was right about evil intentions, I was out of the equation so far as Hugo was concerned. The lady was not up for grabs along with the estate. And therefore nor was the estate.

I retired to my office and scowled at my work for the Hermit's Retreat. I still felt ashamed that it had been Joss who remembered the rose for poor Beatrice, Sinclair sinner or not. After all, I was a Sinclair sinner myself, so I had something in common with her. Where would Beatrice go in the Hermit's Retreat?' And where did I find a photo of her?

Then there was Esther, the one who went to Australia. There was no case for including her in the garden, as usually siblings who left home had not been included. Maybe Esther was still alive? Doubtful, but in theory possible. I wondered whether she had kept in touch. David never mentioned her, which implied he did not write to her. Nor did I recall any Christmas cards flying to and fro. Did that imply she was a black sheep, too? No, for her name remained in the family bible. Somewhere there must be a record about her. I would ask Deborah. The more I thought about this, the better the idea seemed. It gave me a valid excuse to get back to her. Don't go there, she had warned me. Well I had gone there, and there was a missing link – Deborah herself. I could see my phone bill was going to go up. Nevertheless I decided this was the better way to communicate, rather than writing or e-mail. Or was it? On second thoughts I decided to invest time in this problem and send her a letter for her to consider and *then* I'd ring her up.

And so I did. When she answered the phone she laughed which was a good sign. 'It only arrived yesterday, Anna. You don't give me much time, do you?'

'No way, you might go off the boil.'

'If,' she pointed out, 'I am on it in the first place. You wanted to know about Esther.'

'Yes. Was John in touch with her?'

'For a while. She married, had two kids, a boy called Victor and a girl called Jane, and then gradually dropped out of contact after Adelaide died. Esther was eight years younger than John and didn't see much reason for keeping in touch with the old land, he said, or the old family. She's never hit it off with their father apparently, and was having a ball in Australia.'

'Whom did Esther marry?'

'A man named – um – it'll come to me. Yes, Joseph Whittaker.'

So much for Esther as the missing link. I suppose I'd been fostering an idea that Hugo was her long-lost son or grandson, hence his addiction to Fontenay memorabilia.

We chatted for a while, and then I plunged. 'Deborah, I told you Michael Sinclair is still alive.'

'You did.'

'There's also a photograph of you in Waaf uniform outside what looks like Fontenay Place. Was that after you were married?'

'No.'

'During the war?'

'Yes.'

'Were you there at the same time as Michael Sinclair?'

'Yes.'

'I need to know more about him.'

'Why?'

'Half truth is no good. It leaves a bitter taste.'

'What if whole truth is worse?'

'It's a risk I have to take.'

'Ask Michael then.'

'He won't talk. Just as you won't.'

'Drop it, Anna, darling. As your ma-in-law, I do advise it. It will lead to grief.'

'Whose?'

'Mine.'

'*Yours*?' I was taken aback at first, and then realized subconsciously I'd been expecting something like this.

'Let me explain, darling girl, very simply. Then will you drop it?'

'Yes. No – can't promise.'

'Then I won't talk.'

'In that case I'd ferret and that might be worse.'

'Has anyone ever told you you are a prying meddler?'

'Medlar fruit are best eaten rotten.'

A long silence. Then, 'This will not appear in any written form, is that agreed? It will not make a nice paragraph for the family memoirs, it will not be chatted about, written about in letters, it will not appear in your Hermit's Retreat, or used in any way other than for your private information.'

'Yes.'

'Then I'll tell you why the grief would be mine. It is all nonsense that Michael Sinclair was in love with Jennifer, or she with him. It wasn't her he was in love with, it was me.'

Fifteen

I suppose subconsciously I had always suspected there was something wrong with the story of Jennifer and Michael, as I had been told it. It is the story one hears first that lingers longest. The danger is that it sets itself up as truth, and it is for other versions to prove their better claim. Of course, I said to myself when Deborah made her announcement. Of course. Just as one does at the end of an Agatha Christie novel. It's so obvious then, but one has to muddle one's way through to it – as I had done.

It was too late now to blame myself for not pushing Deborah harder when she warned me off. This, she now explained, was for the same reason she had just made me agree to keep her story to myself. Michael was not to be worried, he must still be under the impression she herself was still married. She doubted whether he even had her current address. She hadn't seen him or contacted him since her remarriage after John's death.

'What happened?' I asked her.

'I'll give you the bare facts only, Anna. The full story – as I remember it – is safely locked up in the back of my mind, and there it will rest in peace. It was over, long long ago.'

'Over before you married John Fontenay?'

'I saw Michael after that too – not often, but sometimes.'

'So—'

'Take care, Anna,' she interrupted. 'I said the bare facts. Ready for them?'

'Yes.' I had to compromise. What I was naturally curious to know was whether they remained lovers after her marriage to John. This, however, could not fall under the 'need to know' umbrella.

'Very well. I met Michael at West Malling in '43. I was a Waaf there and one of the drivers. We fell in love. It happens.' Deborah's voice remained matter of fact in order to ram the 'no questions' agreement home. 'He was unhappily married, as you probably know. Meeting Jennifer and working in that rose garden helped him a lot. It saved his self-respect, particularly after he couldn't fly any more. I met Hazel once or twice – she was a hard woman, the original ice lady, and meeting Jennifer led Michael to realize there was a whole different world out there. Jennifer was a lovely woman, warm-hearted, intelligent and understanding. Just what Michael needed at that time – even after he met me. After his accident he needed to be reassured that I wasn't going to go off with the first pilot who cast a glance in my direction. Hazel didn't do a lot for his self-confidence – odd, isn't it? All those Spitfire operations, all that responsibility – and he could still be knocked sideways by her.

'But there was the child, of course, and anyway Michael wouldn't hurt anyone, even Hazel. When he was posted to Fontenay in '44, we both breathed a sigh of relief, despite the agony of being parted. We could see where it was leading, and we were both fighting against it. I wasn't into breaking up homes, and nor was Michael. Unfortunately the powers that be decided otherwise and made me his driver. Since there was no time to go through the usual channels for requesting transfers with D-Day obviously coming up soon, I had to go with him – I must admit it wasn't that hard. We were still in love, we remained in love, and, if you must know, exercised that love. That went on till the end of the war – we were transferred back from Fontenay to Biggin Hill in August '44. West Malling, which had been the main airfield for intercepting the doodlebugs, was suddenly closed. We weren't sorry. Fontenay was a sad place at that time.

'The flying bomb in the grounds shook everyone, even the army officers. We thought Jennifer had died in the Sevenoaks bomb, and that threw another pall of gloom over the estate.'

'What did Michael—?'

'No go area, Anna. And before you ask, I was at West Malling that night. I didn't come back for several days.'

216

I battled with frustration, but I had to play by her rules. 'What happened then?'

'At the end of the war I was demobbed. I went back to my parents in Tonbridge. Michael went back to Hazel. It was a bad time. Michael had been expecting that Hazel would leave him for this other man she'd been seeing, so we had thought everything was going our way. We never doubted it. And then, just at the very end of the war, this man was killed in an air crash – he was on some kind of government inspection team flying to the remains of Europe. Hazel promptly decided that half a loaf was better than no bread and opted to stay with Michael. He was devastated, and so was I, but, in both our books, which read differently to those of today, there was nothing to be done about it, and we parted.

'I got a job, but I was lonely to say the least. John was devastated by Jennifer's death, I knew he liked me, and so I fell into the habit of cycling to Fontenay whenever I could, imagining I could help him. We grew fond of one another and married in 1947.'

'Yet you saw Michael after John's death.'

'We met in London once or twice, that's all.'

'But—'

'I've told you enough, Anna, for your purposes.' Deborah's voice was adamant though kind enough. 'I trust it's enough to show you that Michael had no reason at all to kill Jennifer.'

'Unless . . .' I trod very carefully indeed, 'she seduced him – just once you know – and the baby *was* Michael's, not John's. That would have given Michael a motive.'

A long silence. Then a gentle: 'She didn't, and he didn't. Goodnight, Anna darling.'

By the next morning I was still trying to come to terms with it. I began to think that as a brave researcher of the truth, I was abysmal. I still couldn't get my mind round it. If Deborah was right about Jennifer, then she had either died by accident or at John's hands. No wonder Deborah preferred not to discuss it. But that didn't make sense either. If Michael was in love with Deborah, John had no reason to be jealous so far as Jennifer was concerned. Unless she had another lover, of course. One of the army officers in Fontenay perhaps. But that

217

seemed unlikely, too. Sarah's grandmother hadn't mentioned anyone other than Michael, which suggested Jennifer hadn't told her of any other man. On the other hand, she might not have confided in her sister.

I had slept badly that night. It was the end of February, the sap would shortly be rising – in everything but me. I was only a little further forth in my search to put the rose garden mysteries to rest. I was no further forth in my decision over the top room in the Hermit's Retreat. And we were opening it in three months. True, the public would never miss what wasn't there – but I would. I would know I had failed every time I went into the garden. And linked to the failure would be my relationship with Joss.

Moodily I picked at my muesli. I had to talk to someone, I decided at last, and it could only be one person: Joss. Deborah had grudgingly admitted that he was as concerned in this as I was, and that I could tell him. Though I had deliberately not been keeping him up to date with everything I was doing, this was different (I told myself). After all, he had brought me his treasure trove as a peace-offering.

Just as I was leaving, however, the phone rang. It was Hugo, just to make my day complete. 'My solicitor wants to get on with the lease,' he told me cheerfully. 'For solicitor, also read me.'

'I'm dealing with it, Hugo.' I was on weak ground and I knew it. I'd done precious little except to tell my solicitor it was coming up.

'The lease expires in June, and it's the end of February now.'

'I realize that. I'll get on to it, I promise.'

'It's a good job I trust you, Anna.'

I felt ashamed that I'd let the business side of Fontenay slip while so preoccupied with my own affairs. I couldn't do without Hugo's rent, and he knew it, so I had filed it in my mind as something postponable.

'I'll set the ball in motion this afternoon,' I said, to make amends.

'Try this morning, and I'll take you to lunch.'

'Done.' Did I really want to go to lunch with Hugo, I asked

myself when I put the phone down. No – or perhaps I did. He was a good companion, and would be a good antidote to a tense morning with Joss. I couldn't see it as being anything else, since we were still poised in this halfway house.

It was one of those winter days that tries to pretend it's spring, and it cheered me up. I prowled round the estate until I tracked Joss down. In fact it wasn't that difficult, because he was in his cottage workshop, having a thermos cup of coffee. I tried not to think about the time we had spent in very different circumstances here, as I embarked on my story about Michael and Deborah.

He listened in silence. Then he said, 'That explains it. I guessed as much.'

'So why didn't you share your supposition with me?'

'It wasn't my secret to tell – I just thought it possible there was someone else in the equation.'

'It gets me no further with the Hermit's Retreat,' I pointed out. 'I suppose I could leave the upper room with the two skeletons as an unsolved mystery.'

'It's not like you to admit defeat.'

'I have to. I'm not much further with Gwendolen either.'

'Ah, there I can help you. I left something out of the bundles; they were tucked in with my grandfather's covering letter. I'd been meaning to drop them round.'

Oh, thank you, I fumed silently. Such enthusiasm to see me. How many more excruciating needles can you stick in me, Joss?

'Jennifer gave him a few notes about Gwendolen, since he'd been the one to find the skeleton. She'd been delving into it, and had been in touch with the Sayles family from which Goderic Fontenay's wife Elizabeth came. They managed to unearth evidence that Goderic unexpectedly left Fontenay and came to the Sayles' mansion in the late afternoon of 11th June, the day Charles Fontenay's son St John was born.'

'Implying what?'

'That wasn't too long after the time Gwendolen's baby was born, and Jennifer had found that out, too. Yet when she had the skeleton checked out, there was no mention of a baby's skeleton at her side, and when she checked the parish

219

records, there were no young babies born or died at that time to Gwendolen Sinclair.'

'Did Jennifer say how she thought Gwendolen had died?'

'Yes. She thought it was murder, and that there was only one possible killer: Goderic Fontenay.'

1796

'Mary, have you seen Goderic?' Charles visited her rooms but rarely, and his face was always cold. How could he not understand how badly he had treated her, his wife? This evening, however, his usual icy demeanour was shaken. Mary was delighted.

'No, Charles. If you recall, you forbade me to see him.'

'It is strange. He asked me to accompany him to the rose garden while he bade farewell to Gwendolen. But I am told by the servants he left late this morning, with all his baggage, and bidding them farewell. I cannot understand. He was due to leave tomorrow. Could he not endure meeting her just one last time?'

Mary gloated, hugging her secret to herself, but then doubt crept in. It had been no part of the plan for Charles to go to the garden so soon. Perhaps she had misunderstood Goderic, when he called this morning. How fortunate that even Mrs Pye, her prison gaoler, could not guard her door twenty-four hours a day, and the relieving servants were far more amenable.

'But it is too early, Charles. Nine was the hour Goderic set, not eight. I recall it because I feared since it would be dusk Miss Sinclair would be inconvenienced in coming to the garden.'

'He told me six of the clock, not nine.'

'Then he erred, Charles.' Charles had to be mistaken, Mary knew that. She was quite clear that the hour for Charles to go to the rose garden was nine, *after* the deed had been done. Goderic had said he would pretend to leave Fontenay, but would secretly return to meet that whore and take her bastard

220

from her at eight o'clock. And more than just meet her – he would deal with her as she deserved.

Charles looked at her in silence, and pulled the bellrope. Mary's lady's maid, Sutton, appeared instantly, disconcerted to see Charles. 'Ask Mr Frobisher to come to me,' he requested. Mary displayed no reaction. His questioning the valet would achieve nothing.

Sutton disappeared only to reappear some minutes later. 'He's gone, sir, with Mr Goderic. They left at noon to take the stage from Tunbridge Wells. The coachman, he was in the kitchen, saw them safely on.'

'For where?'

'Banbury, sir.'

Mary's misgivings increased. Goderic had said nothing of Frobisher leaving with him today. He was to follow. And taking the stage with him was strange indeed. Goderic had told her he would return here, and remain secretly in Gwendolen's cottage until tomorrow, when he would leave again unseen.

'He has gone, Mary,' Charles said quietly. 'I will visit the garden at nine, so that Miss Sinclair is not left there alone. I trust you will not misconstrue this gesture.' It was a command, not a plea, and Mary's eyes gleamed hatred.

After he had gone, Mary grappled with her fear that Goderic did not mean to return. He had told her that Charles would go at nine, and that he would murder the whore and take the child at eight. Charles would find what he deserved – the dead body of his strumpet, and Mary's revenge would be complete. But what now? Suppose Goderic did not come back? Was she to be baulked of her triumph? Would Charles meet a living girl, and leave without the child? Why had Goderic's plan gone so amiss? Perhaps, she clung to hope, he had done the deed already after Charles left the garden? Perhaps the girl was already dead? She could not take the risk, and fear and thwarted rage swirled within her. The clock would soon strike eight, and she must act.

To be married to Gwendolen . . . Charles pushed the thought aside. Mary was his wife, and childless or not, must remain so. Once Gwendolen was provided for, Fontenay could settle down again. He himself was but one man and of no importance. The future was. If only he could bring himself to suggest to Gwendolen that he adopt the baby, but that would be impossible with Mary to rear him. He would ensure that Gwendolen reached her uncle's house safely, and then struggle to come to terms with what was left for him in life. He was tempted to go straight to the cottage and be done with it. Tell Gwendolen that Goderic had left and that he would look after her. But he could not. Eight was the hour when Gwendolen fed the child, Goderic had told him, when she most delighted in her time with him, and she preferred to be alone. Very well, he would wait patiently in Fontenay Place until nine. She would have enough to bear in knowing her faithless lover could not even wait to say goodbye. Let her have happiness while she could.

At nine o'clock he entered the rose garden, hardly knowing how he would face the coming scene. He had to tell her Goderic had gone, and she too should leave when she was strong enough. All was heavy and silent as he walked through the gate. There was no feeling of life within, as though a girl and her child awaited him. Perhaps, he thought, she had not yet arrived.

The perfume of the roses was strong in the dying light. It seemed too cloying, threatening to choke him, and he had to fight an instinct to run. And then he saw the folds of a blue dress falling over the steps, in front of the arbour.

Instantly he realized they were still. The girl had fallen, *Gwendolen* had fallen. He ran towards her in terror, and then he saw she did not move. There was a trickle of red as he came near, the blood seeping out, running down the steps, from under the body. Red blood, as red as the roses at her side. He heard himself cry out, but still she did not stir. Gently, moaning, he turned her on to her back, and saw the wound, saw the sightless eyes of the girl he had loved so dearly. She was dead.

Charles sat at her side for three or four hours, until at last his valet came to find him, stopped in horror at the terrible sight, then knelt down beside the body.

'What have you done, sir?' he asked quietly.

'It was not I who did this,' Charles answered. 'Do you see a weapon? There is none. I loved the girl.'

Peters had been with him for many years, and understood these disjointed words. 'It was Master Goderic did it, wasn't it? I know, sir, but none other will. They will think it you. We must bury her, sir.'

Charles looked at him with dull eyes. He knew that it couldn't have been Goderic who had killed the girl he loved, and so would Peters when he thought it through. Though it was right enough in its way. It had been Goderic's plan, little doubt of that. Goderic had worked out exactly how Charles would react.

'He must have returned secretly, Peters,' he said. Perhaps indeed it had been so. Had he somehow come back to kill Gwendolen, and take the baby to kill that, too? Gwendolen would not have left it in the cottage alone. Goderic was ruthless, he would allow no evidence of the child to remain, for fear of word reaching his bride-to-be. Better for his brother to take the blame. The time he had been told to come was six, not nine, and in those hours his beloved Gwendolen had been murdered. Goderic, it had been Goderic, surely, and his terrible suspicion must be unjustified. A tiny flicker of hope remained.

'I cannot bury her,' he said to Peters. 'I cannot do it.'

'Then I will, sir.'

It took most of the night, but at last it was done. 'Shall I cover it now, sir?' Peters asked hesitantly.

Charles could not look down into the makeshift grave, could not bear to see his beloved Gwendolen taken from his sight. Instead he picked one of the red roses. 'Give her this,' he said. 'She was the last of them.'

At daybreak he returned to his room, and lay there until Peters called him three hours later. His valet was as impassive and composed as if that terrible night had never happened. The day brought no relief for Charles, for he knew what he had to do. Hope had to be extinguished before he could begin to battle with the rest of his life. He had to see Mary, for there could be no hiding of truth now. He stopped only to speak to Mrs Pye; on guard in her chair outside the door. It took

223

but a moment to establish that yesterday evening one of the housemaids offered to relieve her for a short while to attend what she had been told was a summons by Charles himself.

It came as no surprise to him, merely confirmed that his greatest fear was true. Sick from the nightmare, he thrust open the door and walked in.

Mary lay in state in her bed, tended only by Sutton. In her arms was a baby. She had been expecting him, for she smiled in her terrible triumph.

'See, Charles. This is St John Fontenay.' She held the child out to him. 'Have I not borne you a beautiful son?'

'No,' I said to Joss. 'Goderic had left on the morning of the 11th. He would never have left while Mary was in labour. I think that's the day Gwendolen died. She would have been up and around by that time.'

'He wouldn't kill and bury her in broad daylight. Too risky.'

'The night before?' Then I reconsidered. 'No. We know from the Blake poem that Goderic was a sneaky villain. He wouldn't do it himself. It had to be Mary. She stole the child and killed the girl.' There was something niggling at the back of my mind that suddenly made me quite certain of this, but I couldn't pin it down.

'Mary was in the middle of childbirth,' Joss pointed out. 'Anyway, what could you do with that story in the Hermit's Retreat? Confess to a Fontenay murder or go along with a cover-up?' Joss was watching me intently, and it threw me for a moment.

'I have no real proof . . .' I began uncertainly.

'When has that ever stopped you?'

I don't think he meant it cruelly but I took it so. He touched my hand lightly, perhaps in apology, but nevertheless it stung. I felt defeated. The thesis I was proposing was terrifying: a woman killing her rival, and then taking her baby, crazed with jealousy. Yet Mary had been pregnant herself, I remembered. Had she lost her own baby some days earlier, and was desperate to get another?

If so, there would be a stillbirth recorded. I checked *The Book of Gertrude's Garden* yet again, when I got back home. My memory had not betrayed me. There was no stillbirth – nor anything that could have disguised one. Nor was there anything on the family tree, but the birth of St John Fontenay. So if I was right, he was half-Sinclair, just as Beatrice Fontenay's child had been.

Odd that the parish registers did not reveal Mary's dead baby. I frowned. Even if the children were swapped, the stillbirth could have been attributed to Gwendolen. It didn't make sense. Why should Mary kill Gwendolen after all? Because Gwendolen was her rival and would have objected to the switch of children? Because she was a threat to Goderic? We knew he must have been a schemer. Did he work Mary up to such a pitch she murdered the girl, or did he do the murder himself and give the child to Mary?

There was one more possibility of course – way out, but not unknown. If Mary's baby's birth had not been recorded, might it be that it had never existed at all? Perhaps Mary's was a phantom pregnancy, born of great desire and longing for a child, like Queen Mary Tudor. Or perhaps there had never been a pregnancy at all, real or phantom. Had the false pregnancy been a lie, a fearful vengeance on her husband whom she thought was keeping Gwendolen Sinclair as a mistress?

I decided I'd take another look at Mary's diary, but it told me nothing new, save that I looked at that entry for 11th June with new eyes: 'The deed is done.'

I couldn't let the matter rest, and decided to look for clues – now I was at least on the scent – at Fontenay Place, and strolled up there straightaway. For some reason I have never felt warmly about the house, but I can't tell why, since it is a lovely building. To me it has something sterile about it, though perhaps it was merely that all those conferences made it impersonal. I had never known it as a home, but it had been one for the Fontenays for two hundred years or more. I felt awkward going in, bearing in mind I should ask Hugo for permission to look at the archive again. It was another reminder that I should get going on the lease, plus its clause about access to all items.

Perhaps it was sheer bloodymindedness on my part, but so what?

I went straight to the library, as there was no one around on reception and no sign of Hugo. With luck I could get at the material there without troubling him. Luck was out, however, as Hugo was in there himself having coffee with an elderly lady I didn't recognize. He was as surprised to see me, as I was him. More than surprised – he looked downright caught out. He recovered himself quickly: 'Anna, how nice to see you.'

There were introductions all round, and to my surprise Jane introduced herself as Hugo's mother.

Why I should be so surprised, I don't know. She seemed rather nice, but he seemed sheepish about it for some reason.

'I've been showing Mother the Fontenay portraits.'

'A fine house,' Jane remarked politely.

I muttered something, then told Hugo casually, 'I came to see the collection again. OK by you?'

'Tomorrow OK?'

I could hardly say now please, so I was forced to be content with that.

After I left, I found myself wondering about Hugo's mother. She had a slight accent that I couldn't place although I've never been much good at them. I dismissed her from my thoughts and settled down to look at the diary yet once more. There *had* to be something. The more I read the entries during her 'pregnancy', the more I was suspicious the baby might be a joke – a cruel and heartless one – played on Charles. Poor old Charles, I thought. Betrayed by his brother, betrayed by his wife and his sweetheart murdered. Only his son would remain and even he was Goderic's.

What, I speculated, would Charles have told his son about his parentage? The truth? Nothing? What had they talked about during the time they worked together over *The Book of Gertrude's Garden* and began the maps and index?

At last my niggle clarified. It had been, as I had realized from the dates, St John who had given Goderic his Crimson Joy *gallica* – a rose that didn't exist – and curt entry in *The Book of Gertrude's Garden*, a way of telling posterity there was a story here without letting down the Fontenay name.

Charles was an honourable man. Therefore, I reasoned, he would not both have lied to St John about his parentage *and* told him what a creep Goderic was. Therefore he told him the truth and left St John to write his own verdict on his true father. St John, I decided, was *all right*! I felt immensely cheered – and I knew the truth about Gwendolen Sinclair's death.

For several days I glowed with my success. I told Joss, who was impressed.

'You're putting that story in the Hermit's Retreat?'

'I don't know,' I prevaricated. Trust Joss to put his finger on the weak point. 'There's still Jennifer to consider.'

'And the full story of Beatrice. Not to mention Gertrude and Edmund. Did Gerard find out anything about them?'

I'd forgotten all about that. 'I shouldn't think so. I'll ask him.'

'It's relevant.'

I couldn't deny that, but I was beginning to think that the more I dug, the more worms I'd find. May was getting very near now.

'I'll ask my grandfather if he knows any more about Beatrice.'

Beatrice could wait, I thought, after he'd gone. She'd got her rose. After all, Esther wasn't represented in the garden, or Hermit's Retreat, and she was probably dead too. It was then that I recognized Hugo's mother's accent. It was not marked, but there was still the faintest twang of an Australian voice. Nonsense, of course. Jane was too young to be Esther, who must have been born in the early 1900s, and Jane's name was Brooks. Then I remembered that Esther had a daughter as well as a son. A daughter called – I scrabbled for the name – *Jane*. Suppose Hugo was *this* Jane's son. It would explain everything. Nonsense, I told myself. You're hallucinating. There's no proof, no proof at all. You're fitting facts into theories, not the other way round, as you should be.

But I could be right, a little voice said. Hugo said he'd been born in England. It could be that the daughter had come back to England with an English husband. I could send for his birth certificate, or look on the Web . . .

227

Or I could ask Hugo. I pondered what to do. My theory would explain a lot of things – his preoccupation with Fontenay for a start. But why hadn't he told us, or told David, about his connection? That was odd and I almost disbelieved my own theory at that, wondering how I could be so mean to Hugo who'd been a good friend to me.

Then I remembered Gerard, and all those hints about Hugo wanting to marry me – and me showing less and less inclination. The insidious voice inside me helped oil my brain: if Gerard were dead, Hugo could be next in the line of inheritance. Fontenay wasn't entailed – I couldn't own it if so, but Hugo knew me well enough to know that I would follow David's wishes that Fontenay remain in the family. If Gerard chose to disregard this, that was up to him, but I wouldn't. Married to me, Hugo would be OK; with Gerard gone, he would be the only candidate, if his uncle Victor were dead and childless.

Stop! I told myself. There is no proof about Hugo's parentage. However, time was not on my side, and there was the lease to think about. I made up my mind. Be blowed to checking out birth certificates, I'd ask Hugo directly.

I had to consider that if I were right, and if Hugo had been behind Gerard's accident, then Gerard might well still face danger, and even I might be in the firing line as I'd declared I wouldn't marry him. So I decided to play it safe, even if I had qualms about its fairness if Hugo was innocent. I asked him to come to my solicitor's office in Tunbridge Wells. Elizabeth Maltingly is a sharp lady and entered into the spirit of the thing, though she clearly thought I was loopy. Perhaps I was. Hugo had done nothing overtly to deserve this, and when we met, I had cold feet about behaving in this way. There was no going back now, however.

I plunged at Elizabeth's nod. 'Hugo, I've been doing some hard thinking about this lease. I'm wondering if you've told me everything about your interest in Fontenay?'

'What?' He looked startled – not unnaturally. 'Is this relevant?'

'Very. Perhaps I've just got a bee in my bonnet, but if so I'd like to shake it out once and for all.'

'What does this bee consist of?' He glared at Elizabeth who did a good impression of a wooden statue.

'That you yourself are of Fontenay descent, probably Esther's grandson.'

I thought he was going to choke at first, then he managed a pleasant smile. One to Hugo. 'Suppose I am, what difference does it make to the lease?'

'Quite a bit, Hugo. Why did you never tell me or David?'

'I did tell David. It rather amused him.' Two to Hugo.

'I'm sure you didn't. He would have told me.'

'Can you prove I didn't tell him?'

Elizabeth was looking interested. She'd always had a secret hankering for criminal law.

'No. Your ancestry certainly explains your interest in the family history.'

'What's wrong with that? Surely that's an advantage for you, especially now.' He seemed puzzled. 'Sorry if I assumed wrongly that David had told you. I still don't see the relevance of this to the lease. Unless of course we're back to Mr Sinclair's insinuations about my wanting to marry you to grab Fontenay through you.'

'No, we're not.'

'Then may we discuss the lease, please. I'm sure Mrs Maltingly has more important things to do than listen to genealogical discussion.'

'Certainly we can talk about the lease. Hugo, I'm sorry but I'm not renewing it.'

That did take him by surprise. He hadn't expected it, and made a big attempt to rally. 'You really have taken leave of your senses, Anna. How on earth can you manage without the rent?'

'That's my business.' I was fighting myself. It would be all too easy to see it Hugo's way. I had to tell myself firmly that I was convinced he had not chatted about his family background to David, and that being so, there had to be some reason for it. The reason could only be that he thought he might have more to gain by keeping quiet, and watching how the cookie crumbled, as they say. Well, *this* cookie was not for crumbling. I intended to stand firm. I had no proof about the attack on

Gerard, but I wasn't going to let it happen again – either to Gerard *or* me.

'Then I'll talk about *my* business,' Hugo retorted. 'The lease requires six months' notice, if it's not renewed. I have bookings up to next year. It's March now and six months takes us to September. However, having sprung this on me, I feel I require a year in view of my previous good record.'

'Mrs Fontenay has taken future bookings into account,' Elizabeth intervened, 'and is prepared to allow you to stay on at the same rent until the end of March next year.'

'No rent at all. I've put enough into the estate recently, assuming I'd be staying as I'd been assured I could. Moreover, if you recall, I'm organizing the opera in the grounds in July.'

Elizabeth looked at me. I nodded: 'Very well. Expenses only from September. Electricity and the like.'

'You will regret this, Anna,' Hugo told me pleasantly.

'Is that a threat?'

'No, a fact. You can't manage without the rent, of course. What else could I mean?'

It was over and yet I was petrified. My knees didn't just wobble, they almost collapsed. How on earth *was* I going to manage? True, I would have an income coming in from the estate from May onwards but that would go to the bank for overdrafts. Fontenay Place would have to be left empty if I couldn't find another lessee, and I'd never find one as good as Hugo. And what mischief might he make in the meantime? And how about upkeep? I was beginning to think I'd been a damned fool.

Nevertheless, the situation seemed to have been resolved. 'I'll make arrangements in due course for inventory-taking again – in case I run off with the family silver,' Hugo laughed.

Laughed? I couldn't believe it would be that simple.

And it wasn't.

Sixteen

A t the gates of Fontenay, Jennifer jumped down from the staff car hurriedly, with no wish to be caught doing so even at this late hour. She would tell John she had taken the bus back, while Michael drove on to Fontenay Place. It was dark now, and with only the masked torch to guide her up the road to the lodge, eerily lonely. There was no sign of any catastrophe from flying bomb damage here to her relief. Even as this went through her mind, however, she heard the noise of an engine coming down on the main drive. Looking behind her, she dimly could make out the silhouette of a covered van or even ambulance. Fear clutched at her, and she quickened her step. The track was too rough to run along in the dark, and she set her thoughts steadily on reaching the one sure rock in her present life, her coming child.

Lucky Michael, with Deborah to love him. They thought it could end happily, but Jennifer doubted that with Hazel and the baby to consider. The war had one advantage, however; it could distance such problems, providing a timewarp for lovers. Not for her, however. Did John love her, or did he love her merely as his possession, a Fontenay wife? Sometimes she wondered. His outbursts of excessive jealousy spoke more of the latter, for surely if he truly loved her, he must know she would never betray him. And with *Michael* of all people. Perhaps she had been rash to continue meeting Michael, but it was helping him and it helped her, to have someone of like mind to confide in in these terrible times. Even though the D-Day landings had been successful, the troops were still pinned down in Normandy and who knew what the enemy might fling at them as they tried to battle their way out towards Paris and Germany itself?

She had loved John so much when they married, and had believed he loved her, but she realized the battering to which jealousy had subjected it was driving love away, perhaps never to return. She clung to the hope that the child would draw them together.

She thought about the love story that Michael had told her in the car, between his father James Sinclair and Beatrice Fontenay. James had been in the Royal Flying Corps in the First World War, posted on defence of London duties. He had met Beatrice Fontenay, newly recruited for the WRAF, at a station dance in April 1918 to celebrate the newly named Royal Air Force. James had been attracted to Beatrice, so lovely with her blonde hair and dancing blue eyes, and to discover she was a Fontenay only increased his interest. Especially when he had announced, 'James Sinclair. One of the Sinclairs.'

'One of the wicked Sinclairs? I've never met a wicked person before. How wonderful.'

'I'm not very wicked. You might even like me, if you danced with me.'

'Do you know,' Beatrice had replied thoughtfully, 'I think I might.'

And she did, and he her. They had continued to see each other for the rest of the war. But when the war ended and Beatrice had to return home to Fontenay, her father had discovered the truth and vented his wrath on her. And so did Adelaide. Jennifer tried to reconcile the image that she had of her mother-in-law in later years with the story that she had been told by Michael, and could not. Michael's story had all the quality of a fairy tale of long ago, yet her mother-in-law had been real, and vulnerable; she and her husband, Jennifer supposed, had been caught by the mores of her times. Jennifer never met Edward who died in 1935, but the same must have applied to him, even though his actions now seemed monstrous.

Beatrice, for all her gentleness, had been a spirited girl and used to the new-found freedom she had discovered in the war. Women's lives had changed greatly in four years. Those over thirty were soon going to be able to vote, and women as young as she had died in the war, side by side with servicemen. War was no respecter of sex or age. Beatrice had felt she was entitled to choose her own path in life.

Her father did not agree. Not only did he forbid Beatrice to see James, but imposed a curfew on her, checking her room at ten at night and eight in the morning, and demanding an itinerary of her day's movements, which he would periodically confirm afterwards. She still managed to meet James, who came up with a solution. She could run away from Fontenay. She was too young to marry without Edward's permission, but she could live with his parents in Buckinghamshire. They would be only too happy to have her, if only to thwart Edward Fontenay.

So that's what they had done, and all might have been well had it not been for Beatrice's younger sister Esther, then fourteen, who had a habit of trailing Beatrice and overheard the plan.

Esther had bided her time, and just when Beatrice believed herself safe, Esther told her father, who went storming up to Buckinghamshire, threatening that if Beatrice did not return he would charge James with the abduction of a minor.

'So she went back?' Jennifer had asked Michael.

'No. They immediately eloped to Gretna Green in time-honoured fashion where they got married.'

'*Married*?' That had shaken Jennifer. 'But that means—'

'That could have meant I'm the true owner of Fontenay if –' Michael had hesitated – 'that little fellow inside you isn't a boy.'

'Or even a girl,' Jennifer laughed. 'Fontenay isn't entailed. The daughter would merely have to change her name or not marry. Only the Fontenay name and lineage are *de rigueur*. It would only have gone to you if I remained childless.'

'Don't worry. Your father-in-law saw to it I wouldn't inherit,' Michael had said.

'How?'

'He found out about the marriage, unluckily for him after I'd been conceived, and had Beatrice forcibly removed. Then he banged her up in an asylum, and had the marriage dissolved on the grounds that she was a minor and insane at the time of the marriage.'

233

'But that's terrible.' Jennifer had been appalled to realize this was only just over twenty years ago, within her own lifetime. How could Adelaide have lived with the knowledge of what her husband had done to which, presumably, she had agreed?

'Fortunately my father is made of stern stuff, too. He's no mean hand at the law either; he claimed his child in the courts – good old Edward tried to prevent him getting me – and William and Louise brought me up. She's been a wonderful mother and I never had a clue that I was in any way different.'

'And Beatrice?'

'Died of a broken heart and flu in the epidemic. Still in the asylum. Edward didn't even come to the funeral, but Adelaide did.'

Jennifer shivered as she approached the lodge. Such passions? Could such hatred be justified? What did a name matter? She could not imagine her own family acting so. And that sneaky Esther. No wonder she'd gone to Australia. Had she ever regretted her betrayal of her sister? Was that why she emigrated, why Adelaide did not talk about her? Had her mother not forgiven her, perhaps even blamed her for Beatrice's death?

Jennifer paused at the front door of the lodge. Inside John would be waiting for her. If only Mrs Pink were living in, but she'd have gone back to the village long since. Jennifer summoned up her strength and went in.

'I'm glad I've caught you, Anna.' Hugo had hailed me as I parked outside the new tea-room, a few days later. 'I wanted a word.'

It was the last thing I wanted, after the session at the solicitor's office, but I could hardly avoid Hugo for the rest of his time at Fontenay.

'I can't discuss the lease, Hugo.' I spoke firmly, because he had to get the message.

'No, I understand that. It's about something else. Coffee? I could drive you up to Fontenay Place.'

His territory? Oh well, why not? If he could play at being rational, so could I.

My sangfroid rapidly and inexplicably vanished as I walked into the normality of the conference centre. Foolhardy was the word that came to mind – putting my head in a very dangerous den. I had enough to worry about in thinking over the results of my decision about Fontenay Place. I was still thinking about where the cash was going to come from to subsidize the estate. True, if the cash was coming from a snake in the grass, I didn't want to spend my life continuously watching my feet. I swung between wondering if I'd had a dose of sunstroke and images of Gerard crashing through that floor. On the whole, I thought I'd been dead right in choosing as I did, and I had several months to sort out the money situation after all.

'Good coffee,' I said brightly as we settled down in the bar.

'You'll miss it.'

'Watch it,' I whipped back sweetly. 'What was it you wanted to tell me?'

'It's not so much telling you something as making you aware of the possibilities. There are a few things you don't know about recent Fontenay history, or if you do, you haven't made the right connections.'

This sounded bad, particularly as the word smug summed Hugo's expression up exactly. 'Go on.'

'You quite rightly deduced that I am Esther Fontenay's grandson – not that she had much time for the Fontenays. Her elder sister was round the bend, and your father-in-law wasn't much better. Esther decided to wipe the dust off her feet. The stories she told about the family fascinated me though, and she had a few pictures that I used to study endlessly. After all, a castle and a few mad relatives are heady stuff for a kid in Australia. I wasn't born in England, incidentally. We moved here later. One of the first things I did then was have a look at Fontenay.'

Very touching, I thought, trying very hard *not* to understand his point of view, just in case it was a ploy to get me to relent.

'It's natural enough therefore that I became attached to the place, and wonder just how rogues and murderers always seem to land up with such beautiful estates.'

'Your logic's wrong, Hugo. Rogues and murderers usually get the rewards they deserve.'

He ignored my brisk response. 'I was particularly interested in the Sinclairs, of course. The way they infiltrated the Fontenay family so secretly time and time again.'

'As you did, you mean.'

'Ouch. Unfair. I'm a Fontenay, *not* an outsider. Did you know for instance that even the pure and saintly Gertrude, the beloved wife of Edmund Fontenay, had Sinclair blood in her?'

'Where is this leading, Hugo?' I wasn't going to reveal that this was news to me, and if true, was fairly shattering. So much for the pure blood of the Fontenays. One, now two, owners who had been at least partly Sinclair.

'I wondered how recently this infiltration had gone on.'

'Leave Joss out of this, if you please.'

'I wasn't referring to him. I was thinking about David.'

Something very nasty here, and totally unexpected. My stomach jolted, and I took a very large sip of caffeine.

'What about David? You're not going to tell me, I hope, that Gerard is illegitimate?' Sarcasm might work.

It didn't. 'No, Anna, darling. You're far too pure. It's David himself.'

'He's the son of John and Deborah,' I began impatiently – *and then I saw*. I was right there with him, having taken a gigantic leap into very deep water.

'Deborah,' Hugo said matter-of-factly, 'knew Michael Sinclair. I've seen photos of them together at Fontenay.'

'They both worked here.'

'Did RAF rules insist every Squadron Leader embrace his driver so closely?'

'*Joie de vivre.*'

'Or take your driver on weekend jaunts to Sussex hotels?'

'Where did you—'

'Find that out, Anna darling? Quite easily, a photograph of them and a bill were in with John's photographs, both marked in red ink "The Test". I don't know what that meant, but it's undoubtedly them.'

Steady, Anna. Was there yet more I didn't know about Deborah? 'My dear Hugo, if every woman who slept with a man before she was married, could later be accused of adultery, the courts would be rather full, don't you think?'

'Rather different in Deborah's case. There's also a photograph of them *after* she was married to John. In London, also marked "The Test". Can you prove David's parentage?'

'Are you *serious*?' I retorted, angry now. 'She only met Michael once or twice after her marriage. I don't have to prove David's legitimate, in any case. If anything, it's you have to prove him illegitimate. And even then – if you still have Fontenay in your beady little sights – I'm not sure that would rule David out from the succession. He's born in wedlock.'

'I seem to remember something in John Fontenay's will – I could be wrong of course – about Fontenay going to his son, David, of the true Fontenay blood line. Now if that's at issue—'

'Get to the point, Hugo.' Uneasily I remembered he could well be right about John's will.

'I'm devoted to darling Deborah, but I don't think she told you the entire truth. Far from only meeting Michael once or twice after her marriage, she saw him frequently, and usually at a hotel.'

'Can you prove it?'

'I have evidence that suggests it, and I could subpoena her to question her in court on oath.'

'This,' I said clearly, 'is ridiculous.' I only hoped it was true. It seemed unlikely Deborah would have confided such things to a paper and then left the paper where Hugo could find it – until I remembered all his long cosy visits to David. I couldn't believe that David would have confided in Hugo what he did not in me, but I couldn't rule it out.

'Perhaps. I would not like to inconvenience Michael Sinclair and Gerard with a DNA test.'

This was getting nightmarish. 'You couldn't force them to have one.'

'No, but as I have other evidence, Michael's refusal would not look good.'

'What's your price, Hugo?' I realized now he was talking of the nuisance element he could introduce. Blackmail, in other words. He knew I wouldn't want Deborah – or Michael, come to that – upset, and was banking on that rather than a flimsy case in court. He was also banking on the fact that I couldn't be *sure* it was flimsy.

He became exceedingly brisk. 'For the moment, forget about that lease expiring. I'm prepared to go on as we have been, same rent, and let bygones be bygones.'

'For the moment?' I asked evenly.

'We'll see how it goes, shall we?'

No, we will not, I wanted to say, but with Hugo that wasn't wise. 'I'll think about it.'

'Not for too long.'

This time I had no option. I asked Joss to come to the lodge that evening, assuming the tone of my voice would tell him this was no lovers' tryst. Not, you understand, that I minded if he got the wrong idea and *still* came, but I would play it fair if I could.

Apparently my tone worked, for he came in, sat down, accepted a drink and waited for me to make the running. I told him the whole story. I had to, since his grandfather was involved.

'It's all threats, of course,' I concluded.

'I agree. He's an odd character, Anna, but it's probably only a bluff to get you to let him stay on.'

'The Fontenays are a ruthless family. I wouldn't put it past him to try to grab the estate.'

'Your son is a Fontenay.'

'He has the benefit of being brought up by me.'

He laughed at that, which released the tension. Inside me, something flickered in hope. I now knew (partly thanks to Joss) the full story of Gwendolen Sinclair. Was it too much to hope that that of Jennifer would soon follow? And if such spring came, could summer be so far behind? Summer being, of course, Joss and me.

'What do you expect me to do?' he queried. 'Do you think there's truth behind it? And if so, do you want me to ask my grandfather if he'll have a DNA test? Or whether he's David's father? I can't do either, since I don't officially know that he had an affair with Deborah. Do you see?'

I saw. 'Yes. I don't know if there's any truth in it. I'll find out, but I agree I'll have to go it alone.' Gloominess descended once more.

'No. We'll go it together. My family is involved whether I

238

like it or not, which puts some responsibility on me, but that doesn't mean I've got to drag them all in. Not till the last resort, anyway. There are other ways.'

'Such as?' Hope rose in me again.

'For a start, when was David's birthday?'

'Fourth January 1950.'

'Which puts conception back to early April '49.'

'With a few weeks either side, if he was premature or late. What difference does the date make?'

'A lot, if Grandfather was out of the country then. He travelled abroad quite a lot in those days, being in the aircraft industry. I might be able to find that out.'

I wasn't optimistic. Hugo might still say Michael was on home leave or Deborah travelled abroad to see him. Joss saw my face.

'Don't worry, Anna. Hugo's bluffing. He *wants* you to worry. He's throwing in a joker in the hope of winning the game outright. Let's play our hand though and see where we get.'

It sounded good but I wasn't convinced. 'I'm going to cut the Gordian knot, Joss. I'm taking a deep breath, and then I'm going to ring Deborah *now*. You can stay if you like.'

It wasn't easy, nor was it quick. She listened in silence while I talked, and then remarked, 'A charming fish, this Hugo. I never met Esther, but John always disliked her. I thought at first he was being hard on her because she'd deserted the Fontenay post, but he said she was a sneaky little thing and that his mother had always blamed her for Beatrice's death. Adelaide told him – since he knew nothing about the true situation – some story that it was Esther who gave Beatrice the flu, and John believed it. I thought he was rather hard on her, but if she spawned the spawn that spawned Hugo he was absolutely right.' A pause. Then, 'I suppose you want to know whether David was John's child or Michael's. The trouble is, Anna, would you believe me if I said John's?'

'Yes.'

'But Hugo wouldn't. And Michael has suffered enough from Fontenay fancies. Does he know about this?'

'Joss won't tell him.'

'Good for him.'

'If Hugo fulfils his threat of the DNA test though—'

'Michael can refuse,' she cut in. 'As I shall. Now leave me to think this through, Anna.'

I put the phone down. 'She's going to think it through.'

'Good for her. It can't be fun when you're – what? – eighty-odd to be accused of having an illegitimate child fifty years ago. Will you let me know what she tells you?'

'Of course. We're together – on this.'

He picked up the pause. 'I think spring's in the air, Anna.' His face was non-committal.

'Another drink?'

'No, thanks. I'm driving home. I'll leave you to the Hermit's Retreat.'

'And Jennifer,' I added. 'Also Gertrude now.' I explained what Hugo had told me and he thought it very funny.

'How much else to crawl out of the woodwork?'

'Don't,' I said in mock hauteur, 'forget that you yourself have only recently emerged.'

He thought that funny too. It was only when he'd gone that the cloud settled in once more. I was beginning to feel haunted by the story of Jennifer and Michael Sinclair, probably because Jennifer was living in this very house at the time she was killed. The house felt very dark suddenly. Almost, like the rose garden, as if it were waiting.

1944

'I'm here!' Jennifer closed the door behind her, checking the blackout, and turned back as John came out of the living room. Her premonitions were confirmed. Something had happened. He looked so strange, so wild.

'I took the bus back,' she began, but he cut across her.

'The bomb, Jennifer, did you hear about the bomb?'

'It was here?' she asked sharply. 'At the house, or the castle?'

'Neither, Jen. It fell in the rose garden. That's gone for a burton, and the Hermit's Retreat with it.'

For a moment she didn't take it in, relieved that the buildings were safe.

'Smashed to smithereens,' John continued, with an odd sort of relish.

'The rose garden.' Jennifer pulled herself together, even as the anguish hit her. Better that than houses, but all her lovely roses gone. All the memories lost. How could she bear it? All that it had meant to her and past generations of Fontenays. Then her agony was quickly dismissed. 'It is only a garden, John. It can be replanted. You have *The Book of Gertrude's Garden* and the maps. At least there was no loss of life.'

'There was actually. George Timms, the undergardener,' John said casually.

Jennifer was appalled, since she knew the Timms family well. 'Oh, his poor parents. That's terrible. I'll go to see them tomorrow.'

'I heard the doodlebug cut out,' John said, still with his strange expression. 'I thought we were for it. I suppose we were lucky it only got the garden.'

He rambled on about the air raid wardens, the ambulance, fire crews and all the onlookers, but it seemed his mind was not on what he was saying, for he gave a strange giggle: 'There was another bomb too,' he said conversationally, 'dropped near your sister's house.'

'What?' Jennifer was gripped by panic. That must have been the sound she and Michael had heard in the distance. 'Is she all right?'

'I telephoned her for you. She's safe, and so are the kids. She was worried about you though. Were you home yet, she asked. You see, Jen, the bus queue copped it, and she reckoned you would have been in it. It was the last bus, Jen, the one you said you caught.'

Jennifer stared aghast, as John's face seemed to change in front of her to that of a stranger. A malevolent, evil stranger. 'I got a lift back this way – a serviceman.'

'Don't lie to me, Jen. It was Michael Sinclair, wasn't it?'

'Yes. I didn't tell you because you're so odd about him. There's nothing wrong though. He saw me there and picked me up.'

241

'And you told him about the baby, I expect? *His* baby?'

She went very cold inside. 'You're not well, John. It's the shock of the bomb. It's not his baby. You know very well it's yours.' She was gabbling in fear now. 'The baby you've always wanted.'

'I don't want a bloody Sinclair in the family,' he yelled. 'How could you do this to me, Jen. *How*?'

She tried to speak calmly. 'I have done nothing to you, John, save to give you the child you want. Michael is a good friend and that is all. He – he is in love with someone he cannot marry – he likes to talk to me about it.'

'That's weak, Jen. Very weak,' he sneered. 'Those Sinclairs worm their way in. "Oh Rose thou art sick". Isn't that how the poem goes? Oh, Jen, *thou* art sick. Sick with the Sinclair taint.' He began to sob, and Jen ran to him in alarm, putting her arms round him. He threw them off and seized her by the wrist.

'The rose was delivered today, the rose you wanted to plant for Beatrice. That I wanted to plant for Beatrice. All Sinclair sinners, *all*.'

'Good,' Jennifer croaked. 'We'll begin to dig the rose garden as soon as we can to show that Hitler can't defeat us. We'll ask George's parents to plant a memorial rose to him—'

'Memorial? We can't wait that long, Jen. I want to plant Beatrice's rose tonight.' His voice rose to a scream. 'Tonight, do you hear?'

'But it's dark, John,' she faltered. He was mad, surely he was mad.

'*Now*. I've got the spade here.' He gave a curious giggle. 'And the rose. Look.' There it was on the carpet, earth, roots and all. It had one flower on it, yellow of course. Yellow for Golden Dawn, and yellow for jealousy. It swam before her eyes.

'Why don't we wait till morning?' She kept her voice very quiet.

'Morning never comes,' he grinned. 'Now, Jen, *now*.' Keeping his grip on her wrist, he seized the plant and torch. 'You carry the rose bush.'

He dragged her outside into the dark and across the grounds to where the rose garden had once been. There was nothing here now but tumbled earth and walls and a huge crater.

Had she not been so afraid, she would have wept to see it.

'There,' he pushed over a pile of earth, and she stumbled on it. She'd been wrong, for she fell on to a rose bush still intact despite the devastation.

'There, plant it between those two rose bushes. They're *still* there, those fucking Sinclairs, grinning at me. Even Gertrude was tainted. Plant Beatrice with her. Go on, plant it. Plant it, you whore.'

'No, John, I will not do it. I will come back tomorrow.' She forced herself to sound calm, as she clambered back to her feet.

'Tomorrow's garden?' he sneered. 'No, Jennifer, not for you. The Sinclair curse has to be erased first.' He picked up the rose, and smashed it with one blow of the spade, then tore off the branches one by one, regardless of thorns and that his hands were bleeding. And then as she tried to restrain him, he turned on her, his hands outstretched. She stumbled again, as she tried to run, was hauled to her feet, and was face to face with a madman. 'Oh, Rose, thou art sick,' was her last thought, as his hands gripped her neck, and all the lost roses of the garden united their rainbow colours before her eyes.

The phone rang at eight thirty and to my surprise it was Joss. Early for him and he wasn't given to phone calls anyway.

'Could you come over to my place this morning, Anna?'

'I could, but—' A summons to his *home* at this hour. I'd never been there before. What was all this about?

'Do so.' He gave me directions how to get there, and at ten thirty I set off towards Sevenoaks. The cottage, in a village to the south-east of Sevenoaks, was a white limewashed Victorian cottage with a garden that did credit to his gifts. Outside there were two cars already parked; one was Joss's, the other one an old BMW, obviously lovingly cared for. I parked the Peugeot, still mystified as to why I'd been asked to come.

As soon as Joss ushered me into his living room – the word parlour came to mind when I saw its snugness, and open fire – the mystery was over. Without a doubt, even without introductions, I knew the elderly, white-haired man who'd risen to greet me must be Michael Sinclair. He had Joss's eyes, the same shock of hair, the same square jaw, an older version of the fighter pilot I'd seen in the photographs. What miracle had brought him here?

'I've caused you some trouble, Mrs Fontenay,' he apologized, when we'd seated ourselves, and I got over the shock.

'I'm not a Fontenay.' I smiled. 'I'm just Anna. My son is the Fontenay.'

'Not according to our friend Mr Brooks, I gather.'

'Joss told you?' I glanced at him appalled, but he shook his head.

'Deborah telephoned me. The first time, Anna, I've heard from her in forty-odd years. Life can still produce happy surprises. I thought about it for a day or two, then drove over here, much to Joss's annoyance. He doesn't think I'm safe on the road. I've tried to put everything behind me, but I've decided it's not possible. First, there are two items you can keep for your archives at this Hermit's Retreat, if you wish. Mary Fontenay's diary you already have. I slipped it into the stuff that I gave Joss from Thomas Sinclair's collection, who never saw it. Jennifer lent it to me, and I never had the opportunity to return it. I didn't want to stir things up with John again.'

He then handed me a plastic bag with a large portrait photograph.

'Who is she?' I asked, though I guessed the answer.

'Beatrice Fontenay on her Gretna Green wedding day to my father. Beautiful, isn't she?'

Oh yes, she was. Joss came to peer over my shoulder. There was nothing to say. All her innocence, youth and high spirits were there in that lovely face, together with hope for a radiant future with James Sinclair. It was almost too painful to look at, and I felt Joss's hand squeeze my arm.

'The Sinclairs have their legends about the feud, as well as the Fontenays,' Michael continued. 'Thomas Sinclair was particularly hot on it. Joss was telling me about Gwendolen. The family didn't take it lightly. Her parents didn't care what happened to her, her uncle raised heaven and earth. He came

244

roaring down to Fontenay, where he was told that Gwendolen had died in childbirth and was buried in the Fontenay grave. The vicar confirmed it, so they could take it no further.'

'The new bells,' I thought.

'It started a whole new round of the feud. I copied that extract about it from Thomas Sinclair's diary of 1882 for you. Good old Thomas was right. The feud was just going to worsen, so it's time to put an end to it,' Michael declared. 'A few things have to be straightened out: one of them is Hugo Brooks and the other is Jennifer. Which first?'

'Tell her about Jennifer,' Joss suggested. 'One leads from the other.'

'Deborah told me you knew most of it, save for that last night. So let me tell you. It's been buried long enough.'

He talked for some while until I felt my face wet with tears. He told us of that last evening with Jennifer, and of a dinner at which John had exploded in irrational anger; he was sure this had happened again.

'John told me next day,' he finished, 'that she'd died in a flying bomb accident, though he must have known I wouldn't believe it. Good riddance, he said, since *my* kid had died with her. I did all I could – bar telling him about Deborah – to persuade him otherwise. I thought he was grieving over her death, and that if I could convince him he would be the happier for it. Was I wrong. He just sneered at me. Deborah tried too, but he wouldn't have it. After she and I,' he paused, 'parted at the war's end, she continued seeing John and went on trying to help him. He was truly distraught once he came to his senses, and realized that he'd lost his own child. I was still horrified though when I found out that she married him.'

'Did you tell Deborah the truth?'

He hesitated. 'Deborah says I can tell you. Not for the police of course. She had begun to suspect, because one or two things didn't add up. So she asked to see me in London, and we talked it through. She was of the opinion that the trauma was so great that John simply blacked out that night, and genuinely had no recollection of what happened, believing afterwards that Jennifer died at the bus stop. Nevertheless, since she knew Jennifer had come back that night, she also knew John

245

must have killed her, and she had to protect herself and any children she might have. She told John about his blackouts and outbursts, though not about his killing Jennifer, of course. Firstly, she insisted he saw a doctor, and it turned out he had a brain tumour. He came through the op, and all seemed well, but Deborah decided to set up her own therapy before she had a child. She told him about our affair, and she told him about meeting me in London. She was taking the most enormous risk, and she knew it, but in her way she loved him. She gave him photos of the two of us, and marked them 'The Test'. He was to look at them every day until he accepted that what was past was past, and that the future was theirs. Amazingly enough it worked, and he put the energy he had devoted to hating me into the Fontenay–Sinclair family trees. I suppose it was my turn to be blotted out. Does that satisfy you?'

'Yes,' I said gratefully. 'It does.'

He sighed. 'I'm glad. It's over now, and whether Deborah and I acted properly or not, no one can now judge. Not even ourselves. There's just one thing left. Joss tells me he's just got Jennifer's rose to plant in the garden. Would you let me do it?'

'Yes.' I couldn't think of anything more fitting.

'Good. You know, I once said to her I might take up gardening after the war. I never did, not professionally anyway. So I'd like to do this for her.' He paused. 'I promised I'd talk about Hugo Brooks.'

'You're not going to have this DNA test, are you?' Joss demanded.

'No. I'm too old for all that twaddle. I'm going to meet this gentleman and put an end to it. What colour are your son's eyes, Anna? Blue, is that right?'

'Yes.'

'Deborah tells me John's were blue. Mine are brown and so are Deborah's. The laws of genetics make it highly unlikely that two brown-eyed people can have a blue-eyed child. Case proven – or as far as Hugo's concerned it is. He bluffs, we bluff. OK with you?'

It was.

*   *   *

246

Hugo withdrew his threat – proving Joss's conviction that his 'evidence' was bluff. In a spirit of co-operation, Michael Sinclair gave him some help in finding alternative premises in the area, and I was generous enough to part with some family mementoes of his mother – or did I do it because I hoped it would speed up and smooth his departure? In return, he carried on with the arrangements for the opera in July, and moreover said he'd depart in September, and rehouse his conferences. That left me with the upkeep of Fontenay over the winter months, but Hugo's absence was worth it.

Early in May, however, I had a landmark phone call from Deborah. I had already thanked her for all her help, and this wasn't her normal time for ringing, so I was taken by surprise. I was even more surprised when she announced, 'I've decided to come back to England to live.'

'Great. Where?'

'With you. Well, in Fontenay Place. I thought you might be able to do with the rent.'

I could hardly believe it, it was such wonderful news. 'Can you afford it? I'd reduce the rent, of course.'

'Yes. I can. Michael's coming to stay there with me for a while. It probably won't work, but we'll give it a whirl. Did you know he flew out to see me? I told him everyone stays the same deep down; we just add layers as the years go by. All we need to do is to peel the layers off and feel the benefit of the central heating.'

Just what Deborah had in mind as the definition of central heating in this context I decided not to ask. If it was sex, good luck to them. I was envious, and put the phone down, feeling a distinct glow inside. I felt like Mole on the river bank, sniffing the air and deciding it was indeed spring. It was time for the rose garden – and Joss.

I had deliberately kept away, partly until the dust had settled, partly because, damn it, I *still* had not decided the most suitable use for the Hermit's Retreat's upper room. It was opening in three weeks' time. I could put it off no longer, however. I was absolved from the past. The present was nicely taken care of in the form of Deborah and Michael coming to Fontenay Place.

Which left tomorrow.

*　　*　　*

The air had that spring sense of sharpened hope, a pale sunshine offering promise of summer, and my boots were sturdy enough to march me through any mud I might stumble into. So that afternoon I set off.

Through the new arched gateway, I could see Joss moving around. Sarah was at college. He was all mine. I dug my hands in my anorak pocket and walked up the path towards him.

It wasn't quite like entering the sudden technicolor of the land of Oz or of the Secret Garden but for me it came close. All the roses so carefully planted, so carefully pruned, were beginning to make their takeover bid for summer. Over the arbour and along the walls, the long tentacles of the ramblers were reaching out, and in what had once been the flying bomb crater, the fountain bubbled and the roses of Gertrude and Edmund were in bud. This time I didn't shrink from them. They offered no threat and I gave them none. It was armistice.

Joss looked up, saw me, dug his fork into the ground so that it stood alone, and came to meet me. Nothing to talk about now, not the roses nor the problem of the last eight months. Just ourselves.

'What do you think?' he asked.

Deliberately I misunderstood him. 'I think there's something missing.'

Taken aback, he looked round the garden in surprise. Every inch seemed to be accounted for.

'What?' He shot a look at me. 'Or am I playing into your hands?'

'You are. We're missing mention of the Sinclairs. There should be a declared Sinclair factor.'

'Planning on planting me?'

'All those who have affected the Fontenays should be remembered. And that –' I produced my coup – 'is what the upper storey of the Hermit's Retreat will be. A Sinclair–Fontenay feud floor.'

A quizzical eyebrow raised.

'And its resolution,' I continued hastily. 'No crass skeleton exhibitions, no Tudor tweeness, but the story of how the Sinclairs have infiltrated—'

He interrupted. '*Infiltrated*? We were dragged in.'

'Very well. How the Sinclairs have enriched the Fontenay story – and bloodline.'

'Not so fast, lady.'

'What's wrong?' Surely he couldn't find anything wrong with that? To my relief, at least he was grinning.

'You'd have the whole collection up here if you did that.'

'No, just St John—'

'And Gertrude.'

How could I have forgotten? My dismay must have been obvious because he laughed.

'Luckily Gerard is a better historian than you.'

'*Gerard* is?'

'Didn't you know he went to see my grandfather in the Easter vac?'

'No,' I said weakly.

'Gramps had lots of stuff on the Sinclair family, and Gerard had done his homework in the university library, as instructed.'

'Well?'

'Gertrude was not only a Sinclair herself, but had an interesting story. She was a great-granddaughter of the randy James IV of Scotland who died at Flodden. Illegitimate line. Her Sinclairs – no relation to the Baron Sinclair who fought at Flodden – objected strongly when she wanted to marry a Fontenay, since there'd always been a dispute as to who actually owned the land. Remember Scott's poem 'Lochinvar', part of his *Marmion*? Apparently there's a family legend that that was based on Edmund Fontenay snatching Gertrude from her shotgun wedding to someone who was a "laggard in love and a dastard in war". The family never spoke to poor old Gertrude again, and she never quite got over the rejection – which is why Edmund began his garden, enclosing his beloved wife away from the sadness of the world.'

'I'm beginning to think,' I observed sadly, 'that nothing is as it seems.'

'Oh, yes it is, provided the thorns are visible.' A pause. 'How do you feel about roses now?'

'No problem.'

'Somewhat cautious, aren't you? Come with me.' He took

my hand, and led me up the steps back to the arched entrance of the rose walk. Green, but still stark now until the tendrils of the ramblers were long enough to cover it. 'Look,' he said, pointing to the rose closest to one side of the arch. It was growing fast, already well up towards the top of the archway.

'A bud opened today,' he said. 'The first in the whole garden.'

'Whose is it?'

'Ours.'

At first I thought I hadn't heard him correctly. Then I saw him grinning.

'I'm afraid I didn't consult you about it,' he continued. 'It's a Madame Alfred de Carrière noisette climber, which is half old *moschata* and half new China blush. It brings the wheel full circle. It's the one Jennifer really wanted for Gwendolen, so it sets the seal on both their stories. But this one is ours.'

Even now I wasn't quite sure what he implied. 'When did you plant it?' I asked.

'Last October.'

I saw now. Oh, how clearly I saw. He'd planted it when we split up. It was his gesture of belief in us. It was my turn.

I cupped the delicate white-pink bloom in my hands, and smelled it. It seemed as though I'd never smelled a rose before – and perhaps I hadn't. Its perfume embraced me. No smothering, no claustrophobia, just a moment of sheer delight and pleasure.

'Our tomorrow's rose?' I turned to Joss. 'Thorns and all?'

'You can order a thornless rose, if you prefer. I'm not one, you know that.'

'I'll make do.'